The Willing Horse

by Ian Hay

CHAPTER I

THE VALLEYS STAND SO THICK WITH CORN

I

A Sunday at Baronrigg is a chastening experience. It is not exactly a day of wrath—though one feels that it might easily become one—but it is a time of tribulation for people who do not want to go to church—or, if the worst happens, prefer their religious exercises to be brief and dilute.

But neither brevity nor dilution makes any appeal to my friend Tom Birnie.

"I am a member," he announces, as soon as a quorum has assembled at Sunday breakfast, "of the old Kirk of Scotland; and I propose to attend service at Doctor Chirnside's at eleven o'clock. If any of you would care"—he addresses a suddenly presented perspective of immaculate partings, bald spots and permanent waves—"to accompany me, a conveyance will leave here at ten-forty."

"Well, we can't *all* get in, that's plain," chirps Miss Joan Dexter hopefully. (The table is laid for fourteen.)

"The conveyance," continues the inexorable Tom, "holds twelve inside and four out, not counting the coachman."

"It's no good, Joan, old fruit," observes Master Roy Birnie. "We keep a pantechnicon!"

"I suppose there's not a Church of England service within reach?" asks little Mrs. Pomeroy, rather ingeniously. "One's own Church makes an appeal to one which no other denomination cannot—can—adequately—doesn't it?" she concludes, a little uncertain both of her syntax and her host. This is her first visit to Baronrigg.

"Now she's done for herself!" whispers Master Roy into my left ear.

"I agree with you. There is an Episcopal Church—Scottish Episcopal, of course—at Fiddrie, three miles from here. I shall be happy to send you over there this evening at half-past six. This morning, I know, you will put up with our barbaric Northern rites!" replies Tom, with what he imagines to be an indulgent smile. "I like to see the Baronrigg pew full."

And full it is.

The longer I know Tom Birnie, the more I marvel that Diana Carrick married him. That sentiment is shared by a good many people, but on more abstract grounds than mine. Tom is a just and considerate landlord, an adequate sportsman, and a good specimen of that class by whose voluntary service this country gets most of its local government done, admirably, for nothing. But there are certain things against Tom.

In the first place—to quote old Lady Christina Bethune, of Buckholm—"no one knows who the creature is, or where he came from." This implies nothing worse than that since Tom represents the first generation of Birnies born in this county, his forbears must have been born somewhere else. In other words—still quoting the same distinguished authority—"they never existed at all." As a matter of fact and common knowledge, Tom's grandfather was a minister of the Kirk, somewhere in Perthshire, and his father an enormously successful member of the Scottish Bar, who bought the derelict little estate of Strawick, hard by here, and settled there in the late sixties with the presumptuous, but, I think, excusable, intention of founding a family. Naturally a family which has resided in our county for only forty-seven years can hardly be expected to have drifted, as yet, within the range of Lady Christina's lorgnette.

Secondly, Tom is a Radical. We are broad-minded people in this county, and are quite indulgent to persons who disapprove of the leasehold system (which does not obtain in Scotland), or who make excuses for the late Mr. Gladstone, or who are inclined to criticise pheasant preserving. That is the kind of Radicalism which we understand, and are prepared to tolerate. That was the sort of person Tom's father was. That is how Tom began. But of late, it must be confessed, Tom has been going it. He supports the present Government; he is for reducing the Army and Navy; he has recently helped to abolish our Second Chamber. (That was no great calamity; but he and his friends have omitted to provide us with a substitute.) He has openly applauded the efforts of a person named George to break up the foundations of our well-tried Social System; while the courses which he advocates with regard to the taxation of Land Values and the treatment of loyal Ulster, surpass belief. That is what the county has against Tom.

But I am neither a laird nor a farmer, and my indictment against Tom is based on more personal and less venial grounds. Firstly, he is not human. He is a calculating machine, with about as much passion as a parish pump. Secondly, he is absolutely destitute of all sense of humour. And yet Diana married him! Her own beautiful person exhaled humanity and humour in equal proportions. In all her short life I never knew her fail to understand a fellow-creature, or miss a humorous situation. Yet she married Tom Birnie. She married Tom Birnie, and she broke off her engagement with Eric Bethune to do it. I am a humble-minded person, and I never professed to understand any woman—not even my own wife, Diana's sister—but I wonder, even now, how any girl could have resisted Eric Bethune as he was twenty years ago, or, having got him, have relinquished him in favour of Tom Birnie. There was something pretty big and tragic behind that broken-off engagement. My Eve knew what it was—I suppose Diana told her about it—but when I asked for the explanation I was tersely instructed not to be an inquisitive old busybody. As for Eric, he never mentioned the matter to me. He simply informed me that my services as best man would not be required after all, and that he would be gratified if I would refrain from asking damn silly questions. (Not that I had asked any.) Also, that he looked to me to prevent other persons from doing so.

And now Tom Birnie is a baronet and a widower, with a son eighteen years old, and Eric Bethune is still an eligible bachelor of forty-three. And how he hates Tom Birnie! However, I will introduce Eric presently. First of all, I must get our party to church.

II

The ancestral hereditary omnibus of the house of Baronrigg deposited us at the kirk door at ten fifty-five precisely, and by the time that the Reverend Doctor Chirnside's Bible and hymn-book had been set out upon the red velvet cushion of the pulpit by a bulbous old friend of mine named James Dunshie—an octogenarian of austere piety, an infallible authority on dry-fly fishing, and a methodical but impervious drinker—we were all boxed into our places in the private gallery of Baronrigg. It is less of a gallery than a balcony, and juts out curiously from the side of the little church, with the public gallery running across the end wall on its right, and the minister on its left. It recedes into a deep alcove, and at the back is a fireplace, in which a fire is always kept burning upon wintry Sundays. The Baronrigg pew—and, indeed, Baronrigg itself—came into the family from Diana's side of the house: she brought them to Tom on her marriage. The pew is rich in Carrick associations. It is reported of old Neil Carrick, the grandfather of Diana and my Eve, that whenever he found himself dissatisfied—a not infrequent occurrence—with the discourse of Doctor Chirnside's predecessor, it was his habit to rise from his red rep chair in the forefront of the gallery, retire to the back, make up the fire with much clatter of fire-irons, and slumber peacefully before the resulting blaze with his back to the rest of the congregation. But no such licence was permitted to us. We sat austerely in two rows, gazing solemnly at the blank wall opposite us, while Doctor Chirnside worked his will upon his flock. Doctor Chirnside is a tall, silver-haired, and pugnacious old gentleman of about seventy. He fears God, and exhibits considerable deference towards Tom Birnie; but he regards the rest of his congregation as dirt. (At least, that is how we feel in his presence.) This morning he entered the pulpit precisely on the stroke of eleven, in deference to the Laird's well-known prejudices on the subject of punctuality—besides, I happened to know that he was coming on to lunch at Baronrigg after service—and, having been securely locked in by James Dunshie, adjusted his spectacles and gazed fiercely at some late comers. Then he gave out the opening psalm.

In Craigfoot Parish Church we always sing the opening psalm unaccompanied. It is true that we possess a small organ, but that instrument is still regarded with such deep suspicion by some of the older members of the congregation that we only employ it to accompany hymns—which, as is well known, have little effect one way or the other upon one's ultimate salvation. But we take no risks with the Psalms of David. These are offered without meretricious trimmings of any kind, save that furnished by the tuning-fork of Andrew Kilninver, our esteemed auctioneer, estate agent, and precentor.

Accordingly, when Doctor Chirnside took up his psalter, the young lady at the organ leaned back nonchalantly; Andrew Kilninver stirred importantly in his seat, tuning-fork in hand; and the choir—highly scented shop-girls and farmers' daughters, assisted by overheated young men in Sunday "blacks" and choker collars—braced themselves with the air of people upon whose shoulders the credit, and maybe redemption, of a whole parish rests.

There is something peculiarly majestic about the manner in which Doctor Chirnside opens his morning service. I believe that, in his view, the unaccompanied psalm is the one relic of pure orthodoxy preserved by him against the modern passion for hymns, organs, printed prayers, anthems, and "brighter worship" generally. That graceless young ruffian, Roy Birnie, gives an imitation of his performance which is celebrated throughout the parish. It runs something like this:

"Ha-humm! Brethren, we will commence the public worrship of God, this Lord's Day, by singing to His praise part of the Seven Hundred and Forty-Ninth Psalm. Psalm Seven Hundred and Forty-Nine. Ha-humm! The Church is full cold. Will Mr. John Buncle, of Sandpits, kindly rise in his pew and adjust the open window west of him? (*Imitation of Mr. John Buncle, petrified with confusion, adjusting the window.*) We will commence at verrse One Hundred and Seventy-Nine:

I, like a bottle, have been

With Thy great maircy filled,

Oh, hold me up, hold Thou me up,

That I may not be spilled!

And so on until the end of the Psalm. Psalm Seven Hundred and Forty-Nine. The Seven Hundred and Forty-Ninth Psalm. *Ping! Ping! Ping!* (*The last is supposed to be Kilninver getting to work with his tuning-fork.*) Tune, Winchester, '*I, like a bottle...*'"

I am a devout person, but I am afraid it does sound something like that.

However, one feels less inclined to smile when the actual singing of the psalm commences. The Metrical Psalms, sung in unison, without accompaniment, and with strong, rugged voices predominating, are Scottish history. They bring back the days when people did not sing them in churches, but on hillsides in remote fastnesses, at services conducted by a man with a price on his head, guarded by sentries lying prone upon the skyline, on the look-out for Claverhouse and his troopers. That is why I, coming of the stock I do, like to hear the opening psalm at Craigfoot.

The start, as a rule, is not all what it might be, for the Scots are a slow-moving race; and naturally it takes a little time to catch up with Andrew Kilninver and his comparatively nimble crew. But about the middle of the second verse we draw together, and the unsophisticated rhymes, firmly welded now with the grand old melody, go rolling upwards and outwards through the open door and windows, over one of the fairest and richest farming districts in the world:

They drop upon the pastures wide,
That do in deserts lie;
The little hills on every side
Rejoice right pleasantly.
With flocks the pastures clothed be,
The vales with corn are clad;
And now they shout and sing to Thee,
For Thou hast made them glad.

I am a soldier, and have been a soldier all my life, so when I encounter an assemblage of my fellow countrymen, I naturally scrutinise them from a recruiting sergeant's point of view. (At least, Eve always said I did.) And what a sight that congregation presented! I have encountered many types in the course of my duty. I know our own Highlanders; I know the French Zouave regiments; a year or two ago—in nineteen-eleven I think it was—I saw the Prussian Guard march past the Emperor during Grand Manoeuvres; I have ridden with the Canadian North-West Mounted Police; I have seen a Zulu impi on the move in South Africa. All have their own particular incomparabilities—dash, endurance, resource, initiative—but for sheer physical solidity and fighting possibilities, commend me to the peaceful yeoman-farming stock of the Lowlands of Scotland. My own regiment is mainly recruited from this district, so perhaps I am prejudiced. Still, if ever the present era of international restlessness crystallises into something definite; if ever The Day, about which we hear so much and know so little, really arrives—well, I fancy that that heavily-built, round-shouldered throng down there, with their shy, self-conscious faces and their uncomfortable Sunday clothes, will give an account of themselves of which their sonsy, red-cheeked wives and daughters will have no cause to feel ashamed.

III

After the psalm we settle down to the Doctor's first prayer. There are two of these, separated by an entire chapter of the Old Testament—a fairly heavy sandwich, sometimes. The first prayer lasts a quarter of an hour, the second, eight minutes. The first prayer takes the form of an interview between Doctor Chirnside and his Maker—an interview so confidential in character and of a theological atmosphere so rarefied that few of us are able to attain to it. So our attention occasionally drops to lower altitudes. The second prayer is more adapted to humble intellects. The Doctor refers to it as the Prayer of Intercession. In it he prays for everything and everybody, beginning with the British Empire and ending with the Dorcas Society. Under the cloak of Intercession, too, he is accustomed, very ingeniously, to introduce, and comment upon, topics of current interest. Occasionally he springs upon us a genuine and delightful surprise. The parish still remembers the Sunday morning in eighteen-ninety-four upon which the Doctor, in his customary intercession for the Royal Family, got in twenty-four hours ahead of Monday's *Scotsman* by concluding his orison: "And we invoke Thy special blessing, O Lord, upon the infant son (and ultimate heir to the Throne of this country) born, *as Thou knowest,*

Lord, to Her Majesty's grandchildren, the Duke and Duchess of York, at an early hour this morning!"

But the first prayer, as already indicated, holds no surprises. I am therefore accustomed to devote this period to a detailed inspection of the congregation below—an occupation which has the special merit of being compatible with an attitude of profound devotion.

Perhaps I ought to explain how it is that I, a mere visitor, should take such a deep interest in Craigfoot and its associations. The fact is, I am no visitor. I was born here, not ten miles away, at The Heughs, a little manor among the foothills, where my brother Walter and his lusty family still flourish. As a younger son I was destined from birth for the Army; but by the time I had passed into Sandhurst, and on to the lordly exile of our Army in India, I knew every acre of the district. I had tumbled into burns and been kicked off ponies all over the county. I knew everybody who lived there, from our local overlord, the Earl of Eskerley, down to Bob Reid, the signal porter at the railway station—who, being well aware that I went fishing every Wednesday at Burling, two stations up the line, was accustomed on those occasions to refuse right of way to the morning train, palpitating for its connection with the junction ten miles distant, until my tardy bicycle swept round the curve of the road and deposited me panting on the platform.

Inevitably, the day came when I fell in love—with Eve. That was no novelty for Eve; for she and her elder sister, Diana, had most of us on a string in those days. Baronrigg was the lodestone of every young spark in the county, except during those dismal months in summer when our twin divinities were spirited away to London for the season. Some were able to follow them there; but I was not. Neither was Eric Bethune. Regimental duty forbade, though we did what we could with the generous leave available in the early nineties.

Ultimately, I was taken and Eric was left. Why Eve took me I have never known. I was only an infantry subaltern, and a younger son into the bargain. But she picked me out from the crowd, and waited for me, bless her! for seven years. My theory was, and is, that a woman only marries a man for one of two reasons—either because he gives her "a thrill," or because she thinks he requires taking care of. There was no doubting Eve's reason for marrying me. She took care of me for one rapturous year; and then she left me, and took her baby with her. To-day both lie in the private burial-ground of Baronrigg. That is why I always accept Tom's annual invitation to stay there at Easter, rather than go to my brother Walter's cheery but distracting establishment at The Heughs.

That is enough about me. Now let us get back to the congregation.

It was a representative throng, yet not entirely representative. For one thing, our chief territorial and social luminary, Lord Eskerley, is a member of the Church of England; and when he goes to church at all—which is usually just after a heart-attack, or just before a General Election—he goes to Fiddrie. For another, no Scottish assemblage can be counted truly representative which takes no account of the adherents of Holy Church—as a peep into Father Kirkpatrick's tightly-packed conventicle on the other side of the glen would tell us. But when all is said, the parish church is still the focus of Scottish rural life, and I was well content with the selection of friends who filled the pews below me.

There was old General Bothwell, of Springburn, a Mutiny and Crimean veteran—altogether quite a celebrity among a generation which knows nothing of actual warfare. (After all, the South African affair touched our civil community very lightly.) Beside the General sits his son Jack, home on leave from India. He commands a company in a Pathan regiment. The General is trying hard not to look proud of Jack.

Just behind the Bothwells sit the Graemes, of Burling—Sir Alistair, his Lady, and their three tall daughters, known and celebrated throughout the county as "The Three

Grenadiers." Across the aisle sits old Couper, of Abbottrigg—the largest farmer in the district, and one of the best curlers in Scotland—with his wife. The old couple are alone now, for all their sons and daughters are married. However, a good many of them are present in other parts of the church, holding a fidgety third generation down in its seat.

Just in front of the Coupers I observe Mr. Gillespie, manager of our branch of the Bank of Scotland, a man of immense discretion and many secrets. With him, Mrs. Gillespie. Also the two Misses Gillespie, locally and affectionately renowned as "Spot" and "Plain." I notice that their son, Robert, who is studying for the Ministry in distant Edinburgh, is with them for the week-end.

Farther back, at the end of a long pew, just under the public gallery, sits Galbraith, our chemist and druggist, a small man with a heavy cavalry moustache and—the not uncommon accompaniment of a small man—a large wife and twelve children. The children fall into two groups, separated by an interval of seven years. The first group—four in number, and somewhat wizened in appearance—were born and reared upon the slender profits of a retail business in tooth-brushes, patent medicines, and dog-soap. The other eight—fat and well-liking—began to appear serially after Mr. Galbraith had amassed a sudden and unexpected fortune out of a patent sheep-dip of his own invention, which has made the name of Galbraith celebrated as far away as Australia.

Over the way from Galbraith, in a side pew, sits Shanks, the joiner. He is a poor creature, lacking in ability either to ply his trade or invent reasons for not doing so. Eve used to say that Shanks never by any chance acceded to a professional summons, and that his excuses were three in number, and were employed in monotonous rotation—firstly, that he had swallowed some tacks; secondly, that he had had to bury "a relation of the wife's"; thirdly, that one of his numerous offspring had been overtaken by a fit.

Behind Shanks sit the Misses Peabody. They are the daughters of a retired merchant of Leith, who died many years ago. They inhabit a villa on the outskirts of our little town, live on an annuity, and exist precariously in that narrow social borderland which divides town-folk from gentry.

Passing on, I note that Mr. Menzies, Lord Eskerley's factor, has at last provided himself with a wife—a stranger to me. Well, Menzies is well connected and has an excellent house; so, doubtless, the lady will be comfortable. But I wish he had not gone so far afield. There is nothing wrong with the girls in this district, Menzies! *Experto crede*!

My eye wanders on over the bowed heads. Finally it reaches the third pew from the front, and I am aware of the handsome presence of my friend Eric Bethune, of Buckholm. Beside him, bolt upright, with a critical eye fixed upon Doctor Chirnside, sits his eccentric lady mother. Eric's attitude is more devout, but I observe that his head is turned sideways, and that he is grinning sympathetically at Tommy Milroy over the way, whose little nose is being relentlessly pressed to the book-board by an iron maternal hand encased in a hot black kid glove.

Eric, although he is as old as myself, is still very much of a boy—or perhaps I ought, in strict candour, to say a child. He was a child at school—in his exuberant vitality, his sudden friendships, his petulance. He was a child at Sandhurst; he was a child as a subaltern—at times, almost a baby. But he has been my friend all my life, and I admire him more than any man I know; perhaps because he possesses all the qualities which I lack. He is tall and debonair; I am—well, neither. He is impulsive, frank, and popular; I am cautious, reticent and regarded as a little difficult. (This is not true really, only there is no Eve now to tell me what to say to people.)

But, above all, Eric is a soldier. In the South African War he was Adjutant of our Second Battalion. They were sent out rather late, and only got to work after Paardeburg. I was with the other battalion, and saw nothing of Eric, but his Colonel considered him the smartest Adjutant in the Division, and recommended him for the D.S.O. He got it, but always declared that he had had no chance to earn it, except by instructing the men very thoroughly in what is vulgarly known as the art of "Spit and Polish." Certainly they were the best turned-out crowd I have ever seen, when they marched through the streets of Edinburgh on their return.

Directly after that we both went back to India. We were anxious to go. Eve had died just before I sailed for South Africa; Diana had broken off her engagement with Eric and married Tom Birnie three years earlier. But I did not stay in India very long. I was restless for home again; and, having decided that the Regular Army could now get along without my services, I sent in my papers and settled in London. When Roy was nine years old his mother followed her sister. She had survived Eve only six years, for the same lung trouble had marked them down long ago. After that Eric felt that he could come back to Buckholm. So he came, and they gave him command of the Regimental Depot, with the rank of Major. The Depot is not far away from here, and he is able to join his mother at Buckholm for much of the time. He is quite his old self now, and he has made the Third Battalion a marvel of smartness and efficiency. But there is one house which he never visits—Baronrigg. I do not blame him. His memories there are not like mine. Moreover, besides hating Tom Birnie, he dislikes Roy. I am surprised at this, because the boy is the image of his mother. Still, I suppose a man may be forgiven for disliking a boy who should have been his own son, but is not. Anyhow, I know I shall not meet Eric during my stay at Baronrigg, so I have arranged to lunch at Buckholm after church to-day.

That covers the congregation, I think. (Doctor Chirnside is working up to his peroration, and in a few minutes we shall be erect again.) I look over them once more. Altogether, a sturdy, satisfactory assemblage, from laird to ploughman. We have not changed much in the last two hundred years, nor will during the next two hundred, so far as I can see. We are Conservatives of Conservatives, although we return a Liberal. We shall go on tilling the fat soil, and raising fat cattle, and marrying young, and having big families, and sending a few of the boys into the Army, and a few to the Colonies, and keep the rest at home to marry strapping girls and have more big families, until the end of time.

We are a little disturbed, to be sure, at the present state of the world outside. A street-bred Government, with both eyes on the industrial vote, has recently compelled us, even us, to disburse our hard-earned pennies upon stamps, to be stuck at frequent intervals upon an objectionable card. We are informed that this wasteful and uncongenial exercise is designed to bestow upon us the benefits of insurance against sickness—upon us, who are never either sick or sorry; and if ever we are, are taken care of (under an unwritten compact of immemorial antiquity) by the employers who have known us and ours for generations back. Other political upheavals are agitating the country, but they leave us cold in comparison with this superfluous imposition of benevolence.

But still, politicians are always with us, and must be endured; so what matter? Our valleys stand so thick with corn that they laugh and sing, and even with Income Tax at one and twopence in the pound, things might be worse. After all, we have our health, and perhaps it is our duty to contribute to the insurance of those sickly city folk. A few stamps are not a very high price to pay for peace and prosperity and sleepy contentment in the heart of the British Empire.

IV.

... I think I must have begun to nod a little. It was a warm morning, and the sunshine and the songs of the birds without, and the confidential rumblings of Doctor Chirnside within, had exercised a soporific effect. But I opened my eyes with a jerk, and observed that the Netherby pew was occupied.

Netherby has stood empty so long that it is quite a shock to see its pew inhabited at all. It is a conspicuous pew, in the corner of the church, to the left of the pulpit, and my unregenerate nephews and nieces call it "The Loose Box." It is built in the form of a hollow square, and is surrounded by dingy red rep curtains, which enable its occupants to gaze upon the officiating clergy without themselves being gazed upon by the congregation. However, the pew is overlooked by the Baronrigg gallery.

This morning the Netherby pew contained seven occupants, humped devoutly round the square table in the centre. Upon the table reposed a gentleman's silk hat, or topper. Now, in this part of the country, gentlemen do not wear silk hats on Sunday. They wear bowlers, or Homburg hats, or even motoring caps. Neither do they wear frock-coats, like the obvious proprietor of "The Loose Box." He was a squarely-built man, and from what I could see of his face, he wore mutton-chop whiskers. There was also a middle-aged lady in a rather unsuitable hat. There were two boys of nineteen or twenty. There were two or three small children, constrained and restless. There was an elderly man with a beard like a goat's, gazing upwards at Doctor Chirnside with an air which struck me as critical. One felt that he would have taken the Doctor's place without any pressing whatsoever. I put him down for a visitor of some kind.

And there was a girl. At least, there was a hat—a big black tulle hat—and I assumed that there was a girl underneath it. I could see her frock, which was white. So were her gloves, which extended above her elbows. Her hands were long and slim. I began to feel curious to see her face.

Suddenly I realised that I was not alone in this ambition. On my left, that young rascal Roy was hanging outward and downward at a dangerous and indecorous angle, in a characteristically thorough attempt to look under the brim of the black tulle hat. Needless to say, in romantic enterprises of this kind, competition, especially with the young, makes one feel merely foolish, so I resumed my normal position and closed my eyes with an air of severe reproof.

Almost directly afterwards the First Prayer came to a conclusion, and we all sat up. Simultaneously the girl in the hat lifted her head. The Parish Church is small and the range was comparatively short. For a moment her face was upturned in our direction. I heard Roy give a gasp of admiration.

"Let us read together," suggested the indefatigable Doctor Chirnside, "in the Fifty-Fifth Chapter of the Book of the Prophet Isaiah. Chapter Fifty-Five. The first verse. *Ho, every one that thirsteth...*"

But I am afraid I was not listening. I was watching the girl's face—as well I might, for it was the face of a flower. She leaned back in her seat against the wall, and composed herself for the Fifty-Fifth Chapter of Isaiah. Suddenly, for some reason, she lifted her head again. This time her eyes encountered Master Roy's honest and rapturous gaze. They fell immediately, but up from the open throat of her white Sunday frock, over her face, and right into the roots of her abundant fair hair, ran a vivid burning blush.

I looked at Roy. He was crimson too.

Spring! Spring! Spring!

CHAPTER II

REBELLIOUS MARJORIE

I

While Sunday at Baronrigg was a day of mild tribulation, Sunday at Netherby was a day of wrath. It was a direct survival of the darkest period of the Victorian era.

Albert Clegg—or, rather, Mr. Albert Clegg—believed in taking no risks with his immortal soul, or with those of his family. He also believed in being master in his own house. Accordingly, when he bade his household remember the Sabbath day to keep it holy, the household, as they say in the Navy, "made it so." The necessary standard of sanctity was attained, firstly, by the removal on Saturday night to locked cupboards of everything in the shape of frivolous or worldly literature; in place of which there appeared a few "Sunday" books—the latest record, mayhap, of missionary endeavour, together with one or two godly romances of a rather distressing character. Periodical literature was represented by *The Sunday at Home*, while unsecular comment on current events was furnished by that brilliantly ingenious combination of broad religion and literary entertainment, *The British Weekly*.

The necessary atmosphere having been duly created, those two powerful engines, Prayer and Fasting, were now set in motion. The latter, to be just, was of little account: its operation merely involved the omission of afternoon tea and the substitution of cold supper for ordinary dinner. But the devotional programme of the Clegg Sunday was an exacting business. It opened with family prayers at eight-thirty a.m., including an extemporary supplication by the master of the house. Catechism came at nine-thirty, Church at eleven o'clock. The household were conveyed thither in the Rolls-Royce. In the course of time, as the glory of that extremely new vehicle faded, and the task of making an impression upon the neighbourhood accomplished itself, the young Cleggs gloomily foresaw a still further extension of Sabbath observance, in the direction of pedestrian exercise. Meanwhile, they covered the three miles to church in the car, and were thankful for small mercies.

After one o'clock dinner, the family sang hymns. Marjorie accompanied—not very convincingly, owing to the presence of a surreptitious novel or volume of poetry propped upon the music-rest beside the hymn-book. You cannot engage in psalmody and mental culture simultaneously with any degree of plausibility. The younger children sang a shrill soprano; brothers Amos and Joe growled self-consciously an octave—sometimes two octaves—lower. Sister Amy—a plain but intensely pious child of fourteen—offered a windy and unmelodious contribution which she termed "seconds." Mrs. Clegg sang—as she did everything else—dutifully, and slightly apologetically. Mr. Clegg sang what he had imagined for more than thirty years to be tenor, inciting his fellow-choristers to continued effort by beating time with his hymn-book, until post-prandial drowsiness intervened, and he retired to bed, with all his clothes on, for his Sabbath nap. During this interval the family enjoyed a slight respite from Sabbath observance—all, that is, but the younger members, who received instructions in Biblical history from two small and not uninteresting manuals, entitled *Peep of Day* and *Line Upon Line*, with maternal additions and elucidations of a somewhat surprising character.

At six o'clock the chauffeur was once more called upon to observe the Sabbath by conveying the family to evening service at the parish church. The small fry, in consideration of *Peep of Day* and *Line Upon Line*, were permitted to go to bed.

After cold supper at eight-thirty, the devotional exercises of the day petered out with a second instalment of family prayers, including what brother Joe (Marjorie's accomplice and pet) was wont to describe as "a final solo from Pa." After that, the exhausted household retired to rest, leaving the master to relax himself from the spiritual tension of the day with weak whisky-and-water.

Albert Clegg had bought Netherby a year previously. He came from the North of England, and was deeply interested in Tyneside shipping. His father had been a small tradesman in Gateshead. Albert's initial opportunities had not been too great, but he possessed two priceless natural assets—superb business capacity and a sincere dislike for recreation or amusement of any kind. At twenty-one he was a clerk in a rather moribund shipping business. At twenty-five he was managing clerk. In that capacity he took it upon himself, unofficially, to investigate the books of the firm—he was the sort of young man who would joyfully devote a series of fine Saturday afternoons to such an enterprise—and was ultimately able to expose a leakage of profits which had kept the venerable and esteemed cashier of the office in considerably greater comfort than his employers for the past ten years. Needless to say, Albert was the next cashier. At thirty he was junior partner and practically dictator. A few years later his exhausted seniors gave up the struggle, and allowed themselves to be bought out. Albert promptly called in his younger brother Fred, who, up to date, had been dividing his undoubted talents fairly evenly between jerry-building and revivalist preaching—a combination of occupations which enabled him to

Compound for sins he was inclined to,

By damning those he had no mind to—

thus marking himself down as an ultimate and inevitable ornament of our National Legislature. Fred was taken into partnership. From that day the firm of Clegg Brothers went from strength to strength.

Albert Clegg's first wife was what Lady Christina would have described as "a young person of his own station in life." She had died a few years after the birth of Master Amos. The present Mrs. Clegg was a member of an aristocratic but impoverished family named Higgie, of Tynemouth, and she came to Albert just at a time when his rising fortunes called for a helpmeet possessed of the social accomplishments which he himself so entirely lacked. On his second marriage, he removed from Gateshead to a large house in the pleasant suburb of Jesmond, and lived there for twenty years, while the Clegg firm prospered and the Clegg family multiplied. As already foreshadowed, brother Fred's combined reputations as a captain of industry and a silver-tongued orator presently wafted him into Parliament, where he established a reputation for verbosity and irrelevance remarkable even in that eclectic assembly.

That is all that need be said about Mr. Albert Clegg for the present. The main purpose of this brief summary of his character and achievements is to provide the reader with some sort of key—in so far as keys are of any use at all where feminine locks are concerned—to the character of that rather unexpected young person, his daughter Marjorie. For it was from her father, most undoubtedly, that Marjorie derived her initiative and determination. From her mother she seemed to have inherited nothing, except her Christian name and her naturally waved hair. Everything else—her superb body, her absolute honesty, her lively sense of humour, her critical attitude towards certain existing things, and, above all, her warm, impulsive young heart—came from that one supreme gift of God which is entirely our own—set high out of reach of those twin busybodies, Heredity and Environment—Personality.

II

On the particular spring morning with which we are already concerned, Marjorie made a bad start. She missed prayers altogether, and was late for breakfast into the bargain. To crown her iniquity, she entered the dining-room whistling a secular air, with her arms full of daffodils.

Whistling is at all times an unladylike accomplishment, even though one whistle like a mavis. Moreover, it was Sunday. Furthermore, Uncle Fred was present on a visit, and one has to keep up appearances before relations, however despicable.

"I am not at all satisfied with Doctor Chirnside," Mr. Clegg was remarking. "But we must employ such instruments as lie to our hands."

"That is very true," remarked Uncle Fred, making a mental note of this apt expression. Uncle Fred was an industrious gleaner of other people's impromptus, with a view to parliamentary requirements.

"As you know," continued Mr. Clegg, "our own Body is not represented in this county. The nearest United Free Church—which conforms most closely to our own beliefs—is fifteen miles away. In any case, I consider that a household should, as far as possible, worship in its own district."

"Quite right," said Uncle Fred. "Like a constituency."

"Besides, we would not get to know people any other way," interposed Mrs. Clegg timidly.

"My dear," said Mr. Clegg severely, "we cannot worship God and Mammon. And I will thank you for another cup of tea. John, my boy, eat up that crust; I know of many a poor lad that would be glad of it. The only other places of worship within easy reach," he continued, "besides the parish church (Established, of course), are a Papist Chapel, Burling way, which I do not go to very often"—Mr. Clegg paused and assumed a wintry smile, to indicate that he spoke sarcastically—"and the English Episcopal Church at Fiddrie—where I would as soon see any belongings of mine trying to disport themselves as in the Church of Rome itself."

Mr. Clegg paused, and Uncle Fred laughed sardonically. Mrs. Clegg, who all her life had hankered after the comfortable consolations of Anglican ritual and the social cachet of an Anglican connection, smothered a sigh, for she knew to what address her husband's remark was directed.

At this moment, as related, Marjorie tramped in, whistling, with her daffodils.

"Hallo! am I late?" she inquired. "I am so sorry: I was out gathering these. Good morning, everybody!"

She sat down amid a deathly silence.

"What were you all talking about?" Marjorie rattled on. "Church, wasn't it? I wonder how many hours old Chirnside will preach to-day? Oh, that awful children's sermon! I don't think it's sportsmanlike to make you listen to two sermons in one morning. My idea is that during the grown-ups' sermon the children should be allowed to go out and play, and that during the children's sermon the grown-ups should have their choice of going out too, or lying right down in the pews and having a nap!" She gazed out of the window, over the sunny landscape. "I know which I should choose!"

"My girl," interposed Mr. Clegg, "if you talk in that strain I shall regret more than ever that I allowed your mother to send you to that school in Paris."

Marjorie had been "finished"—which means "begun"—at Neuilly. It is difficult to understand why her father had sent her there, except that it was expensive. Mr. Clegg had long transferred the blame for this lapse of judgment to his wife.

During those two quickening years, Marjorie, though hedged about by every preventive device known to the scholastic hierarchy, had fairly wallowed in Life—Life as opposed to Existence. She had sucked in Life through her pores; she had scrutinised Life through her shrewd blue eyes; she had masticated Life with her vigorous young teeth. Life in Paris, even as viewed from the ranks of a governess-guided "crocodile" in the Bois de Boulogne, or a processional excursion to the Tuileries, is a stimulating and disturbing compound, especially to unemancipated seventeen. At any rate, Marjorie had returned to her home possessing certain characteristics which had not been apparent when she left it. These were, roughly, three in number:

Firstly, a passionate interest in the world and its contents. She was ablaze with enthusiasm for all mankind. She wanted to do something—to be a hospital nurse, a journalist, a chorus girl, a barmaid—anything, in fact, that would bring her into contact with her fellow-creatures and, if possible, enable her to make herself uncomfortable on their behalf. She was a Giver, through and through.

13

Secondly, an entire lack of sentimentality. Young men made no appeal to her. She had never flirted in her life: she did not know how. She made friendships at a rush—many of them with boys of her own age—but if any young man flattered himself that he had made a tender impression, he was soon woefully undeceived. Marjorie was purely maternal. If she was kind to a young man it was because she felt sorry for him—sorry for his adorable clumsiness, his transparency, his helplessness, his lack of finesse. Young men, as a class, never gave her a thrill. She loved her own sex too, especially the self-conscious and foolish. Marjorie's main instinct at that time, and indeed through all her life, was to interpose her own beautiful and vigorous young personality between the weaker vessels of her acquaintance and the hard knocks of this world.

Thirdly, a strongly critical attitude towards the theory that children owe a debt of gratitude to their parents for the mere fact of having been brought by them into existence. Loyal she was, because it was her nature. Dutiful she was prepared to be. She was impulsively affectionate always; but her inborn sense of equity was strong. Moreover, for two years she had associated with new companions—members of another world than her own—either young girls of the English upper class, who were accustomed to regard their parents as amiable but unsophisticated accomplices in misdemeanour, or maidens from New York and Philadelphia, who appeared to entertain no opinion of their parents, as such, at all. This association had shaken to its foundation the law of her childhood—that children existed entirely for the convenience of their parents, and must expect no consideration, no indulgence, and, above all, no *camaraderie* from those aloof and exalted beings. In the spring of nineteen-fourteen Youth had not yet been called in to rescue Age from extinction.

Such was Marjorie at eighteen—a dangerous mixture, particularly liable to explode under compression.

She had risen early this Sunday morning in order to ramble through the woods and compose her turbulent spirit. The previous evening had witnessed a sleep-destroying interview between her father and herself. After prayers, while Mr. Clegg, according to his custom, was setting the markers in the great family Bible for the following morning's devotions, Marjorie had seated herself beside him at the head of the library table, with the air of one determined upon a plunge. She waited until the servants had filed out and the rest of the family were dispersed. Then she came to the attack with characteristic promptness.

"Father," she said, "may I go and be trained as a hospital nurse?"

"No," replied Mr. Clegg, without hesitation or heat; "you may not."

"May I learn shorthand and typewriting, then?"

"No."

"May I go and take training in some profession? Any kind," she added eagerly, "as long as it is useful."

"No," said Mr. Clegg for the third time. Then with the air of a just person patient under importunity:

"Why?"

"For two reasons," said the girl. "I want to be useful, and I want to be independent."

For answer, Mr. Clegg reopened the Bible, and with the accuracy of long practice came almost immediately upon what he wanted—certain illuminated manuscript pages occurring between the Old and New Testaments. There were six of these pages. Two were allotted to the Births, two to the Marriages, and two to the Deaths of the house of Clegg. Albert Clegg turned to the Births, and ran his finger down the list. There were quite a number of names, for the Bible was a family inheritance.

14

Presently he found what he wanted. A line in red ink had been drawn right across the page under the name of his youngest brother, Uncle Fred, to indicate the end of a generation. Below this line was written, in his own neat business hand:

Children of Albert and Mary Clegg.

This title-heading had erred on the side of plurality, for beneath it came but one entry—that of the birth of Albert's eldest son, Amos, at Gateshead, upon the tenth of March, Eighteen Ninety-two. A second heading followed immediately:

Children of Albert and Marjorie Clegg.

After this came quite a satisfying list. First, Joe's name—it proved to be Joshua, in full—recorded upon the twelfth of August, Eighteen Ninety-four. Then came the entry he was seeking:

Marjorie; born at "The Laburnums," Jesmond, April twenty-fourth, Eighteen Ninety-Six.

Albert Clegg surveyed his daughter over the top of his spectacles, which had been assumed for purposes of perusal, and performed a small exercise in mental arithmetic.

"That makes you eighteen," he observed.

Marjorie nodded. At this point, to her intense annoyance, the egregious Uncle Fred re-entered the room and joined the Board.

"Girls of eighteen—" began her father.

"Young ladies of eighteen," amended the Member of Parliament.

"—have no call to be independent," continued Albert Clegg; "and if they want to be of some use they can stay at home and help their mothers, as God meant them to."

"Mother," riposted Marjorie, "has more servants than she knows what to do with, and she hates interference with her house management, anyway. I have been home now for three months, honestly trying to help, and there isn't a single thing for me to do. There are hundreds of things I can do away from here. I do not ask to go out and do them now, but I do ask to be trained in something useful, so that when the time comes—"

"When what time comes?" asked her father quickly.

"The time when it will be a living impossibility for me to stick it out any longer," said Marjorie frankly. "Do you think I can sit here for ever"—with one comprehensive gesture she summarised Netherby, with its stodgy gentility, its squirrel-cage routine, and its cast-iron piety—"twiddling my thumbs? Every girl has a *right* to make herself efficient, nowadays."

"What comes before our rights," said Albert Clegg, "is our duty—our grateful duty to the parents that brought us up."

"*Honour thy father and thy mother*," chaunted the apposite Uncle Fred, "*that thy days—*"

Marjorie sat up.

"I hope I do honour my father and mother," she said. "I am fond of them both: they have been kind to me all my life. But I do not see why I should be particularly grateful to them for bringing me up. After all"—turning to her father—"you *had* to, hadn't you? You were responsible for my being here, weren't you? It seems to me that parents owe a debt to their children—not children to their parents!"

This amazingly audacious deliverance—and one had to be familiar with the Clegg tradition to realise how audacious it was—produced a stunning silence. Uncle Fred, fumbling in his repertoire for something really commensurate, breathed alarmingly. Presently Albert Clegg's heavy voice broke in:

"A debt? You mean I owe *you* a—a debt of gratitude?"

"Not gratitude," replied Marjorie. "Something bigger—honour. I think that parents owe it to their children, having brought them into the world—and all that sort of thing," she added a little shyly, "to give them a chance to live the sort of life that appeals to them."

Uncle Fred was ready now.

"The French," he announced, "are a giddy and godless race!"

But neither Albert Clegg nor his daughter took any notice. Wide apart as their natures lay, they had one point in common—inflexible determination. Clegg surveyed Marjorie's curving lips and hot blue eyes for a moment, and asked:

"So you want to live your own life, eh?"

Marjorie nodded.

"Yes," she said. "At least, I don't want to rush off and live it right away; but I do think I ought to be given sufficient—" she hesitated for a word.

"Equipment?" suggested her father.

"Rope?" amended Uncle Fred.

Marjorie nodded to her father again.

"Yes," she said, "sufficient equipment. A girl ought to be capable of doing something. I have told you some of the things a girl might learn to do, but there are lots of others. Even if she could support herself on the Stage it would be something."

"The Stage?"

Marjorie had exploded a bombshell this time. Uncle Fred's goat-beard dropped upon his shirt front, and waggled helplessly. Albert Clegg gazed at his daughter long and fixedly. Then he pulled the Bible towards him again, and turned back a page or two in the family record. He twisted the great volume round, and pushed it in his daughter's direction and pointed.

"Look at that," he said.

Marjorie looked. Upon the page of births, near the bottom of the list of her father's brothers and sisters, she saw a horizontal black strip—perhaps a quarter of an inch high—extending the full width of the page, where an entry in the record had been crossed out again, and again, and again, by a thick quill pen. She had seen it before, and had asked what it meant—without success. Now apparently she was to know.

"That," said Albert Clegg, "was my youngest sister."

"Your Aunt Eliza," added Uncle Fred.

"When she was nineteen," continued Clegg, "she ran away from home—to go on the Stage."

"Hoo! Where?" asked Marjorie, intensely interested.

"London, my father thought; but he never enquired."

"He never—? You mean—?"

"He blotted her name out of the Book, and it was never mentioned in our home again."

"And not one of you ever tried to find what had become of her?"

"Certainly not."

Marjorie looked up at her father and drew a long and indignant breath.

"Well—!" she began.

"And now," explained Uncle Fred, "it's coming out in you, my girl."

What was coming out Marjorie did not trouble him to explain. It is doubtful if she heard him at all.

16

"You mean to say," she said hotly to her father, "that your father let his own daughter go right out of sight and mind, just like that?"

"He did. And I want to say to you, my daughter, that I think he was right. This life is a preparation for the next. As we live now, so shall we be rewarded hereafter. A few years' empty pleasure and excitement are a poor exchange for an eternity of punishment."

"That's right! Take no risks!" recommended the sage at the other end of the table. "Safety first!"

"The wisest life," concluded Mr. Clegg, "is the safe life. The safe life is the Christian life, and the sure foundation of the Christian life is family life—united, wisely controlled, family life. So you will stay at home and live that life; and some day you will be grateful. Now go to bed. I appreciate your honesty in telling me what is in your mind, but my advice to you is forget all about it. Good-night!"

"Don't forget your prayers!" added Uncle Fred.

III

Marjorie finished her breakfast without further flippancy, and in due course the family set out for church in the Rolls-Royce. That is to say, Mr. and Mrs. Clegg, Uncle Fred, Marjorie, and the younger children—Miss Amy, already mentioned, and Masters James and John, aged ten and eight—were packed into that spacious vehicle and driven into Craigfoot, with meticulous observation of the speed limit and all the windows up. Amos and Joe followed in the two-seater. The servants had the waggonette.

The parish kirk at Craigfoot has already been described in some detail, but it may be worth while to record a few observations made from a different angle.

From her seat against the wall in the high-curtained Netherby pew Marjorie could see nothing but the last few rows of the public gallery and the Baronrigg balcony. The latter fascinated her, for it was always full—usually of interesting, and always of different, people. Sir Thomas Birnie himself was a permanent figure. He sat in the left-hand corner of the balcony, at the end nearest the pulpit. Consequently, his severe gaze, concentrated upon the preacher, was averted from the other occupants of the pew—a circumstance particularly agreeable to some of the younger members of his numerous house parties. What fun they seemed to have among themselves! How they giggled and whispered! Marjorie longed and longed to be with them and of them, especially the girls of her own age. They were so pretty, so overflowing with life, and dressed so exactly right. For three months, ever since she came back from Paris to find her family at Netherby, and the comfortable hospitality of a Newcastle suburb exchanged for the frigid waiting-list of a county society where one knew either everybody or nobody, she had taken weekly notes of the ever-changing kaleidoscope in the Baronrigg pew—studying faces, studying frocks, studying characters, and weaving histories round each.

Some of the faces were quite familiar. This morning, for instance, in the right-hand corner of the front row, sat Major Laing. He was a frequent visitor at Baronrigg, and was a widower. Marjorie knew that his wife had been a twin-sister of the late Lady Birnie. Then there were Captain and Mrs. Roper. Captain Roper owned horses, and was here—in fact, the whole house-party was here—for the Castleton Races, the largest meeting on this side of the Border. They were constant visitors. Then there was a pretty little woman in a big hat—Mrs. Pomeroy, really—of which Marjorie took mental and quite unsabbatical note. There was Arthur Langley, one of the best-known gentlemen riders in England. There was a tall girl with fair hair—not unlike Marjorie herself. Marjorie decided that this girl was dressed not quite right. She would have been better placed in a fashionable West-end church in London than in this grey, prim, Presbyterian conventicle. Probably her first visit, Marjorie decided. She would know better next time.

Her shrewd gaze passed on.

And then, for the first time in her life, she saw Roy Birnie, home after four months of toil and tribulation at an army crammer's. He had been plucked out of Eton at Christmas to that end, Eton having decided that it was a case for desperate measures. Three months of intensive brain-culture had not affected his appearance, which was healthy, nor his snub nose, nor his cheerful grin, nor the slight curl in his hair, of which his mother had once been so proud and of which he was still so ashamed. He sat on the left of Major Laing, his chin resting on the pew ledge, his grey eyes devoutly closed, and his ebullient spirits throttled down until it should please Doctor Chirnside to conclude the first prayer. He was exactly like hundreds of other clean-run Public School boys of eighteen. Marjorie had observed a dozen such in that very pew during the past three months. But, as already noted, she had never seen Roy.

That usually dependable organ, her heart, missed a couple of beats, and she lowered her head quickly.

Presently, impelled by a power greater than herself (or, indeed, than any of us), she lifted her head and looked up—only to find that Roy was gazing straight down upon her.

For the moment her eyes were interlocked with his. Then suddenly she became aware of the expression upon his face. The result has already been described.

That evening, after prayers, her father motioned to her to stay behind. When they were alone, he said:

"I hope you have given up that idea of yours about going away."

"Well," replied his daughter pleasantly, "I have postponed it, anyhow, father."

"You have decided wisely for yourself," said Mr. Clegg.

Marjorie felt inclined to agree. But it is just possible that the matter had been decided for her.

CHAPTER III

DER TAG

I

I suppose I may be forgiven for having felt a trifle preoccupied upon the first of August, nineteen-fourteen. Most people did. But the European situation, desperate though it was, was not sufficiently desperate to excuse me for forgetting that the first Saturday in August is the inexorable date of Lady Christina's annual garden party at Buckholm. So I blundered right into it.

I am a methodical person, and I like to do the same things at the same seasons. When it comes to revisiting the place of my birth, marriage and, I hope, interment, I make a practice of going to Baronrigg for Easter, Buckholm for the August cricket week, and The Heughs for the woodcock. On this particular occasion I had travelled from King's Cross by the early morning express—it leaves at five o'clock, and is the best train in the day, if only people knew about it—with the result that by four o'clock in the afternoon I found myself rumbling along in the Craigfoot station fly, in lovely, summer weather, *en route* for the Buckholm cricket week. Lady Christina, whose foes—and their name is legion, for they are many—accuse her of parsimony, does not usually send the motor to the station to meet unencumbered males. She expects such guests to cover the last stage of the journey at their own charges and, in addition, to share the conveyance with such parcels and oddments as may be lying in the station office consigned to Buckholm.

On this occasion Mr. Turnbull, the station master, apologetically packed me into the fly in company with half a sheep and three bright new zinc buckets, freshly arrived from the stores in Edinburgh.

In addition to my personal luggage, I was laden with a limp, damp package, smelling to heaven of fish, which had borne me noisome company all the way from my flat in

18

Jermyn Street, having been delivered there by an accomplice of Lady Christina's the night before my departure, with the information that her ladyship had signified my willingness to convey it to Buckholm.

But things might have been worse. Lady Christina had played this fish trick upon me last year as well. (It is one of her most cherished economies.) On that occasion the fish was delivered at my flat five minutes after I had left for Scotland. It was marked "Very Important"; so the lift boy, a conscientious but unimaginative youth, sent for the pass-key and carefully deposited the package in my hall cupboard. I found it there, quite safe, when I returned from Scotland, three weeks later.

The first warning that all was not well came to me when my equipage drew up, to a symphonic accompaniment of rattling buckets, at the lodge gates of Buckholm. These were held, like the bridge across the Tiber upon a famous occasion, by a resolute trio composed of Mackellar, the under-gardener, and Mesdames Elspeth and Maggie Mackellar, Mackellar's daughters, aged about fourteen. Horatius Codes (Mackellar) informed me that by her ladyship's orders it was "hauf-a-croon to get in," adding (quite incomprehensibly at the moment) that it was "on account of the Feet for Charity."

My contention that, as a guest, I was entitled to exemption, or, at least, abatement of entrance fee, was overruled by a dour but respectful majority of three to one. I handed Horatius Codes a reluctant half-crown; Herminius and Spurius Lartius threw open the gates, and the experienced animal between the shafts, unusually braced by the eerie combination of sounds and smells conveyed to his senses by a following breeze, delivered me at the front door, with much spurting of gravel, four minutes later.

My worst fears were realised. Dotted about the wide lawns stood bazaar-stalls, under striped awnings. The band of our Third Battalion from the Depot was making music on the terrace, and fair women and brave men drifted here and there, shying nervously at the stalls. Too late, I understood Mackellar's reference to the "Feet for Charity." I had heard from afar of the existence of this recurrent and gruesome festival for many years. No one knew why it was held, or to what charity Lady Christina devoted the proceeds. I once asked Lord Eskerley if he could tell me. He replied that so far as he was aware it was a charity which was not puffed up, and began at home. But Lord Eskerley is a cynical old gentleman, and has been at war with Lady Christina for forty years.

A sympathetic butler received me and showed me my room. The ceremony was purely formal: I knew the room almost as well as I knew him.

"It will go on until ten o'clock, sir," he announced mournfully, in reply to my anxious query. "The present company will leave about seven; but the townspeople begin to arrive then, when the admission fee is reduced to sixpence. Are we going to have a flare-up, sir?"

"No. What's the use? We shall take it lying down, Bates, as usual. You know Lady Christina!"

"I was referring, sir, to the European situation."

"Oh, sorry! Yes, it looks like it. If Germany joins Austria against Russia, France is bound to come in on the side of Russia; and if France comes in I fancy we shall all come in. And then God knows what will happen! Is there much excitement down here?"

"Very little at present, sir—less than when the South African War was imminent. But I understand that all the officers at the Depot are being recalled from leave. You will find several of them here, sir."

"Mr. Eric is here, of course?"

"For the afternoon, sir, yes. But he sleeps at the Depot now. He is very busy. You will change into flannels, I suppose?"

"Yes."

"It will fill out the time a bit, sir, before you need go outside. Her Ladyship is not aware of your arrival. Shall I bring you a whisky and soda?"

"Please."

By judicious dawdling I staved off the moment of my entrance into the "Feet" for another half-hour. Then, fortified by Bates's timely refreshment, I went downstairs to search for my hostess.

The garden was full of people—sirens in lace caps proffering useless articles of merchandise; officers from the Depot; boys and girls just home for the holidays; local dames talking scandal in deck-chairs. Upon the distant croquet lawn I beheld my hostess engaged in battle. I could hear her quite easily, shouting: "Now then—no treachery, no treachery!" to her partner, a nervous subaltern who was furtively offering advice to a pretty opponent. I remembered Bates's hint, also a maxim to the effect that what is not missed is not mourned. Perhaps it would be wiser—

"Yes, I would if I were you," remarked a raven's voice at my elbow. "She hasn't seen you yet!"

Lord Eskerley is a very remarkable old gentleman, with certain pronounced and rather alarming characteristics. In the first place, he has an uncanny knack of reading one's thoughts, which enables him to begin a conversation without wasting time over preliminaries, which he hates. Secondly, he has a peculiar habit of side-tracking a subject right in the middle of a sentence, sometimes because he is overtaken by a reverie, sometimes because another subject occurs to him—to return sooner or later, but always without warning, to the original topic—like brackets in algebra. I once met him coming out of Brooks's Club, and accompanied him down St. James's Street.

"Just been to a funeral," he announced; and forthwith subsided into a brown study.

I offered a few appropriate observations regarding the uncertainty of human life, and then proceeded to the political situation. He replied with his usual incisiveness. Ten minutes later, as we passed through the Horse Guards into Whitehall, he stopped abruptly, shook me by the hand, and said:

"Good-bye! At Woking. We cremated him. Very interesting!"—and set off at a brisk walk in the direction of the Houses of Parliament.

These conversational acrobatics call for considerable agility on the part of the listener. The strain is increased by the circumstance that, owing to his uncanny powers of memory, Lord Eskerley is able (and usually proceeds) to take up a conversation with you exactly where he left it off, sometimes after an interval of months. I was once walking in the Park on Sunday morning with Lady Christina, whom I had encountered for my sins after church. Near the Achilles statue I was aware of Lord Eskerley, plunged in profound meditation. Suddenly he looked up and saw me. He hurried forward and shook hands, utterly ignoring Lady Christina.

"Courvoisier," he said, "not Martell!"—and departed towards Stanhope Gate.

"What does the demented creature mean?" inquired Lady Christina.

I was able to explain that His Lordship had merely been unburdening himself of a name which he had been unable to recall at the time of our last conversation. Criminology is one of his numerous hobbies, and on this occasion he had been trying to tell me the name of one of the last murderers publicly hanged in England. (Thackeray went to see it.) All he could recall, however, was that the murderer had been a valet in Park Lane, and that his name had suggested liqueur brandy.

Decidedly he is a character. But he is a Pillar of State for all that, and, unlike some Pillars of State, he has done the State some service. He likes me, because I catch his references more quickly than most people.

"Well," I rejoined, "suppose you assist me to find cover?"

"Certainly!" he replied. "By the way"—extending a hand—"how do you do? Wonderful day! Now come and find a seat, and we will smoke."

We doubled a promontory of rhododendrons and sat down on a rustic bench, somewhat apart from the turmoil. The only person in sight was a girl, with very good ankles. (Eve always reproved me for beginning at that end.) She was standing fifty yards away from us, under the dappled shade of a copper-beech, surveying the scene—a little disconsolately, I thought. My companion, as usual, was ready with an appropriate but elliptic comment.

"Doesn't know he's here!" he observed.

"Why don't you tell her?" I asked.

"No need. They'll find one another all right."

"Who is she? And he?"

The question partly answered itself, for at that moment the girl turned in our direction, and I recognised her as the unexpected young beauty of the Netherby pew. Aware that two inquisitive dotards were leering at her, she withdrew out of sight. Lord Eskerley did not answer the rest of my question, because his thoughts had run ahead of the situation.

"There is something particularly cruel and brutal," he said, "about British snobbery. If this had been America, her hostess would have introduced her to every one in sight. (If she had not been prepared to do so, she would not have invited her at all.) On the Continent, young men would have led one another up, and clicked their heels together, and announced their names, with a view to a fair exchange. But here—well, she knows nobody, and every woman in the county will see to it that she continues to know nobody. Practically, that was why she was invited here. Tantalus, and so on!"

"I have often wondered," I said, "why we never go in for introducing. It would save much discomfort to rustic persons like myself."

"I'll tell you. Roughly, our attitude is this. There are only a certain number of people in this world who are anybody—Us, in fact. You are either one of Us, or you are not. If you are, obviously there is no need to introduce you. If you are not—well, an introduction would imply that you are not one of Us! So it is almost more insulting to introduce people than to ignore them. Very ingenious system: I wonder what woman invented it! Still, *she's* all right." (Apparently His Lordship had switched back to the girl again.) "She and her mother only get invited to Gather-'em-Alls and Charity Sales-of-Work, but most of the boys have managed to scrape acquaintance with her by this time. She fairly bowled them over at the Third Battalion Gymkhana a few weeks ago. Looked a picture; won first prize for the motor obstacle race; and fairly had to keep subalterns off with a stick! *And* at least one field officer!"

"You seem to have taken considerable notice of her," I observed.

"I take considerable notice of most things," replied the old gentleman complacently, "even pretty girls. By the way, we are going to fight them."

"The girls?"

"God forbid! Germany!"

"Oh!"

"Yes. I go back to town to-night. There seems little doubt now that we shall come in. We can't leave France in the lurch. For one thing, we should be skunks if we did"—

Pillars of State can be surprisingly colloquial in private life—"and for another, Germany means to gobble the whole of Europe this time, including this pacific little island of ours. It would be playing Germany's game to allow her to take us on one after another, instead of all together. Of course, the peace-at-any-price crowd are yowling; but—if we don't back our friends on this occasion, we can never hold up our heads again. It is just possible that the Germans may be fools enough to invade Belgium, in which case even the Cocoa Eaters and the Intellectuals will have to stop supporting them. But I think we shall fight anyhow. It will be a short war, but it will be the bloodiest war ever fought."

"Why do you think it will be short?"

"Because it will be so expensive in money and men that no country will be able to stand the racket for longer than a few months. Modern weapons are so destructive, and modern warfare costs so much, that before we know where we are one side will all be dead and the other side bankrupt; so we shall *have* to stop! The South African affair cost us a quarter of a million a day, while it lasted. This enterprise may run us into two, or even three millions. Think of that! Twenty millions a week! A thousand millions a year! We can't do it! Neither can France! Neither can Germany! No, it will be a short war. I am bound to admit K. of K. doesn't agree with me. He puts it at three years. I lunched with him two days ago. He was getting ready to go back to Egypt then—sorely against the grain, naturally; but it did not seem to have occurred to anybody to tell him to hold back for a week or two. We can't allow him to go out of the country at present; the thing's preposterous! Let me see, where was I?"

"Lunching with K."

"Oh, yes. He said three years. I asked why, and he replied that before this war finished every single able-bodied man of the combatant nations would be fighting in a national army, and it would take three years for this country to put its full strength into the field. But of course K. doesn't understand economic conditions. He's our greatest soldier, but not an economist. Still, that's K.'s view. I don't agree with it, but it's K.'s view. And if we go to war, K. will probably lead us; so we must expect to provide for war on K.'s scale."

All this was sufficiently stunning and bewildering in its suddenness and immensity; but it aroused my professional instincts.

"How is K. going to set about creating such an army?" I asked. "Raise supplementary Regular battalions; expand the Territorial establishment; or what?"

"I don't think he knows himself. In fact, he said so, quite frankly. In the first place, he hasn't been invited to help, as yet. In the second, he has been absent from England for the best part of fourteen years, and has not been able to keep himself conversant with the recent orgy of Army reform. He knew that the old Militia had been scrapped, but I found he was not sure whether its place had been taken by the Special Reserve or the National Reserve. And, of course, like all Regulars, he regards the Territorials with the utmost distrust. I think he shares the general soldier-man's opinion that the 'Terriers' are the old Saturday afternoon crowd with a new label. His idea seems to be to take no risks with amateur organisations, but to create a *pukka* new professional army on regular lines. He's wrong. He should take the present Territorial Army as a nucleus, and expand from that. The Territorial Associations are a most capable lot, and would build up big units for him in no time. Still, whatever way he does it, he will do it well; he's our great man. And he will need all his greatness. Germany means to smash us this time. She has been calling up her reservists, on the quiet, for the last six months. Her intelligence people have told her that we are all so tied up with the Suffragettes and Ireland that we *can't* come in, and that if we do, we cannot put up anything of a fight. I am almost tempted to believe Germany is right. I don't suppose we have a thousand spare rifles in the country. As for artillery—it takes three *years* to make a gunner! How on earth—"

"Now, then, what are you two absurd creatures conspiring about?" Our hostess was upon us brandishing a croquet-mallet. We rose hurriedly. "Alan Laing, how do you do? Why didn't you come and tell me you had arrived? As for you, Eskerley, I think you are getting into your second childhood. What's all this nonsense I hear about war with Germany? Why, I have a signed photograph of the Emperor in my drawing-room! How can one make war on people like that? And yet there you sit, talking about the thing as if it were really possible, and disorganising my *fête champêtre* by mobilising all my young men! Come and play croquet!"

Croquet with Lady Christina resembles nothing so much as croquet with the Queen in "Alice in Wonderland." It is true that she does not order our heads to be chopped off, but one sometimes wishes she would, and be done with it. Her success at the game—and she is invariably successful—is due partly to the nervous paralysis of her opponents, and partly to the uncanny property possessed by her ball of removing itself, while its owner is engaged in altercation, to a position exactly opposite its hoop. I bent my steps dutifully towards the lawn, leaving Lord Eskerley, who fears no one, not even Lady Christina, to fight a spirited rearguard action with that worthy opponent.

On the way I encountered Eric Bethune, my friend. It always thrills me, even at my sober age, to encounter Eric suddenly. I have never got over my boyish tendency to hero-worship. We shook hands.

"Come along the Green Walk with me," he said. "My car is waiting at the West Lodge; I have to fly back to my orderly room."

"We seem to be fairly for it, this time," I said, as we strode along the avenue of grass.

Eric threw up his handsome head exultantly. The sloping sunlight caught his clean-cut profile and sinewy throat.

"Yes," he said; "we're for it! The Fleet has been ordered not to disperse after Manoeuvres. The Army is mobilising. We are going to have at them at last! It's 'Der Tag,' all right! You are coming back to us, I suppose, Alan?"

"If they will have me," I said.

"Have you? They'll jump at you! They'll give you a battalion! We shall all get battalions! Brigades, perhaps!" He laughed joyfully, like a schoolboy who sees his first eleven colours ahead. "There will be promotions all round—"

"In a month or two," I said soberly, "there will be a lot more."

"Oh, I don't know," replied Eric. "We may finish Fritz off in one big battle. The German soldier is a machine: so is his officer. The whole German Army is a machine."

"A damned efficient machine, too!" I observed.

"Yes, boy; but cumbrous, cumbrous! If we let it get into its swing, it will be hard to stop. But we won't. The little British Army—and mind you, as a result of its South African lessons, it is the best trained, the best led, and the finest body of men that we have ever put into the field in all our history—will get the first move on, and it will chuck itself, like a flinty little pebble, plumb in the middle of the German machinery, and put all its gadgets out of gear! After that, the German, with his entire lack of initiative, will go to pieces, and we'll eat him up!"

Eric's old Scottish nurse was accustomed to say of him that he was "aye up in the cloods or doon in the midden." There was no mistaking his whereabouts to-day. I began to feel the thrill too.

"Are you going back to the First Battalion?" I asked.

"No word of it as yet. My orders are to stay here and perfect mobilisation arrangements. The moment the word goes out from the jolly old War Office, we shall be swamped with reservists: we may have to start a recruiting station as well. Great work! Great work! So long, old son! Run home and polish your buttons!"

He leaped into his car, and disappeared in a cloud of dust—a most characteristic embodiment of the spirit that was flaming in the hearts of all the youth of England and Scotland during that hectic, unforgettable, blissfully ignorant week.

I walked slowly back down the Green Walk, prepared to serve my sentence on the croquet lawn. It was a perfect summer evening. Not a leaf stirred: not a bird chirruped. The shadow of my somewhat square and stocky person preceded me, flatteringly elongated and attenuated by the rays of the setting sun. Deep and abiding peace seemed to brood upon the land. Yet all the land, I knew, was making ready for battle. Well, for my part, I was satisfied. I was a soldier, a widow man, and a childless man. I had no farewells to make, no last embraces—

From among the trees on my right I was conscious of a flutter of white, and a murmur of voices. A man and a woman—no, no, in those days one still talked of boys and girls— were seated side by side on a fallen tree-trunk, with their backs to me. They did not appear to be concerning themselves with war, or strife, or hostilities of any kind. Their present relation, though decorous enough, appeared to be one of most cordial agreement. I recognised them both, and passed on discreetly, silently acknowledging the prescience of that aged but perspicacious student of humanity, my Lord of Eskerley.

"They appear to have found one another all right!" I said to myself.

CHAPTER IV

A TRYST

I

Marjorie lay prone among the bracken in Craigfoot Wood, with her chin resting on her hands, and her insteps drumming restlessly upon the cool earth. Below her ran the road. To her left, beyond the wooded ridge which gave its name to Baronrigg, lay Craigfoot, nestling, like most small Lowland townships, in its own private valley. To her right, out of sight a mile away, ran the branch line of the railway which served that district, and which had furnished material to local humourists for a generation.

By the roadside, on the edge of the wood, stood the two-seater car which was accustomed to carry the overflow of the Clegg family to church on Sundays, and which Marjorie liked to pretend was her own special property. She was never so happy as when her arms were up to the elbows in gear-box grease. There was a good deal of the elemental small boy about Miss Marjorie.

It was four o'clock in the afternoon, and the month was once more August. The war which was to have been over in a few furious weeks had now been in progress for twelve months. The memory of the nightmare campaign of the first winter in Flanders had crystallised into a national epic. And now Kitchener's Army, having characteristically survived that chaotic but inevitable experiment in improvisation, its preliminary training at home during one of the worst and wettest winters ever known in England, had gone abroad. Here it had graduated, with first class honours in endurance and cheerfulness, during a season of trench warfare on the Western Front; and was now bracing itself, with incorrigible optimism, for that heroic mess afterwards known as the Battle of Loos. Everywhere the war was consolidating its position. On land the Boche, in a determined effort to recoup himself for his losses on the Western swings by a profitable exploitation of the Eastern roundabouts, had just captured Warsaw; and Hindenburg and Ludendorff were gloriously smashing their way through Russian armies in which perhaps one man in ten possessed a rifle. At sea, the battles of the Falkland Islands and the Dogger Bank had confirmed the German High Seas Fleet in a policy of watchful waiting—not to be broken, save for the disconcerting experiment of Jutland, until the final abject excursion of surrender more than three years later. Submarines and Zeppelins were beginning to function. Yarmouth and Lowestoft had been bombed, with *éclat*. The *Lusitania* had gone down, with eleven hundred souls; and a certain giant in the Far West was beginning to come out of the ether administered by Teutonic anæsthetists.

At home, the country had settled into its stride; and everyone, in camp, tube, train, and tram, argued—Heavens! how they did argue!—by a simple exercise in simple proportion, that if a mere handful of British soldiers could hold back overwhelmingly superior numbers for a whole winter, what wouldn't we do to Germany when the new British Army found their feet and got busy with the big push which everybody—friend and foe, be it said—knew was coming in September? (The possibility that the enemy might have been unsportsmanlike enough to raise a few new armies of his own did not appear to have occurred to anybody in particular.) The life of the citizen was still fairly normal. Taxicabs were plentiful: theatrical business was booming. One could still buy practically all that the heart desired, provided one had the price. The days when everybody would have money, but there would be nothing to buy, were yet to come.

Marjorie's predominant emotion during the first six months of the war had been that of fierce resentment against having been born a girl. She felt helpless; and whenever Marjorie felt helpless it made her angry. (That was why she was so frequently angry with her father.) All round her the youth of her country were on fire, both boys and girls. Yet the boys were able to stream away to fight, while Marjorie, who was quite as brave, quite as vigorous, and infinitely more capable of leadership than many young men, was debarred by the accident of her sex from doing anything at all. In the year nineteen-fifteen the great conflict was still regarded as a man's war: the inevitability of mobilised womanhood had not yet been recognised. The accepted theory was that men must work and women must weep—for the duration.

The countryside was full of soldiers, in all stages of growth. Marjorie used to encounter whole columns of them, route marching—strange creatures, clothed in apparel which by no stretch of imagination could be described as uniform. But for all their fantastic blends of khaki and tweed, glengarry and billycock, Marjorie's heart warmed to them. They were so boisterous, so childlike, so absolutely certain of what was going to happen to the Boche when they got "oot there."

At their head, as often as not, rode Major Bethune. He and Marjorie had become acquainted under circumstances which will be recorded hereafter, and his punctilious salute never failed to thrill her. He was an inspiring figure, and conspicuously solitary in his present *entourage*. He alone was left of all the cheery, careless brotherhood who had pursued the unexacting peace-time existence of a regular soldier at the depot of the Royal Covenanters—the prop and mainstay of every covert-shoot and tennis-party in the county. They were all in France now. Many of them would never come back. But Eric Bethune remained, to lick recruits into shape—with astonishing speed and efficiency, be it said—and send them out, draft after draft, to stiffen the ever-thinning ranks of the First and Second Battalions. He hated being kept at home, and said so. Marjorie sympathised with him deeply, for she knew exactly how he felt. One day she told him so. After that, Eric took considerable notice of her. He had the simple vanity of a spoiled child, and reacted promptly to all those who took especially deferential notice of him.

The pair met here and there—at Buckholm, whither Marjorie was sometimes bidden with her mother to war relief committee meetings; at entertainments organised for the recruits; at crossroads, where Marjorie's two-seater was frequently hung up by columns of marching men. On these occasions they exchanged greetings—even confidences. Eric was more than twenty years Marjorie's senior—a circumstance which, if anything, heightened their attraction for one another. It gratified Eric hugely to find himself frankly admired by a young girl; while Marjorie, born hero-worshipper that she was, felt pleasantly thrilled at attracting the appreciative attention of a man so distinguished in his record and so much more important than herself. Also, Eric's great age—and to twenty, forty-three and infinity are very much the same thing—made him "safe." Fortunately for Eric's self-esteem, he did not know this.

They had small chance to become really intimate. There were few opportunities for social amenity in those days, and such as survived hardly covered Netherby at all. In that bleak household itself opinion on the war was sharply divided. Albert Clegg came of a stock which had been educated to regard war as a luxury of the upper classes. He believed that all wars were started by collusion between the "military oligarchy" and the armament firms. He maintained that no war had ever been fought which could not have been avoided. The sight of a uniform filled him with horror. He was eloquent—though not quite so fluent as Uncle Fred—upon the iniquity of placing what he called a "musket" upon the shoulder of a growing boy, and setting him for a period of three years to strengthen his body by martial exercises, when he might have been earning dividends for somebody. Finally, he said that the Germans were an industrious, peace-loving, musical nation, and that it was sinful to attack—by which it is to be presumed he meant resist—an army which was merely the involuntary instrument of despotism.

So when the British nation declined, by acclamation, to break faith with France and Belgium, Albert Clegg was sincerely depressed. Moreover, being deeply interested in shipping, he foresaw ruin for the overseas trade of the country. Even when the unforeseen happened; when, as the submarines began to take toll, the market value of tramp steamers shot up a thousand per cent., and freights soared out of sight altogether, he was not entirely comforted. According to his lights he was an honest man, and it was with a twinge of conscience that he found the war accumulating for him profits on a scale which not even a swelling income-tax could altogether moderate. But he compounded with his conscience in the end. He drew his profits, but he drew them under formal protest every time. As Pooh Bah once explained, "It revolts me, but I do it!"

Of the rest of the household, Mrs. Clegg for her part found the war almost pleasantly exhilarating. None of her kith and kin were participating in hostilities, which relieved her from such trifling cares as beset old Mrs. Couper, who was interested in the matter to the extent of five sons and fourteen grandsons; or Mrs. Gillespie, the banker's wife, who had contributed all she had, the *ci-devant* student of divinity, to the cause; or General Bothwell, whose son Jack had arrived in Flanders from India with his Pathans in early December, and had already met the almost inevitable end of a white officer who undertakes the conspicuous task of leading dusky troops into action under modern conditions; or Lord Eskerley, both of whose sons had died at Le Cateau. Bobby Laing, of The Heughs, nephew of our autobiographical Major, had been killed in the landing of the King's Own Scottish Borderers at Gallipoli. Neither of Mrs. Clegg's sons had exhibited any leaning towards what their father described as "this fashionable military nonsense," so Mrs. Clegg's mind was at rest. She left everything, quite cheerfully—like too many of her kind—to the Willing Horse.

Of course, she admitted, there was little going on socially. Still, it was gratifying to roll bandages or pack comfort-bags in company with countesses; and though there were flies in the ointment—in the shape of common persons like Mrs. Galbraith, the chemist's wife, and the Misses Peabody, included in the same gathering by the caste-destroying processes of wartime—there were consolations. Netherby itself, with its spacious accommodation for meetings and committees, was a card which only great social strongholds like Buckholm and Baronrigg could overtrump.

It has been noted that Amos and Joshua Clegg had betrayed no disposition to join up. But while Amos in this matter followed his undoubted inclinations, Joe was restrained only by the bonds of parental discipline. For one thing, Joe was a Public-School boy, and

Amos was not. Joe's school had only been a small establishment in the North of England, but in nineteen-fourteen its little Officers' Training Corps had contributed its full quota of young men. To Amos, Public Schools (to quote his father) were places where boys learned "to take care of their H's and despise their parents": to his younger brother the Public-School tradition was the ark and covenant, not to be lightly profaned by parental sneers or fraternal failure to understand. So Joe kept his own counsel, and ate his dour young Northumbrian heart out for twelve sickening months.

The climax had come that very morning, with the arrival, for Joe, of a circular from his old school, requesting that he would "be so kind as to fill up the enclosed form" with certain specific information regarding his military service, for inclusion in the School Roll of Honour—his rank, his unit, mentions in dispatches, and the like. There was no alternative column to fill in; no comfortable loophole labelled "Civilian war work of national importance"—nothing of that kind at all: nothing but a stark request for poor Joe's military status and record. It had not occurred to the editors that any Old Boy could, in these days, be elsewhere than in khaki.

Consequently, Marjorie had found Joe after breakfast, with his head in his arms, crying like a child in a corner of the unfrequented and cheerless Netherby smoking-room. (Albert Clegg did not smoke.) After comforting him in the only fashion she knew—and a very acceptable fashion any young man but a brother would have considered it—she made up her mind on the spot to accept a certain sentimental invitation somewhat shyly offered by Roy Birnie, and laughingly refused by herself, two days previously. That was why she was now lying in the bracken on the edge of Craigfoot Wood, gazing up the road to Baronrigg.

II

It was Roy's last day at home. At the outbreak of war, to his own intense indignation, he had been refused a commission. Many of his young friends, common civilians no older than himself, had been endowed with what they described as 'one pip' and set to command platoons all over the country. But Roy, as a prospective regular, had been despatched—the victim of a conspiracy in which he traced the hand of every person but the right one—to Sandhurst, where he was compelled to undergo an intensive education in the science of warfare, speculating grimly meanwhile as to the kind of mess his amateur supplanters were making of the British Expeditionary Force. Sometimes he woke at night in a cold sweat, having dreamed, as he had sometimes dreamed before a house match, that the war had come to an end before he had had his innings.

Now, at last, he was emancipated. He was a second lieutenant. He could wear a Sam Browne belt and look an A.P.M. right in the face—instead of hurriedly plunging down side streets to avoid that suspicious official's eye, as he had frequently done when up in London on leave with a crony, the pair of them decked in borrowed trappings to which a cadet's rank did not entitle them. He was an officer, holding the King's Commission; and, best of all, had been gazetted to the Second Battalion of the old regiment, of which his uncle, "Leathery Laing," was now second-in-command. He had completed his draft leave, and was to report at the Depot at six o'clock this Sunday evening, to take charge of a contingent bound overseas to reënforce the battalion at a point on the Western Front as yet unrevealed.

He had made his farewells—in the offhand, jocular fashion affected by our race in cases where the probability of return is more than doubtful. His father had shaken hands with him, and shaken his own head at the same time. Tom Birnie's heart was not in the war: he persisted in his belief that it was started by the Jingoes.

His friends—and Roy had friends in every walk of life—had loaded him with messages to fathers, brothers and sweethearts who were gone before into the pillar of cloud. Mr.

Gillespie, the bank manager, entrusted him with a small package (on behalf of Mesdames Spot and Plain), containing mysterious comforts for son Robert. Jamie Leslie, the organ-blower of the parish church, buttonholed him in the street.

"Mr. Roy," he said wistfully, "you'll tell the boys oot there that I have tried, and *tried*, for to get ower; but they winna hae me! It's because I'm no quite richt in the heid," he added, with a candour which might well have been imitated by others occupying more exalted official positions than his own. "You'll tell them? I wouldna like them for tae think—"

Roy supplied the necessary assurance, and passed on to receive a message from old Mrs. Rorison, whose son John, a giant of six feet four inches, had abandoned the service of the post office in order to join the Scots Guards.

"Tell oor John," said the old lady—it was universally assumed that Roy would encounter the entire Craigfoot contingent, regardless of rank or unit, immediately upon landing—"tae keep his heid doon in they trenches. I ken him! And dinna go keeking ower the top yourself, Mr. Roy!" This, on the whole, was the most practical valediction that Roy received.

Lord Eskerley's farewell was quite characteristic.

"Good-bye! Don't give away any military news when you write to her. It has done a lot of harm already."

There was no one left now to say good-bye to but Marjorie. Like the young sentimentalist that he was, Roy was reserving her for the last. He wanted to bid her farewell at the very final moment—and, if possible, clandestinely. There existed no obstacle whatever to his driving openly to Netherby and delivering his farewell speech on the hearthrug in the library, or among the raspberry-canes in the kitchen garden. But war sharpens our romantic appetites to a surprising degree. At the most ordinary times lovers are accustomed to bid one another good night with an expenditure of time and intensity which takes no account of the fact that they are going to meet again directly after breakfast to-morrow morning. How much more pardonable and ecstatic, then, must that exercise be when it really is good night—when it is more than probable that before the time for reunion comes round again, one of the participants may have blown out his little candle for good.

Roy's preference for surreptitious love-making was natural enough, for another reason. He was a member of the shyest and most self-conscious brotherhood in the world—the tribe of the less-than-twenty-one's. By rights he should not have been in love—matrimonially—at all. A healthy English Public-School boy of nineteen is not entitled to such emotions as inspired Master Roy and his friends in the year of grace nineteen-fifteen. His mind should be set—and in normal times almost invariably is set—upon his biceps muscle, or his first salmon, or his college rowing colours, or (at moments of periodic festivity) the acquisition of souvenirs, like policemen's helmets or door-knockers. Permanent association with one of the softer sex should be to him, for several years yet, a delightful unattainability. He matures late, does our young Briton, and premature responsibility as husband and father usually prevents him from ever developing into the man he was meant to be. But wise old Nature is always ready to modify her own laws in an emergency. In nineteen-fifteen people, especially young people, found their perspectives considerably foreshortened. It is no use taking long views about life at a time when life promises to be more than usually short. There is just one thing to do, and that is to reach out with both hands after such of life's gifts as are normally reserved, especially in this country of ours, for those of riper years.

So, engaged couples who in nineteen-fourteen had taken it as a matter of course that their wedding must be postponed until after the war, suddenly realised that there might be no after the war for one of them, and incontinently got married. Boys and girls whose sentimental exercises in normal times would have been limited to sitting out dances behind a screen in the Christmas holidays not only became engaged, but usually plunged into matrimony a few weeks later. They were governed by forces which they did not entirely comprehend, and which few of them would have been capable of resisting if they had. They had no idea how they were going to live after the war; but they married all the same. It was essentially a case where the morrow must take thought for itself. They capitalised all their stock, both of money and of youth, these happy young gamblers, and lived ecstatically on that capital, stoically resigned to the probability that before it was exhausted their little partnership would have been dissolved. And in too many cases, poor souls, they were justified in their expectations. But who shall say that they were wrong, or improvident, to do as they did? Prudence, perhaps; commonsense, possibly. But not nature, nor patriotism, nor romance, nor the spirit of adventure.

It is not to be supposed that our impetuous Roy had reasoned out these matters with any degree of profundity. All he knew was that he had loved that glorious girl, Marjorie Clegg, from the moment he had first seen her in Craigfoot parish church a year and a half ago; and that now he was called upon to go away and relinquish even his present scanty opportunities of seeing her. Moreover, his battalion had got through twenty-three second lieutenants in the last ten months. One, obvious, course was indicated; but it was a big step for a reserved schoolboy of nineteen. To tell Marjorie, *tout court*, that he loved her frightened him—far more than any statistics about second lieutenants. If it had been peace-time he would have followed the natural path of a boy who falls in love with a girl of his own age. He would have decided to grow up, and become an eligible *parti* at the earliest possible moment. He might, possibly, have declared himself, and invited his beloved to "wait for him." It is within the bounds of probability that the damsel would have promised to do so. The *affaire* would then have proceeded on its innocuous course—spasmodically enough, owing to the interposition of such things as University terms, regimental duties, or vulgar office hours—to its normal end. That is to say, the girl would probably have met and married some one really eligible a few years older than herself, leaving it to the hand of Time to heal the wounds of her late cavalier and unite him in due course to another really eligible girl some years younger than himself, recently the property of a shaveling of nineteen.

But this was not peace-time. The country was at war, and for reasons already indicated waiting and seeing had gone out of fashion. The watchword of the moment, whether applied to munitions or matrimony, was, "Do It Now!" No wonder that Roy felt his heart leap to his throat as the Baronrigg car, conveying him to the Depot seven miles away, surmounted the last crest on the undulating road, and revealed to him Marjorie's two-seater standing in the hollow below, under the lee of Craigfoot Wood. For all her preliminary refusal and offhand acceptance, Marjorie had kept tryst.

CHAPTER V

THE INEVITABLE

Marjorie stood on the bank above the road, knee-deep in bracken. The Baronrigg chauffeur, an elderly gentleman with that perfect repose of manner which is given only to such members of the tribe as are promoted coachmen, drew up beside the two-seater. Roy jumped out and saluted with great smartness. He was in uniform, and was hung about with that warlike paraphernalia professionally known as "the whole Christmas Tree." Having disencumbered himself of this, he threw it into the car, climbed the bank, and joined his lady. His heart bumped.

"You do look nice," said Marjorie. "But what is the matter with your buttons?"

"I have painted them with some black stuff," replied Roy. "Quite the thing—not swank! It is always done on active service: otherwise my twinkling little buttons might attract the eye of vigilant Boche." He took her arm, a little feverishly. "What about a stroll in the shades of the forest? What about it, what?"

This was not the way in which Roy had intended to begin the interview. Upon such occasions of stress no man knows what humiliating tricks self-consciousness may not play upon him. But Marjorie, of the superior sex, appeared quite unruffled.

"All right," she said cheerfully; "come along! I am so glad you are here."

"Are you, Marjorie?" exclaimed Roy, much encouraged.

"Yes. I want to consult you about something."

Roy drew back an overhanging branch.

"Step inside the consulting room!" he suggested.

Marjorie seated herself upon a ledge of rock in the snug nook which the branch had concealed. Roy lay down on the grass at her feet. There was silence. At last Marjorie said:

"When must you be at the Depot?"

"Six." Roy glanced at his new, luminous, dust-proof, non-breakable wrist-watch. "That gives me twenty minutes. What did you want to talk to me about, Marjorie?"

"About Joe."

"Oh!" There was a certain lack of enthusiasm about the interjection, but Marjorie did not notice it. Roy looked up at her. Her brow was puckered, and her eyes were troubled. She was very fond of brother Joe. Roy, resolutely disengaging his attention from the high lights in her hair, said gently:

"Tell me."

Marjorie blazed out suddenly.

"He can't stand it any longer! He has done his best to be patient, and obedient to father, and all that; but it's breaking his heart. Why, only this morning—"

She related the pitiful incident of the school circular and the Roll of Honour. There were tears in her eyes when she had finished.

"So," she concluded, "he has made up his mind to join up."

"Good egg!" observed Roy. "Is he going to apply for a commission, or what?"

"That was what I wanted to consult you about," said Marjorie. "You are so clever about these things, Roy."

"Fire away!" replied Roy, much inflated.

"Commissions," asked Marjorie—"can you get them easily?"

"Not so easily now. The authorities are beginning to sit up and take notice. The first lot of officers in the new armies were mostly all right. They didn't know much, but they were sahibs, who played the game and handled their men properly. Now they are getting used up, and some pretty strange fish have been given commissions lately. The voice of the T.G. is heard in the land. Here is a letter from my uncle, Alan Laing—our second-in-command. You know him?"

"No, but I have seen him."

Roy chuckled.

"Yes," he said, "and he has seen you; and you fairly knocked him flat! But never mind Uncle Alan now. He's a wicked old man, anyhow. About this T.G. business. Uncle Alan wrote to me the other day. He said that some of the officers lately sent out were about the stickiest crowd he had yet handled. Here's the letter."

Of course, among ourselves in the Mess, he read, we make allowances, and try to get the best out of them; for after all, most of them are plucky enough and efficient enough. Unfortunately, the rank-and-file, with the true British passion for inequality, do not share our democratic sentiments. They say, in effect: "This blankety blighter is no better than we are. Why should we salute him, or obey him, or follow him?" The T.G. too often confirms his own sentence; I caught one of my subalterns trying to stand a corporal a drink the other day. I hear they are going to start officers' schools soon. The sooner the better!

"Of course," said Marjorie, flying, woman-like, to the personal application of the subject, "Joe wouldn't behave like that."

"Good Lord, no! Of course he wouldn't," said Roy.

"Amos probably would, though," added honest Marjorie. "He has never been to a proper school, so he has had no chance to have his Clegg manners improved. But we aren't troubling about Amos: it's Joe. Would they take him into a Cadet Officers' School, do you think?"

"I am sure they would," said Roy confidently. "Only, it might require a little time, you know."

"That's a drawback," replied Marjorie. "Once father knows what Joe is trying to do, his life at home won't be worth living. It'll be a fight all day long: he will be lectured, and badgered, and prayed over. I shouldn't wonder if they sent for Uncle Fred!"

A thought struck Roy.

"I say," he enquired, "how old is Joe?"

"Twenty."

"That hangs the crape on Joseph!" announced Roy—"for a year, at any rate. They won't give a commission to a minor without his father's consent." He wriggled. "Don't I know it! If they did, I'd have been in the show a year ago."

"In that case," said Marjorie, "we must fall back on our second plan."

"We?"

"I mean Joe and I."

"Oh, sorry. I was hoping you meant you and me! What is the plan?"

"It's a secret just now," said Marjorie. "Perhaps I'll tell you about it, when I write."

Roy looked up eagerly.

"You *will* write to me?" he said. "Often?"

"Of course I will!" said the girl. "It will be wonderful!"

What she meant was that it would be wonderful to have, in future, a personal interest in the British Expeditionary Force. As already indicated, the circle in which Marjorie had been born and bred was not very heavily represented in France—nor would be until conscription came. But now Roy would be there. She would have a personal outlet for her imagination, and a peg to hang her prayers on. Women hate abstract patriotism, as they hate all abstractions. Roy would supply the human, personal element, upon which a woman's visions must always be founded. Male orators might volley and thunder about the common cause and the redemption of civilization; but to most women the Great War and its issues were usually embodied in the person of a single undistinguished individual in a tin bowler.

Roy, of course, did not understand.

"How glorious of you to say that, Marjorie!" he exclaimed.

31

"You do not know," continued Marjorie rapturously, "how I have longed and longed to have some one to write to, and send parcels to, and everything—some one I really knew!—instead of a bundle of things to be distributed among a whole platoon!"

"And you are going to make me that particular person?" said Roy, joyfully.

"Rather! You see," explained Marjorie with fatal frankness, "I don't know anyone else. At least, I shan't, until Joe—"

Roy's face fell. "I thought there was a catch about it!" he said woefully.

"About what?"

"About what you said. I didn't understand that all you wanted was some one to write to; and any old thing would do—even me! I did hope, for a minute—"

Marjorie was all repentance at once.

"Oh!" she cried. "How hateful of me! Roy, I didn't mean it! What must you think of me? I must seem like a common little war-flapper. But I'm not, am I? Roy, you *know* I'm not! Will you forgive me?" She extended a hand impetuously.

It fired the train. Next moment Roy had caught it in both of his, and was kissing it rapturously.

"Marjorie—dear!" he murmured. He was kneeling before her now, with his arms crossed upon her knees. He looked up into her face, and suddenly realised what he was leaving behind. A great sob shook him. Perhaps the thought of the twenty-three second lieutenants had something to do with it. After all, he was only nineteen, and love and life were very sweet. His head sank on to his arms; his shoulders heaved.

There followed a brief interval of silence—perhaps three minutes. But within that interval something happened to Marjorie.

Presently a slim hand removed Roy's glengarry bonnet, and began to stroke his obstinately curly hair. Next, Roy was conscious of a warm splash, somewhere behind his right ear—followed by another, and another. Marjorie was shaking now. Roy looked up at her again, and the sight of her wet face suddenly braced him against his own weakness. He sprang up.

"You poor, poor, poor!" he said. "Let me—"

He produced a khaki handkerchief from his sleeve, and dried her eyes, Marjorie meekly submitting. After that, inevitably, he kissed her. It was not a very successful kiss: first kisses seldom are. Then he sat down upon the grass again with his head against her knee, and her hand against his cheek. He sighed, long and rapturously. Marjorie stroked his hair with her free hand. Children both, they were living through a moment for which others, less fortunate, have sometimes waited a lifetime, and which in no case ever comes to man or maid a second time.

Presently they began to talk, employing the two inevitable topics of the newly-betrothed—"When did it begin?" and, "Do you remember?"

They recalled their first glimpse of one another—that May morning in church, more than a year ago.

"Uncle Alan was very witty on the subject," said Master Roy. "Oh, most diverting! It's my belief the old ruffian was having a good one-time-look-see at you himself, and that was why he caught me at it. Well, I can't say I blame him!"

They wandered on to the second subject. Here they had much ground to cover.

They had not actually met until three weeks after the glimpse. During those weeks Roy religiously attended dances, tea-parties, political meetings, even a church soirée, in the hope of encountering his divinity; but in vain. Once he bought three numbered and reserved seats for an amateur theatrical entertainment in the Town Hall, and sent two of these to Netherby, "With the compliments of the committee." But Mrs. Clegg, knowing that her husband did not hold with theatrical entertainments, and that under no circumstances would she or the family be permitted to attend this one, had passed the tickets on to a more emancipated quarter, with the result that Roy witnessed the performance in the giggling company of two Netherby housemaids. He told the story to Marjorie now, and was rewarded with tears and laughter.

But they had met at last—at the local Hunt Steeplechases. Marjorie was present, privily, in the two-seater, with brother Joe. Roy had spied the pair from the regimental enclosure. He was due back at his crammer's in two days' time, and was a desperate man. Summoning his entire stock of audacity—it was considerable, but he needed it all—he left the enclosure, pushed his way through the crowd, and addressed himself to the male member of the rather forlorn couple standing by the rails.

"I say, sir, aren't you Mr. Clegg, of Netherby?"

Joe, quite unequal to the situation, murmured something inarticulate; but Marjorie came to the rescue.

"How do you do?" she said. "You are Mr. Birnie, aren't you?"

"Yes. We are your next-door neighbours—your nearest little playmates, in fact," replied Master Roy. (Netherby is some four or five miles from Baronrigg; but no matter.) "My father has been meaning to shoot cards on you for a long time. Meanwhile, would you care to come into the enclosure? Bracing air! Gravel soil! Commands a distant prospect of the Cheviot Hills, and so on! Highly recommended! Do come!" He waited breathlessly for her reply, fearful of having gone too far. But the invitation was accepted.

"What a moment!" he said. "*What* a moment!" He looked up at Marjorie again. "I was afraid you would turn me down, for cheek. You hesitated a bit, didn't you?"

Marjorie laughed, joyously.

"My dear, that was for manners! I wouldn't have let you go at that moment for anything in the world!" She played a gentle arpeggio on the brown cheek under her hand.

"By gum, I wish I had known that!" observed Roy, with sincerity.

Once inside the enclosure Marjorie created a profound sensation. It is true that not many of her own sex addressed themselves to her, but this omission was more than balanced by the *empressement* of the gentlemen.

First of all, naturally, she was introduced to the senior officer present—Major Eric Bethune, who, in the secret view of his subordinates, proceeded to take an unsportsmanlike and unduly prolonged advantage of his superior rank. Duty called him at last to the side of a lady of riper years. Thereafter, Marjorie, almost invisible for second lieutenants, was escorted about the course, shown the jumps, plied with tea, and invited to back horses at other people's expense. She had driven home in a dream, with her exhausted relative slumbering beside her.

After that a few mothers and sisters, hounded thereto by clamorous menkind, had left cards at Netherby. The calls had been duly returned, with the result that some of the sisters added themselves, quite voluntarily, to the ranks of the brothers. Marjorie possessed the supreme quality in a woman of being attractive to her own sex. Mrs. Clegg and her daughter began to be seen at subscription balls and the more comprehensive garden parties; presently at more intimate entertainments. In the end, Netherby usually received a card for any function that was going, always excepting such—formal dinner parties and the like—as necessitated inviting Albert Clegg.

"The girl is a peach," was the local verdict, "and mother does her best; but the old man merely suggests eternal punishment!"

And wherever Marjorie appeared—at ball, function, fête, bazaar, gymkhana, or tea-fight, Master Roy Birnie, home for good from the crammer's, was usually visible in respectful attendance.

Not that she had not other adherents. Even Major Bethune himself, the handsomest man and the most eligible *parti* in the county, did not consider it beneath his dignity to sit out a dance or two with the daughter of Albert Clegg. But Roy's devotion was marked by its unflagging and conscientious continuity. He was a regular visitor at Netherby. It was his habit to ride over every morning—usually about eleven, when the master of the house was engaged in transacting business in the library, mostly over the telephone to Newcastle—where he would play tennis, perform tricks on the billiard table, give the children riding-lessons, pick roses for Mrs. Clegg—do anything, in fact, which afforded him a reasonable excuse for remaining on the premises. Being British, and only eighteen, his passion had not declared itself in words; nor would have for many a day, but for the quickening influences already indicated. Even when the coming of war suddenly laid a man's responsibilities upon his young shoulders, and removed most of his rivals, real and imaginary, *en masse*, to the other side of the Channel, he did not look higher, for the present, than the foot of Marjorie's pedestal. His intention was to leave his lady perched upon the summit thereof for the duration; and then, if and when he returned safe and whole from castigating the Boche, to invite her to step down to earth and start, under his escort, upon the adventure of life. To do more at present struck him as unsportsmanlike. He would be forcing her hand unfairly; he would be taking a sentimental advantage of the military situation. But the last ten minutes had entirely upset his plan of operations. He had kissed Marjorie; Marjorie had indubitably kissed him back; and now they were sitting side by side in Craigfoot Wood, in an attitude which twelve months ago would have outraged both his susceptibilities and his sense of humour, facing the prospect of indefinite separation. What was the next step? What about it, what? Pending a decision, he saluted his lady afresh.

From the road below them came a respectful toot from the horn of the Craigfoot motor, suggestive of a faithful attendant coughing a discreet reminder behind his hand. Roy glanced at his watch, and rose to his feet with a heartrending sigh.

"Time to go!" he groaned.

He held out his hands to Marjorie, and raised her up. For a moment those two young people looked one another bravely in the face—for the last time, for aught they knew. They were very much of a height; Roy had the advantage of perhaps an inch. Then that direct young maiden, Marjorie, put both arms round Roy's neck.

"Good-bye, dear," she said. "Take care of yourself, and come back safe to me!"

"I'll come back," replied Roy stoutly, forgetting all about the twenty-three second lieutenants. He had no doubts about anything now. Then:

"Marjorie," he asked, "when will you marry me? As soon as the war is over?" He waited, expectant.

Marjorie's answer took the rather puzzling form of a little choking laugh, accompanied by two large tears.

"As soon as that?" she asked.

The young of the male species possesses no intuition.

"Yes," replied Roy earnestly, "just as soon! Or"—with the air of one conceding a point—"pretty soon after." He came closer. "Marjorie—will you?"

This time Marjorie smiled without any tears at all—a purely maternal smile.

"Leave it to me, little man!" she said.

Then she kissed him again, and sent him off to fight for her.

That night Joe Clegg crept downstairs, out of the house, and thence (per two-seater) to the railway junction twelve miles away. Here he caught the early morning train to London, where it was his intention to enlist. He was accompanied by his sister Marjorie, who, after a final and tempestuous debate with her father upon the subject of filial duty and feminine usefulness in war-time, had decided to burn her boats too, and enlist in the gallant sisterhood of those who were Really Trying to Help.

CHAPTER VI

SOLO

The lights sank low again, and a flickering announcement appeared upon the screen, to the effect that the next picture would be a further instalment of that absorbing serial, *The Marvels of Natural History*—upon this occasion, *Still Life in the Frog Pond*. The majority of the audience took the hint, rose to their feet, and shuffled out. But Marjorie stayed on. Some of us go to the pictures to see pictures, others to hold hands, others to sit down and rest. Marjorie belonged to the third class. Not even the prospect of a quarter-of-an-hour in a frog pond could induce her to concede to the management the chance of selling her seat once more before closing time. She sat on, in a tired reverie.

Marjorie had arrived in London three months ago, to find that overcrowded metropolis fairly evenly divided between two classes—the people who had taken up war work, and the people who were doing it. The chief difficulty of the latter was to push their way through the unyielding ranks of the former. Things righted themselves later, under the unsentimental *régime* of necessity; but in November, nineteen-fifteen, the road to victory was blocked with good intentions.

Having invaded London, Marjorie and Joe devoted two days to exploration. Marjorie had been in London twice before—going to and returning from school in Paris—her stay upon each occasion being limited to a single extremely domestic evening at Uncle Fred's house in Dulwich. This experience naturally qualified Marjorie (being Marjorie) for the role of guide and courier to that unsophisticated yokel, brother Joe. They put up at the Grand Hotel, because Marjorie considered Trafalgar Square a good *point d'appui*, and a difficult place to lose altogether even in the howling wilderness of Central London. They pooled their money. Marjorie had drawn the whole of the savings of her dress allowance—about one hundred pounds—from the custody of Mr. Gillespie shortly before the day of her departure, and Joe had a quarter's salary intact. They dined, went to the play, sat in the Park, lunched at the Carlton, and generally had their fling (but not of) a world composed entirely of elegantly dressed females and uniformed officers of every grade.

After keeping carnival for forty-eight hours, Marjorie conducted her brother to a recruiting office, where the authorities were unfeignedly glad to see him, business at that period being lamentably slack. There, having kissed him, she left him and returned to the Grand Hotel. At the end of half-an-hour she rose from her bed, dabbed her eyes with a cold sponge, sent for her bill, paid it with a bright smile, and removed herself and her effects to a self-contained flat near the Brompton Road. There she sat down to make a plan. She had several sketched out, but her choice depended, like so many other choices in this life, upon sordid financial considerations. If her allowance were continued, she could afford to do war work for love. If not, she must perforce do war work for money. So she wrote to her father, telling him frankly why she and Joe had left home, giving her new address, and concluding her letter:

So now you know where I am. If I don't hear from you I shall know that you don't intend to have anything more to do with me. But I hope I shall hear from you. Love. Marjorie.

35

Upon the question of her father's financial intentions she refrained from inquiry, for she knew full well what the result of such directness would be. Her intention was to hold on until the September quarter, and then try the experiment of a cheque to her own order on Mr. Gillespie's bank. Her hope was that the allowance would continue automatically, as it might not occur to her father to stop it—presuming he wished to do so.

"If he does," she said to herself, "I must just go and work in an ammunition factory, or something—that's all! Still, I don't believe he will. Father's a hard man, but he does try to be just. He can't punish me for simply wanting to work now, of all times!"

In this she did her father no less, and as it ultimately proved, no more than justice; for a *ballon d'essai* despatched northward to Mr. Gillespie at the end of September was received by him with the honour due to a credit balance.

But September was a long way off. Marjorie methodically reviewed all the avenues of occupation open to her. Nursing attracted her most; but she knew herself to be pathetically ignorant of the elements of the craft, and furthermore doubted (rightly) if her combative nature would endure the complete subservience to the professional element inevitable in the life of that plucky, much-enduring, self-effacing Cinderella, the V.A.D. Stenography and typewriting were unknown to her. Munition-making at this time was but an infant industry—as the occupants of the trenches had continuous occasion to note, with characteristic comment. There were a number of minor Red Cross activities open to her—bandage-rolling, parcel-packing, and the like—but these pursuits were too sedentary for ebullient Marjorie. Other forms of war activity, such as selling programmes at charity *matinées*, or pestering total strangers in 'buses and tube-trains to purchase flags to relieve the contingent wants of hypothetical Allied babies, were pushed contemptuously aside as war work *pour rire*. It was not too easy, either, to know where to apply, with adequate results. Upon the Olympus whence the country was being directed to victory, the Organisation of Womanhood still lay in the tray—much the biggest tray on Olympus—marked "Pending." Those quaint but proud expressions, "Wren," "Waac," and "Wraf" had not yet been added to the English language.

Marjorie finally decided to try canteen work. Vicarious service had no attraction for her; to get as close as possible to the human side of an enterprise was all her aim. At the canteen she would see and wait upon the most human member of the human family, one Thomas Atkins. A single fear made her hesitate. She wanted to spend herself utterly upon the Cause. Might not this canteen business prove just a little too trivial; a little too like playing at work?

She tried it for a week. After carrying tea-urns from the kitchen to the counter for eight consecutive hours she decided, without any hesitation whatever, that her apprehensions were groundless.

Month by month, Marjorie bent her giant's spirit and her straight young back to her task. The Canteen, near Waterloo Station, was never closed, and was full at practically every hour of the day and night. But, day-shift or night-shift, fair weather or foul, good news or bad, nothing made any difference to Marjorie. She was always on time, always cheerful, always perfectly ready to perform tasks left undone by the Undertakers of War Work. She set herself a standard of endurance and privation approximately as nearly as possible to that which she understood prevailed on the Western Front. This seemed to her the least that a stay-at-home person like herself could do, in consideration of the fact that no bodily risk attached to her duties. (As yet, Zeppelin frightfulness was merely one of London's gratuitous entertainments.) Consequently, after six months' unceasing drudgery, Marjorie was beginning to feel very tired, and just a little despondent.

The spirit of despondency stalked abroad in those days: it was the natural reaction from the wave of enthusiasm which had carried the country so highheartedly through the anxieties and uncertainties of the first twelve months. It was becoming increasingly obvious that "K" was right; that the war was going to last for a term of years; and that the country could not reach the goal on its first wind. Pending the arrival of the second, a slump in martial enthusiasm was inevitable. Tubes and omnibuses no longer carried men in uniform for nothing. Civilians no longer offered their seats to soldiers and sailors. Patriotic flappers no longer presented white feathers to wounded officers in mufti. It was no longer considered *de rigueur* for the orchestra in public restaurants to bring a docile public to its feet by periodical excursions into patriotic melody. The Battle of Loos had demonstrated once more that the young British soldier never fights better than in his first battle; also, alas! that when a nation goes to war free from the taint of "militarism," soldiers must die that Staffs may learn. Gallipoli had been evacuated, when with a little luck and good management the evacuation might have taken place at the other end. Bulgaria had recently joined our enemies, and it was felt that with more skilful handling she would have come down upon our side of the hedge. Early in December figures to date of British casualties in all theatres of war were officially announced for the first time: they reached a total more than five times as great as the numbers of the original Expeditionary Force. A shortage of men was becoming apparent: although nearly four million had joined the Colours, the cry was still for more. The Voluntary system was at its last gasp. Despite the honest and ingenious Derby scheme for a more even distribution of the burden, it was plain that an intolerable and increasing weight was being borne by The Willing Horse. Conscription, long overdue, was clearly on the way, with the result that the voice of the Conscientious Objector was now heard in the land. On the top of all this the No-Treating Order had come into force, and another injustice was inflicted upon that section of the community which preferred that its refreshment should be paid for, as its battles were being fought, by some one else. Even Marjorie's spirits sagged a little during that black winter. Her sense of oppression was increased by two potent factors. In the first place, she was underfed. It was entirely her own fault, or, rather, that of her first parent, Eve. In their hearts, all women cherish a profound contempt for what men call good food. Formal meals, consumed at leisure and with comfortable ritual, are to them a mere pandering to gross male standards of self-indulgence. A woman hates sitting at a dinner-table through a meal of thoughtfully varied courses. To her the perfect repast is, was, and always will be an egg on a tray, on a chair, in any room but the dining-room.

Marjorie was not exempt from this failing. Too often her principal meal of the day was eaten in a tea-shop, and consisted of food that satisfied quickly and nourished not at all. The meals at Netherby had been irksome, but they were at least wholesome. Furthermore, in her desire to emulate the soldier's lot, she imposed upon herself a voluntary rationing scheme—which if applied in military circles would have undoubtedly produced a mutiny. She had the zealot spirit, too. After the twelfth of October, the day upon which Edith Cavell died, Marjorie ate neither butter nor jam for a fortnight. Less sincere tributes have been paid to our great dead.

But, above all, she was desperately lonely. If it is not good for man to be alone, it is far worse for woman. And Marjorie was very much alone. It is surprising what a small acquaintance most of us really possess. Such as are occupied every day in earning a living—and who is not in these times?—are almost entirely dependent for human companionship upon the people with whom they work and the people with whom they share a home. Of course, there is a certain type which makes sociability its life work; which is eternally busy with visiting-cards and engagement-book; scraping acquaintance here, exchanging addresses there—the type, in fact, which entertains a not altogether unreasonable dread of being left alone with itself. But if you possess neither the inclination nor the leisure for these amenities, and do not live at home, and do not happen to work in company with a throng of your fellow-creatures, you can be a very lonely individual indeed, especially in a great city.

Marjorie, fortunately, had the canteen. She formed acquaintanceships quickly, as all attractive people do. Some of these, owing to her natural discrimination, were short-lived, and none made an abiding impression. Marjorie was more interested in things than people in those days. But the soldiers appreciated her. Sometimes their appreciation took the form of tips. One Canadian presented her with half a crown, and commanded her to buy "candy" with it; but the majority of her patrons furtively thrust a penny or twopence—and twopence meant a good deal to Tommy in those shilling-a-day times—under the saucer, adjusted cap, and said awkwardly, "Well, so-long, miss!" hurrying out before the delinquency was discovered. Many of them sent her post cards, from Flanders, or Egypt, or India, addressed as often as not, if they had lacked the courage to ask her name beforehand, to the "Young Lady with the Tea Urns."

But Marjorie's leisure hours were not exhilarating. That moment at the end of the day's work, when every member of the human family ought to be provided by law with some one or something to go home to, was the worst. Still, it was all part of the game, and she played up sturdily. She invented amusements for herself—such as could be indulged in by one person, gifted with imagination and a sense of humour. London itself was her playground. Most of the picture galleries and museums were closed by this time; but London's real attractions are ever in the street. Walking home on a fine morning from night duty, Marjorie would frequently look in at St. James's Palace to see that the Guard was properly changed. Sometimes she trudged as far as Buckingham Palace with the relief. She bought a little book which dealt with London landmarks, and sought out for her own amusement the Old Curiosity Shop, London Wall, the site of Tyburn Tree, and the birthplaces of numerous historical celebrities. She acquired a store of useless but pleasant knowledge: for instance, that the wooden slab with iron legs, which stands by the railings of the Green Park in Piccadilly, was originally set up to enable ticket-porters to rest their bundles for a moment before breasting the gradient—more perceptible to a ticket-porter than a modern taxi—that leads to Hyde Park Corner.

The great railway stations were a perpetual feast to her, especially Victoria and Waterloo. Many an evening found her at the barrier at Victoria as the leave train drew up at the platform, to disgorge a wave of bronzed, boisterous, mud-caked, unshaven children into the arms of demonstrative relatives. Sometimes, too, in the early morning, she attended this same train's departure, upon the shortest run in the world—the run in the opposite direction was the longest—the journey between London and Folkestone. With swelling heart and tightening lips she watched the crowd of returners to duty—all curiously silent, and all smiling in the most unanimous and resolute manner for the benefit of those who had come to see them off. The silence and the resolution broke sometimes when the warning whistle sounded—perhaps for ten seconds. As soon as the train began to move, Marjorie always turned and walked rapidly away before the women came wandering aimlessly back from the empty platform. She could bear most things, but not that.

There were few amusements upon which she could afford to spend money. The theatre generally was beyond her reach, but the cinema was an abiding boon to herself and countless others—a fact to which the attention of intellectual despisers of common pleasures is respectfully directed. The cinema was always open; one could go in when one had time, and come out when one had had enough. One could go there alone without looking or feeling conspicuously alone, which is not possible in the ordinary theatre; there were no waits, and no noise; and the darkened auditorium, whether one regarded the screen or not, was a rest-cure in itself.

Then there was the recreation of correspondence. Marjorie wrote to Roy every day, and Joe once a week. She had received no letter from Netherby in answer to her own; so she decided to make no present attempt to repair the rupture of diplomatic relations in that quarter. Joe was now a private in the Royal Engineers, undergoing intensive training in the north of England. She had not seen him since his enlistment, nor expected to, for leave was difficult. Moreover, Joe referred frequently and appreciatively in his letters to local hospitality. Marjorie scented a romance, but Joe gave nothing away.

And there were Roy's letters. They arrived with amazing regularity—the postal service of the British Expeditionary Force was one of the unadvertised marvels of the war— written in pencil upon the thin blue-squared sheets of a field dispatch-book, with the censor's triangular stamp in one corner of the envelope and Roy's own name scribbled on the other. They contained little military information, and a surprising amount of irrelevant foolishness. Roy told Marjorie about life in billets. He reported upon his progress with the French tongue. He told her of Madame *la fermière*, in whose loft he slept, and with whom he practised elegant conversation, but who was unfortunately only intelligible upon Sunday, that being the one day in the week when her false teeth were in actual use. For the rest of the week they reposed thriftily in a drawer. He told her how he visited a French Field Hospital, and had committed the solecism of addressing the nurse—an elderly Sister of Charity—as "Mademoiselle Nourrice." He wrote, as a schoolboy might, of some extra good "blow-out" at an *estaminet*; of his small amusements; of his small grievances. He wrote, as a lover does, of his lady, and how much he loved and missed her, and how greatly the thought of her inspired him. But of tactical operations, or the joy of battle—and there is such a thing—or the privations and horrors of war, there was nothing. The whole aim of the man in the trenches at this time appears to have been to maintain the morale of the people at home. It was during this very month that Forain, the French cartoonist, epitomised the psychology of the entire war in a single drawing—two gaunt, mud-caked *poilus*, crouching waist-deep in the water of a devastated trench during an intensive bombardment, gasping anxiously to one another: "*Si les civils tiennent!*"

Of Roy's whereabouts Marjorie knew little. He had come safely through the Battle of Loos—more fortunate than the majority of his colleagues. He had served in Belgium for a space; after that the Division had been transferred to France again. He was fond of indicating his position on the map by cryptograms insoluble by friend or foe, or codes which not even their author could decipher the day after their invention. But occasionally he succeeded:

Of course we are not permitted to say where we are, but it would be harmful to blub about it.

The latter half of this sentence sounded so more than usually idiotic that Marjorie felt sure it conveyed some subtle message. But though she applied every solution known to the amateur detective, she could make nothing of it. It was not for many weeks that it occurred to her, during the night watches, to cease probing for key-words or transposing vowels, and to try paraphrasing the sense of the text. By this means she reached the conclusion that there was "harm in tears"—and a "buried town" immediately sprang to view. But more often she was trapped in the pitfalls of ambiguity.

"*This is a pleasant old-world spot,*" Roy had remarked in a recent letter. "*You would love the Vicar.*"

"The Vicar! The Vicar? The Vicar of what?" Marjorie spent half an hour poring over the *Daily Mail* map of the Western Front which decorated the greater part of her bedroom wall, in a vain search for a place called Wakefield, or anything like it. She wrote back:

By the way, the Vicar you are so enthusiastic about is an entire stranger to me.

To-night another letter had come, conveying enlightenment:

Sorry you don't like the Vicar. He used to be a good chap. An up-river man, and some singer in his day.

Two minutes later, Marjorie's pencil was on the map, underlining Bray-sur-Somme. Dear Roy! She leaned back in her cheap little stall in the darkness, and chuckled softly to herself. How wonderfully these foolish trifles lubricated the grinding wheels. But oh—!

Spots and splashes appeared upon the film, and it began to rain ink—an infallible sign in the world of moving-picture romance of the less expensive kind that the end of the tale is approaching. Marjorie rose to her feet, pulled on her hat, and felt her way out into the Earl's Court Road. She was sufficiently well known to the asthmatic Admiral of the Fleet—at least he looked like that—who guarded the portals of the Electric Palace to receive from him a gracious good night.

"O reevoyer, miss! I 'ope to see you on Thursday. We shall 'ave a fresh picture then— Charlie Chaplin, the new screen comedian. Everybody's talking about 'im. Very comical, 'e is!"

Not far from Earl's Court Station, in the obscurity of the discreetly darkened street, Marjorie came upon a motor-car. A girl chauffeur was endeavouring to jack up the off-hind wheel. Marjorie ranged up alongside at once.

"Let me help you," she said.

"Thanks," gasped the girl. Together they wrestled with the stiff jack.

"A puncture?" inquired Marjorie.

"Yes. Rotten luck! I am only a mile from home, and this old tyre has gone on the blink. I must put on the spare rim."

"I know this kind," said Marjorie, fired with characteristic enthusiasm at the prospect of a thoroughly irksome job. "Let me do it!"

"You're welcome!" said the girl, who was white with fatigue. "I don't mind the driving and the long hours," she continued sociably, settling down on the running board while Marjorie deftly removed the unserviceable rim; "but changing tyres, and oiling the engine, and filling up grease-cups, and all those messy things—that's what I can't stick!"

"Is this your—your work during the war?" asked Marjorie, suddenly interested.

"Yes—The Women's Legion. We haven't been started long. It's hard work in all weathers; but it's helping—a bit. I'm trying to keep my husband's job open for him."

Ten minutes later, utterly exhausted, Marjorie let herself into her tiny flat in a by-street off the Brompton Road. It was half-past nine. She set the alarm clock for half-past five, and went to bed with Roy's letter under her pillow. She dreamed that Roy had been promoted—suddenly, but not unexpectedly—to the rank of Commander-in-Chief, and that it was her privilege to drive him to battle every morning at five-thirty, in a motor-car with the off-hind tyre punctured.

CHAPTER VII

DUET

I

In one respect her dream came true.

Shortly after nine o'clock next morning, as the breakfast rush eased off, Marjorie was aware of the flushed features of the lady superintendent of the canteen, Miss Penny— "The Mouldy Old Copper," in the unregenerate language of the junior staff—angrily visible through a mephitic fog to which steaming tea, frying bacon, and moist humanity had all contributed. (Even in the crispest weather Tommy Atkins is a most hygroscopic individual.)

"We are for it, my dear!" announced The Mouldy Old Copper.

"What—Zeppelins?" inquired Marjorie, setting her tenth urn in position.

"Worse! Inspection! They are coming at twelve. The Government have suddenly decided to inquire into the feasibility of making the Canteen Service an official affair—a branch of the A.S.C., or the R.A.M.C., or the Q.M.G., or some other futility. So they are coming to inspect us, as 'a typical example of a canteen maintained by voluntary effort and service.' I got it over the telephone just now."

"It was decent of them to warn you," said Marjorie.

"That's just what they haven't done! I got the news by a side wind. It's to be a surprise inspection. They want to see what a show run by women is like when it's off its guard. I like their impudence! What do they expect to catch us doing, I wonder—arranging the tea-cups in the wrong formation; or not keeping accounts in triplicate; or flirting with the men; or what!" The Mouldy Old Copper turned a bright bronze colour. "I'll jolly well talk to them, if they start any of their old—!"

"Don't you think," suggested Marjorie, "that it would be a good plan to telephone round at once to make sure that there are enough waitresses? You know what a bear-garden this place is when the men can't get served."

Miss Penny considered.

"Yes, you are right," she said. "At least, we will warn some of them. Not all—oh dear no, not all! There are women connected with this place who haven't allowed their so-called work here to interfere with a single tea-fight or subaltern-hunt since they joined. Of course they would sell their souls to crush in to-day. Well, they shan't! They shall hear all about it to-morrow, instead! I shall love telling them—especially the Toplis girl, and Lady Adeline, and Mrs. Napoleon Jones—or whatever the name of that horror with the pekineses is! You run along, dear, and telephone to about a dozen of the decent ones, and tell them to be sure and turn up by ten-thirty."

The result was that at high noon, when the Olympians descended upon Waterloo Road, they found the canteen crowded with happy warriors partaking of nourishment from the hands of a bevy of attractive and competent Hebes. The Committee of Inspection consisted of a much-beribboned Major-General, two or three lesser luminaries proportionately decorated, and an elderly civilian in a shocking hat.

The Mouldy Old Copper conducted the procession round the canteen. Here and there a halt was called at a table, where the Major-General, having made the diners thoroughly comfortable by commanding them straitly to "sit at ease," inquired, in the voice of a Bengal tiger endeavouring to coo like a dove, whether there were "any complaints." There were none, which was most gratifying, but not altogether surprising.

Marjorie, greatly diverted by the *sotto voce* remarks which reached her from tables in her neighbourhood, rested her tired arms upon the speckless counter and looked demurely down her nose. Upon her ear fell a raven's croak:

"Very good—with such a short time for rehearsal! But these damsels must come here *every* day, you know! By the way, does he write to you regularly? I told him to."

Marjorie turned, and gaped in the most unladylike manner. The elderly civilian in the bad hat had strayed away from his escort, and now stood at her elbow—revealed as Lord Eskerley, to whom she had once been presented at a regimental gymkhana at Craigfoot. Apparently he was aware that the Olympian deputation were being treated to a display of "eyewash." Apparently, also; he knew Marjorie. Not only Marjorie, but Marjorie's most private affairs. Altogether, he seemed to know too much.

"By the way," continued his lordship characteristically, "how do you do? I forgot." They shook hands. "Lovely day, isn't it? You look overworked. What are your hours here?"

Marjorie told him.

"What is your particular *métier*?"

Marjorie introduced the tea-urns.

"No woman, however young or muscular, should carry heavy things about," said Lord Eskerley. "Razors to cut grindstones; as usual! Would you like a change of occupation?"

"Indeed I should," replied Marjorie—"so long as it was helping things along, you know."

"What can you do?"

Marjorie fingered the dimple on her chin dolefully.

"Not much, I'm afraid. I don't know anything about nursing, or shorthand, or anything useful."

"You can drive a car, though."

"How do you know that?"

"How does the trembling fawn know that the wolf is not a vegetarian?" The old gentleman glared at Marjorie over his spectacles.

"I expect its mother warns it," hazarded Marjorie, a little guiltily.

"Ah! Possibly. My mother, unfortunately, never saw you, though I am sure that if she had she would have warned me. But there are other ways—instinct, to a certain extent; also experience. You and your two-seater once missed me by inches in the Craigfoot road. You were on your way to keep an appointment, I thought: I forbore to speculate with whom. But never mind that. Now—my chauffeur very properly joined the army to-day. Would you care to step into his shoes? He wears large fourteens, and your appointment would probably wreck my prospects as an eligible widower; but I think those are the only two objections. Will you give me a trial? Thank you very much! Report this evening."

II

Marjorie's labours henceforth were as arduous as ever, but were mainly performed in the open air—which to her meant all the difference between work and play. Each morning she drew up before Lord Eskerley's gloomy mansion in that aristocratic slum, Curzon Street, at nine o'clock sharp, and conveyed her employer upon his daily round. First to the Ministry of Intelligence, an unobtrusive mansion in the purlieus of Whitehall Gardens. Then, about eleven, to Downing Street. Then back to the Ministry. About one, to Curzon Street, for a brief luncheon. In the afternoon Marjorie ran errands: that is to say, she conveyed visitors to the Ministry from all quarters of London—from other Ministries, from the House of Commons, or from remote private addresses. At seven she conveyed his lordship home to Curzon Street, where, day in, day out, in victory or defeat, he dined at seven forty-five precisely.

"Give your digestion fair play," he once suddenly advised his chauffeuse, as she tucked him into the car on a bitter January afternoon, "and the world is yours!"

Marjorie promised to do so.

"Have a clear understanding with your stomach in early life," his lordship resumed, the moment Marjorie reopened the door of the car twenty minutes later. "Remember he *rules* the rest of your internal economy. Socially, we never meet him, or speak of him; but he is the whole show! And—he is as sensitive as an upper servant! Give him the consideration due to his position; don't ask him to work at unusual times, or do things that are not part of his duty; and he will not only serve you for a lifetime, but will keep your heart up to its work, restrain your brain from more than usual foolishness, and put the fear of death into the organs below stairs! But treat him casually, or give him odd jobs to do—and he will let you down, as sure as fate! Call for me at the usual time, please."

Marjorie's duties did not end at dinner-time; for war knows nothing of the eight-hour day, or early closing, or Sabbath observance. Lord Eskerley frequently went out about nine in the evening—sometimes to Downing Street, occasionally to Buckingham Palace, not infrequently to an unpretentious house in Dulwich, where he found it convenient to interview persons whom it would have been undesirable to receive officially at the Ministry or Curzon Street. The house stood in the same road as Uncle Fred's. The fact gave Marjorie, gliding past in the wintry darkness, a pleasant sensation of escape from futility.

One bleak and muddy day in February she drove Lord Eskerley down to Bramshott Camp, to assist at a review of two new divisions. Somewhere outside Godalming the gears began to burr and slip. Finally, Marjorie pulled in at the side of the road and descended.

The window of the car was let down and Lord Eskerley's head appeared.

"How long will it take?" he inquired, avoiding superfluous questions, as usual.

"About ten minutes. The lever has worked loose; I can't get my gears in properly," replied Marjorie.

"Do you want any help? I have with me"—his lordship leaned back and exhibited his fellow-passengers—"General Brough-Brough; his A.D.C., Captain Sparkes; and Mr. Meadows. The General and Captain Sparkes, as you will observe, are all dressed up in review order, and I cannot have them tarnished or made muddy, or I should be bringing contempt and ridicule on the King's uniform; also rendering aid and comfort to the enemy, which is not allowed in war time. So that disposes of them. I shall not insult a lady of your capabilities by offering my assistance. That leaves Meadows. Do you want him?"

"No, thank you," said Marjorie, swiftly removing the floor boards above the gear box. The window was drawn up again, and Mr. Meadows, Lord Eskerley's private secretary, a young man debarred from warlike exercises by acute astigmatism and valvular murmurs, looked very much relieved.

Ten minutes later, Marjorie, somewhat flushed and not a little oily, resumed her place at the wheel, and deposited her passengers at the stroke of the appointed hour at Divisional Headquarters at Bramshott.

Her employer, stepping out of the car, surveyed her grimy features quizzically.

"Habakkuk!" he chuckled.

Six hours later, at the end of the return journey, he inquired:

"Do you read your Voltaire at all? Probably not: I'll send you his 'Life.'"

The volume reached her next morning. Therein Marjorie discovered a marked passage, in which it was recorded that Voltaire found Habakkuk "*capable de tout*." Thereafter, Lord Eskerley habitually addressed her as Habakkuk.

III

Still, Marjorie was not entirely happy. As already stated, any form of outdoor occupation was, in her view, play; and the present was essentially a time for work. She belonged to that zealous breed which is never really contented unless it is uncomfortable—to whom congenial occupation is merely idleness under another name. She enjoyed her present employment so much that she felt ashamed: she felt that she was not pulling her weight in the war. Probably a short conversation with a sensible person would have cured her of these illusions; but Marjorie had no one with whom to converse. She might have confided in her employer; but she argued, with some reason, that he would merely make an apposite and caustic reference to the gentleman who is reputed to have painted himself black all over in order to play Othello. It did not occur to her to mention the matter to Roy in a letter. Roy, for the present, belonged to his country, and was not to be diverted from his duty by domestic or personal trifles. What Marjorie needed and longed for at this time was a confidant.

If we desire a thing urgently enough we usually get it. Sometimes we get more than we bargain for.

One day Lord Eskerley came down his front-door steps arm-in-arm with an officer in uniform. His lordship's *chauffeuse*, who prided herself upon her soldierly restraint, did not look round from her wheel as the pair entered the car, but she heard her employer say:

"You can drop me at the office, Eric, and the car will take you on to the club."

Eric Bethune's voice replied that this arrangement would suit its owner top-hole.

When Lord Eskerley alighted at Whitehall Gardens he turned and addressed Marjorie.

"Habakkuk," he announced, "inside the car I have left a D.S.O. on a fortnight's leave. Please deposit him at the Army and Navy Club in Pall Mall. He is a Scotsman, so there will be no gratuities."

"Very good, my lord," replied Marjorie, looking rigidly to her front. She and the old gentleman made quite a speciality of these solemn little pleasantries.

The portals of the Ministry had hardly closed upon the Minister when his guest emerged from within the interior of the car and climbed into the front seat beside Marjorie.

"May I come and sit here?" asked Eric, shaking hands. "I recognised your back view through the front window-glass."

"It's against regulations," replied Marjorie, smiling, "but I can't disobey a colonel. Besides, I want to hear all about the Western Front. How are the Royal Covenanters?"

"I am commanding the Second Battalion now," replied Eric. "I have been with them since October."

"Yes, I know," said Marjorie thoughtlessly.

"How did you know?" asked Eric, not altogether displeased.

Marjorie, carefully negotiating the cross-currents of Trafalgar Square, bit her lip. She was beginning to give herself away already. But she replied, looking steadily before her:

"I get letters sometimes."

"I hope your correspondents report favourably on me," said Eric lightly. "Do you know many of my officers?"

"Not many—now. Let me see." Marjorie decided swiftly not to be evasive, but to reply to Eric's naïve inquisitiveness as naturally as possible. "Major Laing—I have met him once or twice. Is he still with you?"

"'Old Leathery'? Yes. He goes on for ever. Who else?"

"One hardly likes to ask these days, for fear—you know?"

"Yes, I know. But we've been lucky lately. We are in a quiet sector of the line. We have had no officer casualties for two months. Wait while I touch wood!" He tapped the mahogany dashboard. "Do you know Kilbride, my adjutant?"

"I don't think so."

"He's a stout fellow. Let me see. Do you know young Birnie? He comes from your part of the world, and mine."

"Yes, I know him," said Marjorie. "Is he quite well?" For the life of her she could not help asking.

44

"Yes, he's all right." Eric gave Marjorie a sudden sidelong glance. He possessed the curiosity of a child, and not a little of a child's jealousy. He had certain things in mind—rumours, nods, innuendoes, elephantine jests in the mess. Marjorie's eyes were fixed steadily upon the road ahead of her, and her face expressed nothing more than polite interest. But if Eric had been a really observant person—a woman, for instance—he would have noticed that her hands were gripping the steering-wheel until the nails were white.

"Whom else do you know?" he continued. "Garry—Balfour—Carruthers—little Cowie?"

"No." Marjorie knew none of these. They were a later vintage.

"Laing and Birnie seem to be all of your friends that are left," said Eric. "Which of them is your correspondent? Not old Leathery, surely?"

"No; Mr. Birnie. We are quite old acquaintances," said Marjorie, thoroughly annoyed at the unfair tactics which had isolated Roy.

"Well, all that I can say is that I am thoroughly jealous of Master Birnie!" announced Eric, smiling. "Now tell me all about yourself. What are you doing here in London, driving a car?"

"Here is your club," said Marjorie, putting on her brake.

"Confound it!" Eric's annoyance was quite genuine. "We had so much to discuss. Can't you lunch with me somewhere?"

"I never know when I shall lunch. It depends on Lord Eskerley."

"Well, can you dine? Surely you don't work all night as well!"

Marjorie hesitated. As it happened, she was free that evening, for she knew that two cabinet ministers were dining and conferring with her employer. There was no reason whatever why she should not accept Eric's invitation. But for a moment some instinct held her back. Then she thought of the eternal solitude of the flat.

"Thank you very much," she said. "I will."

They dined together and went to a play. Eric made a charming host and a decorative escort. For the rest of the week—he was spending six days of his leave with Lord Eskerley—Marjorie saw him constantly. She drove him about London, and they went upon more than one exhilarating excursion together. By the time that Eric departed to Scotland to visit Buckholm she knew all about the regiment—its exploits, its smartness, even its private jokes. Her general impression was that the regiment had improved greatly since Colonel Bethune had taken command.

On the subject of Roy, both exhibited considerable reticence. When Eric mentioned his name, he did so in a manner which jarred—"Your little friend Birnie"; "Cowie, Douglas, Birnie, and other riff-raff of the mess." Colonel Bethune might almost have been trying to belittle Roy intentionally. So Marjorie, afraid of losing her temper and giving away the position, carefully avoided Roy as a topic—an omission which Eric may or may not have noted, but made no attempt to correct.

But the week was soon over, and Colonel Bethune and cheery nights out were no more. Marjorie fell back into the old routine with an inevitable sense of reaction. She realised next afternoon, as she sat waiting in the rain at her wheel in Curzon Street, how improvident it is to accept happiness or distraction from sources outside one's normal environment. She knew now that the only permanent happiness is the happiness that comes from common things. More than ever she yearned in her heart for a regular companion—a crony, a confidant, a pal—as lively and as "safe" as the companion she had just lost.

As noted above, it was raining—raining on a dismal afternoon in March. It had been an anxious and busy week, for the Boche had fallen like an avalanche upon Verdun, and the French resistance was in the preliminary and uncertain stages of what was to prove one of the most heroic defensive actions in history. Allied Councils of War had been frequent, and Lord Eskerley's department had been heavily engaged.

Word had just been sent out to Marjorie that his lordship would be detained another hour at least, and that Miss Clegg, if she pleased, was at liberty to take the car back to the garage. But Miss Clegg was pleased to remain where she was. She sat on, with the rain dripping off her peaked cap and down the bridge of her nose, sedulously nursing a theory that in so doing she was getting a little nearer to the Western Front.

It never rains but it pours. Suddenly, from round the corner of Queen Street, there came to Marjorie a new factor in her life—a humid but quite alluring vision of attenuated skirt, black silk stockings, and inadequate fur stole. The rain was working its will upon the vision: she had not even an umbrella. But she pattered bravely along upon her absurd heels, taking what shelter the lee of the houses afforded, and keeping her head well down—presumably for reasons connected with her dazzling complexion.

As she passed Marjorie she looked up, and Marjorie saw that she was little more than a child, and a not very robust child at that. With Marjorie, to think was to act.

"I say! Wait a minute!" she cried, and began to rummage under the cushion of her seat, extracting ultimately a spare raincoat of her own.

"You must put this on," she announced to the girl: "you are soaking." She bustled her new protégée into the garment without waiting for permission. Then another thought occurred to her.

"I have half an hour to spare," she said. "May I take you anywhere? Nobody"—indicating her employer's mausoleum-like residence—"will mind."

Appealing blue eyes looked up at her. An enormous but attractive mouth broke into a grateful smile.

"It's jolly decent of you," said a voice of incredible childishness. "Are you sure?"

"Rather!" said Marjorie. "Will you get inside, or sit by me?"

"By you, please."

"All right! Come along!"

Marjorie cranked her engine, and took her place at the wheel. Her new little friend snuggled down beside her.

"You *are* strong!" she said admiringly. "And yet you don't look very hefty. Your hands are lovely. How do you keep them so nice, doing this kind of work?"

"They are my vanity!" laughed Marjorie. "I sit up half the night trying to keep my nails in order. I wonder if it's worth while: I sometimes feel inclined to let them rip—for the duration! Where can I take you?"

"The Imperial Theatre, if you don't mind. I have a rehearsal at three, and it's after that now. I shall get a telling-off, as usual, I suppose. Well, I'm not worrying: such is life!"

"Are you on the stage?" asked Marjorie, genuinely thrilled.

"Yes. We open in about a month, with a new musical show."

"What's it called?"

"I never can remember: they change the title about once a day. Not that it really matters. 'Too Many Girls' is the latest; and pretty suitable, too! My dear, you simply can't get men for the theatre nowadays! The good ones have all joined up, and the rotters daren't walk on. You ought to see our chorus men! They are all about seventy, or else they have one lung, or one rib, or one ear, or something. Still, we carry on somehow. Are you driving a car for war work?"

"Yes. I don't really feel that I ought to be doing it; it's too much like fun. I was in a canteen at first, but I got rather run down and hard up, and I was offered this job as a chauffeur, so I took it. I think I should go back to the canteen if I could afford it. I never see any soldiers now. At the canteen one could do something for them, poor things."

"They're lambs!" agreed the passenger—"especially the young officers. Are you engaged?"

Marjorie, very much occupied in negotiating Piccadilly Circus, nodded.

"An officer?"

Marjorie nodded again.

"My boy's an officer, too. What's your name, by the way?"

"Marjorie Clegg."

"Mine's Liss Lyle. (It's Elizabeth Leek really, but in the profession one has to think of something better than that.) There's the Imperial there. Just shake me off at the front entrance, and I'll slip round to the stage door."

"Oh, but I want to drive you right up to the stage door!" said Marjorie frankly. "It will be wonderful!"

The little woman of the world at her side smiled indulgently.

"Very well then, dear, you shall! Round that corner, and then round again."

Marjorie set down her passenger with a genuine pang. She was certain now what was wrong in her life. She had no one to gossip with.

The two girls shook hands.

"Thanks awfully!" said Liss. "Also for Little Willie Waterproof." She took off the raincoat.

"Stick to it just now," said Marjorie: "it may be raining when you come out."

"Can I? I love you for that. I'll come round and leave it for you somewhere, shall I?"

Marjorie dived impulsively into the opening offered.

"Come to-night!" she said. "We might go and have some dinner somewhere. I can always get off for an hour—sometimes for the whole evening. I have a lot of evenings to myself," she added.

Ultimately the pair dined together, *chez* Lyons, and Marjorie spent her happiest hour since her invasion of London. She found her little friend a characteristic medley of childishness and maturity—featherheaded, affectionate, naïve, with far more worldly wisdom than herself, yet with all a child's dread of being laughed at for ignorance.

She came from Finchley—and apologised for doing so. She had no mother, and her father, overburdened, it seemed, with daughters, had raised no particular objection to Miss Elizabeth's theatrical predilections. She was at present living at a boarding-house near Paddington. Did not like it much. Said so—apparently to every one, including the other boarders. But nothing troubled her long. Her thoughts, birdlike, hopped to another twig, and her cheery little song of life was resumed. She was not deeply concerned with how and why. She pecked carelessly here and there at what fortune offered, without pausing to reason why or count the cost; but so far appeared instinctively to have avoided what was unwholesome. Her chief passions were dress, gossip, and expensive confectionery. Her conversation was a blend of theatrical shop and military slang—including many parrot-phrases which could have conveyed no meaning to her whatever—and was chiefly remarkable for a certain confiding frankness and a glorious contempt for what Mr. Mantalini would have called "demnition details."

"You must meet my boy," she said to Marjorie, as they walked homeward. "You'd love him. He's a *pukka sahib*!"

"What is his name?" asked Marjorie.

"I am not quite sure of his name," replied Miss Lyle, with characteristic candour; "but I think he's in the Yeomanry. His Christian name's Leonard. I met him with two other fellows at a party, and I got all their surnames mixed up—I always do—and I can never remember which of the three is his."

"You will find out before you marry him?" suggested Marjorie respectfully.

"Oh, rather! But there's plenty of time for that. Besides, he's going out soon, and then it won't matter."

"It won't *matter*?"

"No. We are not so potty about one another as all that. I could see the lad wanted to be engaged—after all, poor things, they can't afford to wait, these days—so I let him. He's nice, and clean, and it looks well to be called for after rehearsal. I shall miss him awfully when he goes. It's rotten to be by yourself in this world—isn't it?" A pair of pathetic eyes were upturned to Marjorie's.

Next moment Marjorie's arm was round the waif's shoulders.

"Liss, you shall come and live with me!" she said impulsively.

"Righto!" replied Liss. "I was dying to be asked, but it seemed too wonderful to be possible. I shall have to sponge on you for a bit, though. I haven't a bean until the show opens."

"That's all right," said Marjorie.

"Now, where shall we have our dug-out?" asked Liss, becoming terribly busy.

The pair spent a rapturous evening building castles in Kensington.

CHAPTER VIII

CHORUS

I

Finally they found an eyrie—a flat, somewhere in the sky at the back of Victoria Street, consisting of a big bedroom, a tiny sitting-room, a gas stove, and a surprisingly modern bath. They bought furniture at unpretentious establishments in Tottenham Court Road, laying their own carpets and hanging their own curtains. (The latter were the only really essential articles of domestic furniture in those days of aerial visitation.) Marjorie hung up a few reprints and photographs; Liss contributed a portrait of her nebulous and anonymous fiancé, together with seventeen picture post cards of stage celebrities; and the ideal home was opened.

Still, Marjorie's hunt for happiness was not yet complete. There were two crumpled rose-leaves. Firstly, her implacable conscience continued to inform her that her war work was too easy. Secondly, her evenings were as lonely as ever. As soon as rehearsals finished, and "Too Many Girls" started upon its nightly and tumultuous presentation, Liss disappeared regularly every evening about half-past six; to return, sometimes exhilarated, sometimes gloomy, sometimes affectionate, sometimes quarrelsome, but invariably hungry and inexorably talkative, about midnight. Supper was then served. The two ladies rarely ate at a table: as already noted, the keynote of a feminine meal is its passionate avoidance of anything in the shape of ceremonial routine. As often as not Marjorie would take her supper to bed with her, while Liss, munching and babbling, plied back and forth between the sitting-room and bedroom, in progressive stages of disrobement, bearing fresh supplies and relating the experiences of the day—continuing long after she had shed her flimsy garments over two rooms and a vestibule, arrayed herself in night attire, and crawled into bed.

"My dear, we had the most wonderful house to-night. Seven *legitimate* calls after the first act! What an audience these boys on leave make! (Here are a couple of sardines: the bloater paste is nah-poo.) They gave Phyllis Lane such a reception! She had to do the dance after 'Pull Up your Socks!' three times; (and if you want any more cocoa tell me, because I am going to turn out the gas-ring.) Her husband has been mentioned in dispatches. Leonard wasn't in front to-night—selfish pig! I'll tell him off for that, to-morrow. (Oh, you darling, did you put this hot-water-bottle in my bed? I must give you a kiss for that. There! No, it won't hurt you, it's only lip salve.) Mr. Lee came behind to-night, and spoke to us all. Said the show was a credit to everybody, and he was very pleased to hear how brave we all were during the raid the other night. Yes, he's the managing director. (Have you finished? Very well, then! Give me the tray. Here's a cigarette for you.) By the way, I was talking to Uncle Ga-Ga to-night. Oh, didn't I tell you about him? He's one of the chorus gentlemen—about a hundred years old, and simply mad to get into the war. But they won't take him. He keeps changing his name, and dyeing his hair a fresh colour, and trying again; but they turn him down every time. Seems queer, doesn't it, that when a man wants to go he can't, while there are so many who should and won't? (Can I use your cold cream, dear? I can't find mine.) Lee said they would probably put on a second edition about August: we start rehearsing the new numbers next week. Why don't you come and get a job in the chorus? It wouldn't interfere with your other work. There's two or three other girls doing the same as you, and Lee lets them off with one *matinée* a week. He's very patriotic. A-a-a-h! Oo-oo-oo! Ee-ee-ee! What a *lovely* warm bed! Well, as I was saying—Marjorie Clegg, what is the use of my wearing myself to a shadow waiting on you at supper and then the moment I get into bed and begin to chat for a couple of minutes before lights out you start snoring like a grampus? Very well, have it your own way. Live and let live, *I* say.... That's all.... As for that little toad Leonard—!..."

Miss Lyle's baby eyes closed, her small nose buried itself in the pillow, and her little tongue was still for several hours.

But Marjorie was not asleep. She lay awake thinking, while outside London, shrouded in the blackest obscurity, snatched such slumber as that endless, flaring, muttering line of outposts in Flanders could guarantee. For all her splendid vitality, Marjorie was a highly-strung girl—with a conscience. That morning Colonel Bethune, passing through London from Scotland on his way back to the Western Front, had invited her to a "farewell luncheon." She had accepted, gladly—and had repented ever since. For behold, over the coffee, Colonel Bethune had asked her to marry him!

He had asked her very charmingly, and with obvious confidence—a combination which made it an ungrateful and difficult business to say no without offence. At first Marjorie had been too taken back to say anything at all. When her answer came its sincerity was unmistakable; and poor, vain Eric was obviously and deeply mortified. With a vague idea of consoling him, she had mentioned that her affections were already engaged. He had asked her for no name, but she knew that it had been written in her face, and that Eric had read it there. Then a new and disappointing characteristic of the man had cropped out. He had turned and reproached her—had told her that she had flirted with him, and led him on—which was a base lie. But for all that, she was filled with remorse. In her selfish desire for a good time she had been thoughtlessly inconsiderate of Colonel Bethune, and almost disloyal to Roy.

She and her host had parted miserably ten minutes later, each having learned a bitter lesson—Eric, that in the field of love, especially under stress of war, callow youth can be more than a match for dazzling maturity; Marjorie, that where a pretty girl is concerned no man can be regarded as 'safe' until he is dead.

Well, she would expiate her fault in the only way she knew. This decided, she fell asleep.

II

Next morning Marjorie, depositing her noble employer upon the steps of the Ministry of Intelligence, inquired:

"May I speak to you for a moment, sometime, Lord Eskerley?"

"Twelve-twenty-five," was the prompt reply—"after Downing Street and before signatures. But I will not exert my influence to have him made Commander-in-Chief!"

At twelve-twenty Marjorie presented herself to Mr. Meadows, in the secretary's room, and was passed through double doors into the presence of the minister. His lordship looked up over his spectacles and indicated a chair.

"Habakkuk! Good! Sit down. Four-and-a-half minutes! Well?"

"I want to say," announced Marjorie, plunging head foremost into her confession, "that I can't stay here any longer."

"Why?"

"I am not happy in my mind. I must go away."

"Good gracious! Don't say Meadows has fallen in love with you! I will not permit my subordinates to encroach upon my prerogatives! No—not that? Proceed, then!"

"I think I ought to leave you," Marjorie continued, quite unmoved by her employer's senile quips, "because I am having too good a time. I have been feeling all along that I ought to be doing something else."

"So I have observed. Well?"

"The only trouble is that if I go back to the canteen work (where they want my help very badly), I shan't get paid for it; and I can't afford to work without pay of some kind. I have a small allowance from home, but it doesn't go far, and the girl I share a flat with was pretty hard up when I first picked—became acquainted with her."

"Oh! Ah! So you keep a foundling hospital, too?"

"Only one!" explained Marjorie. "She's a dear," she added warmly. "She's on the stage. She was badly in debt before the new piece started—they don't get paid during rehearsals, you see—and she is only just beginning to get on her feet again; so I can't afford to work for nothing during the day just now, unless—"

"Unless you go on the stage yourself at night? Is that it, O *Capable de tout*?"

"I was thinking of it," confessed Marjorie; "but I don't know how you guessed."

"It's the first thing every pretty girl thinks of when confronted with the necessity of earning a living. Go on."

"And I want to ask you: Is it playing the game to be on the stage *at all* in war time? I mean, ought the men to be encouraged to go to revues, and things like that, when they are on leave? Is it all wrong, and demoralising, and unpatriotic, as some people say?"

Lord Eskerley sat up, and took off his spectacles.

"Unpatriotic fiddlesticks!" he remarked with great vigour. "In war time there are just three things that matter. The first is morale. I have forgotten the other two. The maintenance of purely military morale can safely be left in military hands; but civilian morale—and that includes the morale of the men on leave of course, rests mainly on the triple foundation of the Church, the Press, and the Stage; and, as things are to-day, I am not sure that the Stage doesn't have the biggest say in the whole business. (Don't tell

50

Doctor Chirnside I said that, will you?) So you are thinking of joining your foundling behind the footlights. Chorus, I presume?"

"Yes. They would give me three pounds a week."

"They would get you cheap! And you want me to satisfy your conscience that the life of a galley-slave in a vitiated atmosphere all day, followed by vocal and calisthenic exercises in an even more vitiated atmosphere for three hours every night, is a sufficiently close approach to hard work to exonerate you from all suspicion of lukewarmness with regard to the war?" The old man stood up and shook hands. "Donna Quixota Habakkuk, the certificate is granted! I suppose you will stay on for a week or two, until I find a successor—I won't say a substitute? Don't forget me, altogether. Come and see me sometimes. I am less busy, and more solitary, than you suppose. You know when to come: you are familiar with my goings out and comings in. And—good luck, my dear!"

III

Life behind the scenes, as usual, falsified expectation. Marjorie's first visit to the theatre was paid a few weeks after her interview with Lord Eskerley. They entered by the stage-door, Liss explaining to a taciturn but benevolently disposed person in a glass box, whose name appeared to be "Mac," that her companion had an appointment with Mr. Lee. Thereafter, Marjorie was conducted through an iron door, which commanded the thoughtless, by stencilled legend, to close it gently; through a mass of ghostly scenery, past whitewashed walls bearing notices extolling the virtues of Silence; and out through another iron door (marked, somewhat paradoxically, "*Not an exit*") into the auditorium, rendered dimly visible by the overflow of light from an economically-illuminated stage.

Liss turned back the holland covering from two stalls at the end of a retired row.

"Sit there, dear," she said. "I will grab hold of old Lee some time, and tell him you are here. I can sit with you for a bit. This rehearsal is for principals; the chorus aren't called until twelve."

The rehearsal of the principals consisted, for the moment, of an altercation between a fat man, standing in the middle of the stage, and the musical director, sitting at his desk in the orchestra. It was a most friendly—one might almost call it an affectionate—altercation. No epithet ever fell to a lower level of mutual esteem than "Old Boy!" or "Old Man!"—or, under extreme provocation, a "Dear Old Boy!" As is not unusual in these cases, it was difficult for the casual outsider to discover:

(*a*) What the argument was about.

(*b*) Which side of the argument was being sustained by whom.

In the front row of the stalls stood an ascetic-looking man in black tortoise-shell spectacles, apparently acting as umpire. Seated upon a partially dismantled throne beside a step-ladder, up stage, sat a pretty girl in a pink tam-o'-shanter, placidly perusing a crumpled brown-paper-covered manuscript. Other persons were dotted about the auditorium—fat men, cadaverous men; men with tortoise-shell spectacles, and men without; an occasional female. All were conferring in monotone. Round the bare walls of the stage, at present destitute of scenery, sat the ladies of the chorus, most of them wearing rehearsal dresses of unpretentious design—knitting socks of khaki, and occasionally exchanging a guarded confidence. Altogether the atmosphere struck Marjorie as more domestic than theatrical—almost ecclesiastical in its dullness and drowsiness.

"Who are these people sitting about in the stalls?" she asked Liss.

"Oh, just odds and ends! The author, and the lyric writers, and extra lyric writers, and costumiers, and photographers, and people like that—all waiting to catch Mr. Lee, and

51

start an argument with him about something. That's Tubby Ames on the stage. He's having a row with Phil Kay; he has about two a week. I bet you he's trying to get Phyllis Lane's song cut. (That's her, in the pink tam; she's sweet.) It's been going too well lately. Tubby was kept waiting for his entrance in the Second Act last night while she did her third encore dance. Trust Tubby to step on other people's fat! Yes, I thought so."

The comedian's voice was heard again. The gist of the dispute was emerging from a cloud of verbiage.

"Phil, dear old man," he exclaimed earnestly, "I should be the last person in the world to interfere with a brother or sister artist; but really, I am only saying what every one feels. After all, we must all pull together in these days, and I feel instinctively that unless the way is kept *ab-so-lute-ly* clear for that entrance of mine, the action will drop—and flop goes your Second Act! And where are you then?" He leaned right over the footlights.

The conductor, apparently a man of peace, flinched visibly.

"Old boy," he began, "it's this way. I quite see your point—"

The comedian pressed his advantage swiftly.

"I thought you would," he said. "I have had a good many years' experience in this sort of work—more than you, perhaps. For instance, when I was with Charles Wyndham—"

"It's the Story of his Life!" whispered Liss despairingly. "We get it about every second rehearsal. He's out of pantomime, really. It's only because there's nobody else to be had that he's here at all. He has varicose veins, and—"

But the ascetic referee in the stalls broke in upon the autobiographist.

"Mr. Ames," he commanded—his voice was strong and harsh, and was obviously extensively employed in shouting down other discordant noises—"talk sense!"

"That's Mr. Lancaster," whispered Liss excitedly. "He's the producer. We are all frightened to death of him. He's a wonder!"

"Miss Lane's song cannot be cut," continued the wonder, "and it cannot be transferred elsewhere; so you must lump it! Now, Miss St. Leger, come on, please, and try your 'Plum and Apple' duet with Mr. Ames."

Miss St. Leger, the leading lady, was standing in the wings. Her face was round and childish; her eyes were brown and pathetic; her whole appearance suggested timidity and helplessness. Hearing her name called, she walked obediently down to the footlights, favoured the producer with a dazzling smile, and began:

"Say, listen, Mr. Lancaster! I got a kick coming too! That duet I am putting over with Mr. Ames in the Second Act of the present show is practically a solo! When we started in singing it, way back in last fall, it was a duet, I'll allow. But somehow I got a kind of crowded feeling, now. I don't seem to belong in that duet when Mr. Ames is around. And I want to say right here that I am not going to stand for that kind of rough stuff any more!"

By this time the languid chorus were sitting straight up on their chairs. The scattered figures in the auditorium had ceased their muttered incantations, and were leaning forward, all ears. The pacific Phil Kay was squirming in his seat. Marjorie and Liss gripped hands ecstatically; the ecclesiastical atmosphere had evaporated.

"I understand team work," continued the ethereal Miss St. Leger, "as well as any artist; and you won't ever find me stepping on any other folks' laughs or business. But one thing I will not do, and that is feed fat to a dub comedian all the time—especially a guy that's too fat already!"

There was a roar of laughter from stage and stalls. Even the austere Lancaster grinned sardonically. Mr. Tubby Ames, gaping like a stranded fish, surrendered abjectly, as was his invariable custom when firmly handled.

52

"All right," he said, with a pathetic smile. "Carry on! Nobody loves a fat man! Chord, please!"

Said an Apple to a Plum;—
"Seeing how this War has come,
Join me in the stew-pan, do!"

Miss St. Leger, flushed with victory, took her demoralised opponent in an affectionate embrace, and replied:

Said the Plum, "I guess I will!
I am fairly stony; still,
I will do my bit, like you!"

"There's Mr. Lee now," said Liss—"just by the stalls entrance. Let's catch him!"

Our two conspirators descended upon the great man. He proved to be much less formidable than Marjorie had feared.

"We can make room for you, girlie," he announced paternally, "and"—with a glance at Marjorie's face and figure—"a hundred more like you, *if* they can be found, which I doubt!" He patted her shoulder. "Now—where will you fit in? Let me think! You are too big to go prancing about the stage with Baby Lyle, and the other little people. Your life's work is to stand well down stage in a stunning frock, and fill the eye! Take her along to Mr. Lancaster, Baby, and say I sent you. I must be off."

"I ought to tell you," said Marjorie, "that I may find matinées a difficulty. I am working at a canteen. I have only one free afternoon a week."

"That will do," said Mr. Lee. "I believe in helping girls who are doing war work. I'm a special constable myself. Not bad for an old man of fifty-four, eh? But we all try to do something here. Now, run along to Lancaster, girls! I have to report for duty at Vine Street at three o'clock."

With a gracious smile, Mr. Lee disappeared through the stalls entrance. Liss squeezed Marjorie's hand excitedly.

"My dear, you have made a *tremendous* hit with him! He can be horribly grumpy when he likes. Come and be introduced to Lancaster."

The producer was found dismissing the rehearsal of principals. The plum and apple had become jam in the last verse, so both romance and patriotism were satisfied.

"Very good," he said. "It all goes all right now, except the dance. Mr. Kosky will take care of that." He raised his voice. "Principals, same time to-morrow! Good morning, Miss St. Leger! Good morning, Tubby, old man!" His voice boomed louder. "Now then, chorus ladies and chorus gentlemen, please!"

The damosels round the stage laid down their khaki socks, hitched up their own stockings, and gathered in groups in the wings. Simultaneously a procession of six gentlemen appeared from the direction of the stage-door, extinguishing cigarettes.

Liss hurriedly introduced Marjorie. Lancaster shook hands.

"I think we can find a place for you in the show," he said, regarding her with critical approval. "Can you sing?"

Marjorie, with a sudden and incongruous recollection of the harmonium at Netherby on Sunday afternoons, smiled, and replied that she could sing a little.

"Mr. Kay will try your voice after rehearsal. No previous experience, I suppose?"

"No."

"It doesn't matter. You had better sit and watch this rehearsal this morning, and try to learn our language. Baby, my dear, run along and get into your place."

Liss, who appeared to be the *enfant gâté* of the establishment, scampered away, and presently appeared among the chattering throng on the prompt side. Mr. Lancaster clapped his hands. There was silence.

"Now, ladies and gentlemen," he explained, "we are going to try the first new number in the Second Act—'Honolulu Lulu.' Places, please, and try to put some ginger in it this time! You come on laughing and chatting. Now—*commence*!" He clapped his hands again. "For pity's sake, everybody, *desist*! Gentlemen, gentlemen, remember that you are happy South Sea Islanders, without a care in the world—not welshers coming back from a dirty day at Kempton! Again, please! And ladies, don't come bolting on in that panic-stricken way. You aren't taking shelter from an air raid; you are young village belles, come to participate in the Annual Festival of the Sun! You are joyful! You are glad! You are going to sing about it! For the Lord's sake, *smile*! Phil, old man, the symphony once more, if you please! All come in at the end of six bars. La-la! La-la! La-la! *Now*, all together! No! no! no! *no*!" Mr. Lancaster clapped his hands and beat his breast alternately. "Ladies, ladies, *ladies*! Let me tell you, for the last time, that it is a human impossibility to sing with the mouth shut! It can't be done! For generations and centuries people have been trying to sing out of their noses, and their ears, and the back of their necks; but no one has ever succeeded yet. Open your little mouths! Open them wide! And *keep* them open, for the love of Mike!"

And so on, until a standard of approximate harmony was attained.

IV

Next day Marjorie walked on at her first rehearsal, and practised the new numbers with the rest. Mr. Lancaster's attitude towards her was the same as Mr. Lee's. That is to say, he addressed her much as an old gentleman of seventy might address a little girl of six.

"Now, dear, I know you are feeling nervous, and aren't going to do yourself justice, just at first—"

"I am not a bit nervous, thank you," said Marjorie.

"Oh, yes, you are," said Mr. Lancaster. "But remember that I understand about that, and am making allowances all the time. So don't be frightened; but keep your head up, and sing out, that's a good girl!"

"He's a hard nut," remarked her next-door neighbour into her ear—"but he never swears at you. At least, if he does, he always apologises afterwards. He's quite a gentleman."

In a few days Marjorie was admitted an accepted member of the choral sisterhood. She found her colleagues, for the most part, young, friendly, talkative, excitable, and as improvident as grasshoppers. Most of them possessed a "boy" of some kind—usually a callow subaltern of the one-star brand, with a vocabulary largely composed of the expressions "priceless" and "pathetic." Some of them were married. A few had husbands actually out in France, or farther afield. One or two had babies, and talked about them a good deal.

Of the principals, Miss St. Leger, with her magnetic personality and tough little Chicago voice, was a prime favourite with everybody. Her hold over the audience was wonderful: she could galvanise a Wednesday matinée into enthusiasm. Compared with her, the second girl, Phyllis Lane, was no more than an attractive amateur. But both were kind to their humbler sisters. Indeed, nearly everybody was kind to everybody in those days. The theatrical profession is conspicuous for its big generosities and petty jealousies. In August, nineteen-sixteen, the former had almost entirely obliterated the latter. A huge daily casualty-list is a very levelling—indeed, binding—influence, especially in such a community; there was not a girl in the chorus at the Imperial who had not an interest, actual or prospective, in that casualty-list.

The male members of the company, as was only natural at the time, were remarkable neither for their youth nor their physical fitness. In addition to the phlebitic Ames, there were—Jack Hopeleigh, a well-preserved hero with a light baritone—he was registered under the Derby Scheme in group forty-three; Hubert Hartshorn, a comic manservant, who owed his irresistible wheezy laugh to the fact that he had been badly gassed at Ypres more than twelve months previously, and was now discharged permanently unfit; and one Valentine Rigg, a stage lawyer, who for forty years had earned a modest but steady income by arriving in the Third Act with a black bag, and clearing up all misunderstandings just before the clock struck eleven.

To the student of humanity the chorus gentlemen were really more interesting than the principals. There was a dismal individual named Chivers, who now kept a stationer's shop in Brixton, but had once been in grand opera—Carl Rosa's chorus. He contributed a reedy tenor to the ensemble. There was a plump little man with a round face and little tufts of white whisker, invaluable in scenes of revelry where guests of the "jolly old uncle" type were required. This was his first theatrical engagement for fifteen years. In the interim he had supported life with invincible cheerfulness, as a bookmaker's clerk, a traveller in hymn-books, and head-waiter in an old-fashioned Brighton hotel. There was a discharged corporal of the Machine Gun Corps, with lungs of brass, the D.C.M. ribbon on his waistcoat, and twenty-seven fragments of German H.E. in his left leg. There was an unpleasant-looking youth named Mervyn, with bobbed hair and a patronising manner—debarred from volunteering his services to his country by reason of a susceptibility to chills upon the liver. Popular rumour located these elsewhere.

And there was Alf Spender—"Uncle Ga-Ga." His age was a mystery. His own estimate, for war purposes, was forty-one. The ladies of the chorus put it among themselves at a hundred and fifty. It was possibly fifty-four, or thereabouts. He was a frail creature, with a simple soul, and what Americans call a "single-track" mind. He had been a super or chorus man ever since he could remember; and until the year nineteen fourteen had never relinquished a humble ambition to achieve a speaking part. But now all that was cast to the winds. His single track was carrying other traffic. Somewhere within his ill-nourished frame burned the pure white flame of genuine patriotism. His one desire was to be admitted to the privilege of khaki, and to do his humble part in "teaching those dirty Germans a lesson." He never rested in his efforts to qualify. He dyed his scanty locks; he endeavoured, by daily study of a manual of Swedish exercises, to school his feeble limbs and sickly body to the requisite pitch of efficiency. He offered himself at every recruiting station in London, giving a different name at each. But all in vain; no one would accept him. He could pass no physical test; a big heart was not enough.

"Still, I haven't given up hope," he confided to Marjorie. "I have just discovered a really admirable hair-tonic; and there's a new strengthening-food come on the market, which may help. Of course, the chief difficulty is my teeth; an M.O. turns me down the moment he examines them! I haven't many, you see, and what I have don't fit together very well; and good dentistry runs into money—a fiver, at least. But I don't despair—not by any means. They will want me in time! It seems inhuman to say so, but I do trust this battle that's just started on the Somme won't finish the war right off. I couldn't bear to see the troops coming back victorious, and feel that I did nothing to help!"

Here was another Willing Horse. Marjorie's heart warmed to him; they became friends. They shared a newspaper at rehearsals, discussing Sir Douglas Haig's daily bulletin word by word. They read between the lines, and decided that, despite newspaper heroics to the contrary, the gigantic offensive of July the First had only been partially successful.

"We never got through on the left at all," said Alf. "Look at that place on the map—Thiepval. We were meant to carry that bang off, and we didn't! They don't say so, but we didn't! We have broken their line all right, but the trouble is that we have broken it on too narrow a front—and I think it's all because of that Thiepval place. We must widen the gap, or the attack fails. Shall I tell you what I would do if I were head of the Army Council?"

"Yes—do," said Marjorie, eagerly.

"I would secretly construct some sort of contrivance that would protect our troops as they dashed across No Man's Land. That's the most dangerous moment. I'm not worrying about artillery fire, mind you! You may dodge that, or you may not; anyhow, there's a sporting chance about it. It's those machine guns! The Germans have them fixed in such a way that when they are all fired at once there is not a yard of ground that isn't a running river of bullets. Now mark you, once we get across that bullet zone, we have the Hun at our mercy. We British"—Alf's emaciated frame stiffened exultantly—"can do *anything* with the bayonet! But we must get across first!"

"But how?" Marjorie sighed despairingly.

"I don't know: I haven't enough technical knowledge. But some sort of armour-plated motor 'bus would be the idea. I'll bet old Kitchener would have fixed it, if he'd been alive. Oh, dear!" (The *Hampshire* had gone down some six weeks previously.) "By the way, have you heard from Mr. Birnie of late?"

Then Marjorie would tell him all Roy's news. Naturally it contained little of military value, but our two enthusiasts read it—or rather, approved portions thereof—with all the solemn deference due to the Authority on the Spot.

"He may get home on leave some time soon," Marjorie said. "He went out last August, and it's July now. Leave is long over-due, but they stopped it all for weeks before the battle. His battalion was in the opening attack, I think, but they are out now, refitting."

"It must have been an anxious time for you while they were in," said Alf. "Did you know?"

"Yes—at least, I knew a few weeks before that they were at Bray-sur-Somme; so when the news of the attack came I felt pretty certain."

Alf's mild blue eyes flashed.

"I wish I had been with him," he said, "instead of"—he glanced disparagingly downstage, to where Phil Kay, entrenched in the orchestra, was resisting Tubby Ames's bi-weekly offensive—"*this*! It must be a grand moment, coming back to rest, right out of a battle—all mud-splashed, and exhausted, knowing you have made good! Did he give you any details when he wrote?"

"The only detail that mattered," said Marjorie with an unsteady little laugh, "was this!"

She produced a field post card—muddy, crumpled, evidently dispatched by the grimy hand of a stretcher-bearer or a ration orderly. On the back were printed certain alternative statements, familiar enough by this time, designed by the authorities to cover all the chances incident to the life of a soldier in the field. They were all deleted with a blunt pencil, save the first:

I am well.

"That was the nicest letter I ever had from him!" said Marjorie.

"And I bet that's saying a good deal!" replied Alf, with a stately little bow. "Now, touching this Delville Wood, on the right—"

But here the battle-call of Mr. Lancaster was heard in the stalls; and our strategists turned reluctantly from the prosecution of the military campaign to the maintenance of civilian morale.

V

The Second Edition was produced in due course, with the success inevitable in that enthusiastic, unsophisticated, *carpe diem* period. Marjorie appeared successively, and with distinction, as a Lady Guest at the reception of a most unconvincing Duchess, where she flourished an empty champagne glass painted yellow inside; as a Bird of Paradise in the chorus of an ornithological ditty entitled, "If my Girl was a Bird, I would Build Her a Nest," contributed by the well-preserved light baritone aforementioned; as a damsel of the South Sea Islands, participating, with somewhat improbable ritual, in the Annual Festival of the Sun; and in other less exacting roles. Her most distinguished appearance was in the Finale (in a tableau of the Allied Nations), as The Spirit of France. In this she was entrusted with a separate entrance, a solitary walk down stage, and the deliverance of a rhymed couplet of a patriotic nature, in which General Joffre suffered the indignity of rhyming with "Our hats we doff," "nasty cough." She was quite composed, and offered her outrageous contribution with such *aplomb* as to arouse frantic applause. Liss was a dancer, and her activities were mostly linked with those of seven other little creatures like herself. She was whole-heartedly delighted with her friend's successful graduation.

Next morning the company were called at eleven, to be photographed. The morning after, Marjorie reported for duty at the canteen, and was received with open arms by the Mouldy Old Copper. With renewed enthusiasm she settled down to the old drudgery. She was supporting herself; her long and dreary evenings were over; and, best of all, she was really Doing Something to Help.

VI

One morning a few weeks later Mrs. Clegg was deposited by the Rolls-Royce at the front door of Buckholm, and was ushered by Mr. Bates into the amber drawing-room. She entered with the uneasy self-consciousness of the visitor to a great house who has come, not to pay an intimate call, but to attend a committee meeting.

"The other ladies have not yet arrived, madam," announced Bates; and added, in stately reproof: "It is not quite eleven o'clock. Her ladyship will be down presently. Will you please to be seated?" He deposited the flustered and untimely caller upon a sofa, handed her a magazine, and left her alone.

Mrs. Clegg mechanically turned over the pages of the magazine. It was one of those periodicals which was doing its characteristic best at that time to compensate our warriors in the field for compulsory severance from domestic felicity by a weekly display, on a generous—nay, prodigal—scale, of the forms and features of loved ones far away—particularly of such as happened to be connected with the lighter walks of the lyric drama. Mrs. Clegg's eye was caught by a photograph on the middle page—of a tall, slender girl, draped from head to foot in what looked like a flag, with the Cap of Liberty perched upon her fair head. The face seemed familiar. Mrs. Clegg adjusted her tortoise-shell lorgnette—at home, when reading, she wore simple spectacles—and examined the photograph in greater detail. Then she perused the journalistic effusion underneath. It began:

One cannot have *Too Many Girls* of This Kind, Can one?...

Mrs. Clegg was a dutiful wife. On her way home she stopped at the railway station and bought a copy of the magazine at the book-stall. After dinner she showed the middle page to her husband. It was a courageous act, for no such literature had ever been introduced into Netherby before.

That night, when the household had retired to bed, Albert Clegg reopened the Family Bible, lying since prayers at the head of the dining-room table; turned to the Births, Marriages, and Deaths and sent his fountain-pen scouting down the first column. Presently he came to the name he wanted. He scored it out—scored it, and scored it, to complete obliteration. When he had finished, Marjorie had joined Aunt Eliza in the ranks of the Legion of the Lost.

CHAPTER IX

THE BOOK OF THE WORDS

We were due back in the line that night, and I was struggling, in company with one humid orderly-room sergeant and several hundred houseflies, to clean up the usual orderly-room mess—indents, returns, and other nuisances which, in the absence of the adjutant, usually fall upon the patient shoulders of that regimental tweeny, the second-in-command.

I was seated at the kitchen table of a farm-house in Picardy. The weather had been wet and misty for weeks—the weather at critical moments in this war was invariably pro-Boche—but this afternoon the sun had reappeared and summer had come back with a rush. Still, on the overworked highway outside mud still lay deep. At the farm-gate two transport men were admonishing two mules, in the only way they knew, for indicating reluctance (in the only way *they* knew) to hauling the headquarters company's field-kitchen out of the oozy ruts where it had reposed for ten days. Through the open door, looking east, I could descry the wrecked spire of Albert Church, with its golden Virgin and Child projecting horizontally from the summit, like the flame of a candle in a steady draught.

To my ears all the time, through the heavy summer air, came the incessant muffled thunder of guns, and guns, and more guns—British guns, new British guns; hundreds of them—informing Brother Boche that he, the originator of massed artillery tactics, was "for it" himself at last. The bombardment had begun systematically about the middle of the month, all up and down the Western Front. Last Saturday it had intensified in the neighbourhood of the Somme and Ancre Valleys; I had lain awake in my billet, listening, and recalling that summer afternoon, less than two years ago, when Lord Eskerley had gloomily explained to me that it took at least three years to make a British gunner. This afternoon the whole earth trembled; the final eruption could not be much longer delayed.

For Britain was ready to strike at last. True, she had struck before, both recently and frequently; but that had been mainly in self-defence, or for experiment, or to create a diversion. Now she was in a position to strike home. For nearly two years the Willing Horse had stood up indomitably under the strain, while a nation, mainly willing, but shamefully unready, was getting into condition. To-day that nation was ready; every man worth his salt was at last a trained soldier. Never before in our history had such an army been gathered, and never again would such an army be seen, as strained at the leash behind that twenty-five mile front on the thirtieth of June, nineteen sixteen. True, we launched greater armies, and won greater victories in the two years that followed; but—the very flower of a race can bloom but once in a generation. The flower of our generation bloomed and perished during the four months of the First Battle of the Somme. We shall not look upon their like again. It is to be doubted if any generation will—or any race.

Sometimes, in these later days of reaction and uncertainty, we are inclined to wonder whether that sacrifice was justified; whether it would not have been better to wait just a little longer. But in truth we had waited long enough. Strategy might advocate delay, but honour could not. For four months Verdun had stood up like a rock against the rolling tide of assault; it was time we took some weight off Verdun's shoulders. For two years the half-equipped armies of Russia had maintained a suicidal offensive on our account; even now fresh German divisions were streaming away from the Western Front to the Eastern. It was time we called them back. Strategy or no strategy, we meant to accomplish those two purposes. And we did—with something over. Perhaps the Flowers who sleep by the Somme to-day feel, on that account, that what they perished for was worth while. They kept the faith.

I had just dictated provisional Battalion Orders for the morrow; made the usual mistakes in the weekly Strength Return; and was wrestling with an incomprehensible document—highly prized by that section of the Round Games Department which sees to it that wherever the British soldier goes, whether singly or in battalions, his daily rations and weekly pay are diverted from their normal course to meet him—when there came a scuttering of hooves, and Master Roy Birnie, our esteemed sniping and intelligence officer, came flying round the corner on a borrowed horse (mine), as if all the Germans in Picardy were after him. However, this was merely Roy's exuberant way of coming home for his tea. He descended, hitched his steed to the farm-pump, and came striding into the kitchen with blood in his young eye. I dismissed the sergeant in quest of tea. Roy favoured me with a formal salute, then sat down, and began:

"Uncle Alan, I wonder why every battalion in the British Army (except ours) is entirely composed of damn fools!"

"I have heard that speculation so often upon the lips of members of other units of the British Army," I replied, "that I have given up trying to find the answer. Tell me your trouble."

Roy accepted the invitation at once.

"Well," he said, "I had a peach of an observation post up in the front line. It was an old derelict mill-wheel affair—one of those contraptions you see on the end wall of every farm-house in this country, with a poor brute of a mongrel dog inside, treadmilling away to work a churn, or play the pianola, or something. It lies out flat in front of C Company's sector, on top of a little rise, looking like nothing at all. You know it?"

"Yes," I said. "It has been there for months; it is one of the accepted features of the landscape by this time."

"That's right; the Boche has never suspected it. Well, I have been using it as an O. Pip for six weeks. There is a private covered sap leading out to it, and once you're inside you can stand in a pit, with your little circular peep-show all round you. Why, through one loophole I can see right away to Beaumont Hamel! Now, as you know, ten days ago we handed over to the Late and Dirties. This morning, when I went up into the line to see about taking over again to-morrow, what do you think I found—in my own special private O.P.?"

"I don't know," I said. "A hairpin?"

"Uncle Alan, for the Lord's sake don't play the fool! I'll *tell* you what I found; the whole floor of the post—*my* post, mind you—was covered with empty cartridge cases! Some Late-and-Dirty perisher had been in there with a rifle, firing volleys—no, *salvoes*—out of it! With an oily barrel, too, I'll bet! Of course the Boche has the place registered now; and next time there is any general unpleasantness brewing, up it will go! And I hope the Late-and-Dirty dog who gave it away will be inside, that's all!"

"It's rotten luck, I admit, boy. But in this case it doesn't particularly matter. In a day or two, we hope, your observation post will be far in rear of us. Perhaps some clerkly gentleman from the base will be making his nest therein."

Roy's face brightened suddenly.

"When do we push off?" he asked eagerly.

"That is a secret known only to the powers above. But I shouldn't be surprised if it were to-morrow, or the next day. The Colonel is away at a Brigade Conference now—the last, I dare say. He will probably call an officers' meeting when he comes back."

"Is Kilbride with him?" asked Roy quickly.

"Yes. Why?"

Roy smiled awkwardly.

"Well, *you* know!" he said. "Addressing you as Uncle Alan, and not as second-in-command, it's a little difficult sometimes for us Hoy Polloy to gather from the C.O.'s account of the proceedings what really *is* settled at these Brigade pow-wows. That is why we find it so useful to pump old Kilbride afterwards. The Colonel is such a fire-eater that he loathes all this chess-board warfare, as he calls it. His idea of fighting is to go over the parapet about a hundred yards ahead of his men, rush straight at the nearest German, and bite him to death. A pretty sound plan too, in many ways. The men would follow him anywhere."

"You are right, Roy—they would. And addressing you, not in your official capacity, but as my nephew, that's just what makes me anxious."

"You mean you are not sure where he *will* lead them?"

"I am not sure where he *won't* lead them! However, we must not criticise our superiors. Go and have your tea, you disrespectful young hound, and then come and help your uncle to wrestle with B.213. Hallo, here is the Colonel!"

There came a fresh sound of hooves; a neigh of welcome from the bored animal already tethered to the pump; and Eric Bethune and his adjutant rode into the yard.

Eric had been sent to us after Loos—our first commander, Douglas Ogilvy, having been killed in a bomb-fight near Hulluch. (I remember the day well. The Germans were furnished with bombs which exploded on impact; ours were of the Brock's Benefit type, and had to be lit with a match. Unfortunately, it was raining at the time.)

I need not say how joyfully the coming of Ogilvy's successor was greeted by the second-in-command. Eric came to us with a reputation. For nearly twelve months he had ruled an overcrowded and under-staffed depot at home, containing never less than two thousand turbulent ex-militiamen, and had licked into shape and self-respecting shape some of the toughest material that our country produces. After that, he had achieved his heart's desire and been sent out, to be second-in-command of our First Battalion. His first proceeding on arrival was to organise a successful attack upon a valuable sector of the line lost by another unit ten days previously. He led the attack in person, and was mentioned in Dispatches.

He came to us, inevitably, with a halo—or should it be nimbus?—and set to work to make us the smartest battalion on the Western Front. Physical fear appeared to be quite unknown to him. For my part, I confess quite frankly that I do not enjoy an intensive bombardment in the least. I really believe Eric did. So, I think, in soberer fashion, did his predecessor. But we were soon conscious of the change of regime in other directions. Where Eric differed from Douglas Ogilvy was in his passion for the spectacular side of soldiering—the pomp of ceremonial, the clockwork discipline, the perfectly wheeling line, the immaculate button in the midst of mud and blood. Eric was at last in a position to model a battalion on his own beliefs. The result had been an ecstasy of worship at the shrine of Spit and Polish.

"A dirty soldier," he was fond of telling his followers, "means a dirty rifle; and a dirty rifle means, in the long run, a dead soldier. Go and shave, and save your life!"

And there was no doubt that, within limits, he was right. That mysterious and impalpable entity, which we call morale, is apt to languish without the aid of soap and water, and a certain percentage of officially fostered *bravura*. The chief difficulty about this war was to prevent it from degenerating into a troglodytic game of stalemate. Everything that maintained morale and stimulated pride of Regiment was welcome.

But there are other things; and if these be lacking, look out for danger—especially under modern conditions. And it was this fear which possessed my slow-moving, uninspired mind as I took tea in that Picardy farm-house that hot and fateful afternoon with my superior officer and lifelong friend.

"Well," Eric began, filling his pipe, "we have had our last pow-wow, thank God! The Brigadier was in his element. He had the whole affair worked out in a little time-table—like a Jubilee Procession. Salute of twenty-one guns at dawn—procession to move off in an orderly manner at six a.m.—buffet luncheon at noon—carriages at five-forty-five, and everything!"

"Did old Kilbride take down a copy of the time-table?" I asked.

"I don't know. Probably he did: it's the sort of thing he would do. As for me, the whole business nearly made me weep. Why are we treated like children, or amateurs in charge of a Territorial Field Day? Don't these chuckle-headed Mandarins realise that we are fighting under conditions of actual warfare, when at any moment things may happen which no time-table can cover? Don't they understand that you *cannot* control the course of a battle by drawing up a niggling time-table any more than you can control the weather by buying a barometer? There are only two things that count in a soldier. The first is initiative in attack; the second is a complete understanding with his officers. Thank God, my men have both. Show them the objective; send them over the parapet; and they will see to the rest of the business without any time-table or book of the words whatever, thank you very much! Discipline! Discipline! Discipline! That's the only thing that matters!"

"Did you communicate your views to the meeting?" I asked.

"I took that liberty. In fact, I have been taking it for the last three weeks. I fancy I am getting slightly unpopular among the higher forms of animal life; but some one has to take the lead in these matters. Most of the men are too newly promoted—too recently gazetted, for that matter—to intrude their opinions. Good fellows, but amateurs—and diffident amateurs at that! Of course they regard everything the Brigadier says as gospel—and he did worry them so! He explained over and over again to each Battalion Commander the exact route by which he was to lead his men to their objective, and what he was to do when he got there. He was to dig in, and consolidate, and mop up, and re-establish communication—with Brigade Headquarters first and foremost, of *course*!—make arrangements for a ration dump—fancy *thinking* of food at such a moment—!"

"'An army fights on its stomach.' *N. Bonaparte*,' I observed.

"Trust you to remember yours, old man! Then he told us a lot more things, mainly about keeping touch with the Gunners, the Machine-Gunners, and the Signallers, and the R.E., and the Ammunition Column, and the Dry Canteen, and the Old Folks at Home—everybody, in fact, except the enemy. After that, a Gunner Brass-Hat stood up, and spoke *his* little piece. He rubbed in the time-table business; said we must adhere to its provisions *very* carefully; otherwise his guns would invariably be pooped off into the stern of the Brigade instead of the bows of the Boche. He didn't put it quite so baldly as that, but he waffled about the urgent necessity of observing the greatest exactitude, especially when the Gunners proceeded from bombardment to barrage. Then the Brigadier pronounced a sort of benediction, and asked, as a kind of after-thought, if there were any further points he could elucidate for us."

"That, no doubt, was where you put your little oar in!"

"It was. I asked him straight—and I could see half the fellows in the room agreed with me—if he had considered the effect of such paralysing exactitude upon *morale*? Our tradition—at least the tradition of my Regiment—was, and always had been, to seek out the enemy and destroy him. My men had not had a Staff College education; they did not understand or cotton on to this business of limited objectives, and working to a time-table. Their objective was Berlin, and their time-table was the limit of physical endurance; in other words, they were sufficiently disciplined to go until they dropped. Wasn't it rather a pity to cramp their style, and so on? I am afraid I rather riled the Brigadier; for the moment I forgot he had been through the Staff College himself."

"What did he say?"

"He mumbled something to the effect that my suggestions, if adopted, would involve a radical rearrangement of the plan of operations of an entire Army Corps; and that if my men didn't understand the tactical requirements of a modern battle it was my job to explain them to them. He said that—to *me*! Offensive old bounder! But of course, discipline is discipline, so I said no more. One cannot humiliate these old boys in the presence of long-eared subalterns; I remembered that."

"It's a pity you didn't remember it a bit sooner, old man!" It was a rash observation, but I was thoroughly alarmed.

Eric flushed a dusky red.

"Look here, Alan," he said, "I can't take criticism from any officer of mine, however old—"

"Sorry!" I replied. "But do be careful, Eric! You know what these people are. For God's sake, don't get sent home!"

Eric wheeled round upon me.

"What do you mean?" he snapped. "What gossip have you been listening to?"

I began to feel my own temper rising.

"I am not in the habit of listening to gossip," I said stiffly—"especially about my Commanding Officer. But the Brigade Major dropped me a pretty broad hint the other day, to the effect that your independent attitude was causing alarm and despondency among the Brass Hats; and—well, I think it's only fair to mention the fact to you."

But Eric was in no mood for sage counsel that day. He smelt battle; he was "up in the cloods."

"Pack of old women!" he exclaimed impatiently. "Wait till they see what we do in the show to-morrow, compared with the notebook wallahs!"

Then he glanced at my troubled face, and the old boyish smile came back—the smile which had held me captive for thirty years or more. He leaned over, and clapped me on the shoulder.

"Cheer up, Alan!" he said. "It was good of you to warn me; but I *must* use my own judgment in this matter—and I take full responsibility for doing so." He rose, and knocked out his pipe. "Now, I suppose I must have an officers' meeting, and let old Kilbride read to them the Brigadier's impression of how this picnic is to be conducted. They are a very earnest band. They will take it all down—they'd take down the multiplication table if you recited it to them—and read it to their N.C.O.'s; and the N.C.O.'s will misquote it to the men; and to-morrow I shall see my battalion, guide-book in hand, methodically advancing to victory, chanting elegant extracts from Orders, to encourage themselves and frighten the Germans! It's a mad war, this! Now, where is the orderly sergeant?"

"Sit down a minute," I said, "and listen to me." I was imperilling the foundations of an ancient friendship, but I could not leave matters like this. Eric dropped impatiently into his chair.

"Well, what about it?" he asked.

"Eric, old man," I began, "I was at Loos—the only show which we have put up in any way comparable with to-morrow's unpleasantness—and you were not; so I am going to improve the occasion. The great ones above us are quite rightly trying to fight this battle on the basis of the lessons taught us by Loos—and they were pretty considerable lessons. May I give you the experience of your own battalion?"

"Go ahead!" said Eric, resignedly filling his pipe again.

"We went off like a bull at a gate, and bundled the Boche out of his front and second lines in a few hours. I am only giving you our own experience, mind you. Other people weren't so well placed, and got practically wiped out crossing No Man's Land. On the other hand, a Division farther along on our right went slap through everything, up Hill Seventy and down the other side. (They say a platoon of Camerons penetrated right into Lens. Of course they never came out again.) Anyhow, by noon on the first day we were cock-a-hoop enough, right up in the air on perfectly open ground behind the Boche reserve line, without the foggiest notion where Brigade Headquarters was, where the next unit was—as a matter of fact, the people on our immediate left were farther ahead still, while the people on our right hadn't got up, and never did—where our artillery was, where our next meal was to come from, and what we were going to do now! We did all we could, which wasn't much. We tried to reverse the captured trenches, without tools. The Sappers turned up, as Sappers invariably do, just when they were wanted most, and performed marvels in the way of improvising defences; but we were still in a pretty precarious position. For the next twenty-four hours nothing in particular happened. Then the Boche, who had been regularly on the run, rallied, and came stealing back. He found our victorious line echeloned in the most ridiculous fashion all over the place, without any semblance of co-ordination, full of gaps you could march a battalion through. He made all the notes he wanted, called up his reserves, and delivered an extremely well thought-out counter-attack. Strung about as we were, he had us cold. We couldn't get up any ammunition or bombs. Special one-way communication trenches *had* been dug for the purpose, but they, of course, were jammed with traffic going the wrong way— stretcher-parties, prisoners, and details of every kind. (Fifty thousand wounded went back to Bethune in the first forty-eight hours.) We had nothing to hope for from the people farther back. Our gunners were there all right, ready and willing; but they didn't know where we were, and dare not fire for fear of hitting us. Whole Divisions of reinforcements were trying to get through, but the roads were packed with transport. In multiplying our artillery and machine guns we had overlooked the fact that for every gun you put into the line you add at least one limber or waggon to the general unwieldiness of the Divisional Ammunition Column. The country for miles behind the line was like Epsom Downs on Derby Day; nothing could get through at all. It was forty-eight hours before a really adequate scheme of reinforcement could be put into effect, and by that time we were practically back where we started. Up to a point, Loos was a well-conceived and splendidly executed operation; but after the first rush everything got out of gear. We had been told our final objective was Brussels! With a little luck and management we might have got Lille. As things turned out we got one pit-village. Luckily we got a lesson too; and to-morrow's show is going to be fought on that lesson. We are to advance to a fixed line and stay there, so as to eliminate gaps; we are to work to a time-table, to enable our gunners to fire with confidence; and we are to maintain communication from front to rear by a very carefully prepared scheme of one-way trenches and armoured telephone cables. Hence all the pow-wows and the little notebooks, Eric!"

But Eric was not convinced. He was in his most childish mood.

"It won't work! It won't work!" he reiterated. "It sounds all right at the pow-wows, and reads all right in the book of the words, but you can't perform these chess-board antics of peace-time under actual war conditions. There is only one way to win big battles, and that is by initiative, resting on perfect *discipline*—by having each separate unit disciplined and disciplined to such a pitch that its commander can handle a thousand rifles like a single pocket-pistol. I am vain enough to believe that my men are disciplined to that extent. Some of the other units are not; and not all the pow-wows and guide-books in the world will help them!"

He rose, and began to buckle on his equipment, whistling through his teeth. I knew that sound, and I dropped the subject.

"Is the kick-off hour fixed?" I asked.

"Yes. About three hours after dawn to-morrow; Kilbride has the details. We are going in from our present sector. I suppose the battalion are all ready to move?"

"Yes; they are parading now. They are timed to pass through Albert after dark, and take over from the Mid-Mudshires just before midnight."

"Good! They may as well know at once that they are going to attack, if they haven't guessed it already. I shall say a word to them before they move off. Are they all going together?"

"No. By companies, at twenty minutes interval."

"Well, let them parade together, anyhow. After I have spoken to them I shall go on with the leading company, and take Kilbride with me. I want you to stay here and clean up. Is another unit taking over this billet?"

"Yes—the Mid-Mudshires; we are simply changing places with them. I am expecting their advance-party at any moment."

"All right. When you have handed over, come along with the Orderly-room staff and join me. Have you much left to do here?"

I glanced round the littered table.

"A fair amount. You are taking Kilbride yourself?"

"Yes. Do you want help?"

"If you could spare me an odd subaltern—"

Eric glanced out of the window, to where the Headquarters Company were parading in the muddy road. His eye fell upon Master Roy, who, a little apart, was inspecting his own particular beloved command—a workmanlike squad of snipers. Eric swung round.

"If you want a really odd subaltern," he said, "take young Birnie! Appoint him Assistant Adjutant for the occasion, and tell him to send those pop-gun experts of his back to duty!"

I fairly gasped.

"You will break their hearts!" I said. "Can't you use them as scouts, or—"

Eric blazed right out this time.

"For God's sake, Laing, allow me to command my own battalion!" he cried. Then—characteristically—"I'm sorry, old boy! You mean well, I know; but really I must do things my own way. We don't require Bisley specialists in a hand-to-hand battle. As for Roy Birnie, a little less sniping and a little more intelligence won't do him any harm at all. Now I'm off to harangue the battalion. Sergeant, is my groom outside? I want my horse."

CHAPTER X

DISCIPLINE! DISCIPLINE! DISCIPLINE!

Exhortation before Action was a form of military ceremonial exactly to our commander's taste. I had heard him address his followers many a time. Nearly thirty years ago I had formed one of an audience of fourteen—shivering in shorts and jerseys in an east wind at the back of the school pavilion what time we were addressed by one Eric Bethune, about to lead us into a Final House Match which, owing to the size, speed and prestige of our opponents, could be regarded as little else than a forlorn hope. We won that Final House Match. I decided then, and have never departed from that belief, that no more gallant and inspiring leader of a forlorn hope than that same Eric could have been found among the manhood of our race. And here we were again, eight hundred strong this time, gathered in hollow square for the same purpose.

Eric spoke to us for perhaps five minutes, sitting his horse like a graven image, with the last rays of the setting sun glinting upon his burnished equipment. ("Protective dinginess" was anathema in Eric's battalion.) Around him, steel-helmeted, perfectly aligned, motionless, stood his men. It was characteristic of their commander that he did not preface his address with the order that they should stand at ease. All ranks remained rigidly at attention while he spoke.

I need not repeat his words. It is enough to say that, having heard them, I, for one, would willingly have followed the speaker anywhere he chose to lead me, without a thought (for all my fundamental convictions on the subject) of limited objectives, or artillery time-tables, or other mechanical hindrances to free fighting. He moved his men, too—representatives of the dourest and most undemonstrative element of the dourest and most undemonstrative nation in the world. I could see the effect of his words, in the glow of tanned faces, in the setting of square jaws, in the further stiffening of sturdy, rigid bodies. It was hard to decide which to be most proud of—the leader, or the men. I glowed inwardly as my eye ran down the motionless ranks. Great hearts! Great stuff! And, above all, representative stuff—truly representative, at last! They were not of the Regular Army type, nor the Territorial type, nor Kitchener's Army type. They were of the National Army—Britain in Arms—voluntary Arms—The Willing Horse, reinforced and multiplied to his most superlative degree.

Five minutes later A Company were streaming down the road in fours, Eric striding at their head with the company commander and adjutant. He had sent his horse back to the transport lines, and was "foot-slogging" exultantly with his men. I returned to the farm kitchen. I entered rather suddenly. Our newly-appointed assistant adjutant was sitting at the table, with his head buried in his arms. His back was to the door.

I tripped heavily upon the door-sill. Roy sat up hurriedly, and busied himself with the papers before him.

"Everything cleared up now?" I asked briskly, slipping off my heavy marching equipment.

"Yes, sir," replied a muffled voice—"very nearly."

"In that case," I continued, with great heartiness, "we can get away almost immediately. I am expecting our relief here in five minutes."

I babbled on a little longer, to give him time to recover. Presently he turned upon me, and spoke. His face was flushed—absurdly like his mother's when something had roused her chivalrous indignation.

"Uncle Alan, it's a rotten shame! I had a wonderful scheme all mapped out! It was in Orders, too! We had marked down all sorts of cushy spots for sniping Boche machine guns from. I had an aeroplane map of our sector, with Thiepval, and Beaumont Hamel, and everything! Now, my poor chaps are all sent back to their companies, where they will be treated like dirt; and—I am given a job as assistant office boy!"

It is impossible to furnish adequate comfort to a man who has been deprived unexpectedly of his first independent command. I merely patted Roy's shoulder, and said gruffly—

"Discipline, Discipline, Discipline, lad! That's the only thing that matters!"

Roy sat up at once. He was a soldier, through and through.

"I beg your pardon, sir," he said. "I am afraid I was mixing up Major Laing with Uncle Alan! That wasn't the game, was it? My error! It shan't occur again." He smiled resolutely. "I think everything is in order now. Shall I hand these files over to the Orderly-room sergeant?"

"Righto!" I said. "Was that a despatch rider I saw at the door just now?"

"Yes—from Brigade Headquarters. He left two messages."

"Did you give him a receipt for them?"

"No. He slung them in and bolted off. I expect Brigade Headquarters are on the move, and he didn't want to lose touch with them."

"Never mind! See what they are about."

Roy opened the first envelope, and extracted a field despatch-form. He glanced at it, and grinned.

"It's lucky we got this before going up into the line!" he observed; and read aloud:

The expression "Dud" must no longer be employed in Official Correspondence.

"It's a memo from Olympus," I explained: "They mean well, but their sense of proportion is not what it might be. And the next article?"

Roy did not reply. I looked up. His face was as white as chalk. He was breathing heavily through his nose, staring in a stupefied fashion at the flimsy pink slip in his hand.

"My God!" he muttered; "My God! It'll break his heart."

"What on earth's the matter, old man?" I leaned across the table. Roy thrust the despatch towards me.

"From Divisional Headquarters," he said, mechanically. "The Brigade Major has sent it on."

The message was quite brief:

Lt.-Col. E. F. B. Bethune, D.S.O., commanding Second Battalion, Royal Covenanters, will return home forthwith and report to War Office.

Pinned to the despatch was a hastily scrawled covering slip from the Brigade Major:

Passed to you, for immediate compliance, please.

The next thing that I remember was Roy's voice:

"They've done it on him! The dirty dogs! They're sending him home! Did you—know?"

"No! Yes! Well, I was half afraid of it. I knew the people higher up were getting a bit restive: in fact, I tried to warn him only this afternoon. But I never dreamed they would strike back at a moment like this. You are right, Roy—it will break his heart." (It was the second occasion upon which I had employed that phrase within the last hour.)

Another thought struck Roy.

"You are in command now!" he said.

"I suppose so; but not until this despatch is actually delivered to the Colonel."

We were silent again. We were both picturing the same scene, I fancy. Presently Roy said:

"If only it had been delayed in some way!"

I nodded.

"Even for a day!—"

"Even for an hour!—"

66

"Even for ten minutes! We should have been gone out of this place, and they would not have got us until the show was over!"

Our eyes met, then dropped hurriedly. We had read one another's thoughts. Discipline, Discipline, Discipline!

Roy picked up the two despatches, folded them, and put them mechanically into the pocket of his field despatch-book. Then he cleared his throat huskily. I found myself doing the same.

"Look here!—" we began both at once.

A cheery voice interrupted us:

"Good evening, sir. Is this Caterpillar Farm?"

We both jumped, like detected conspirators.

In the doorway stood a subaltern, saluting, with the totem of the Royal Mid-Mudshire Regiment stencilled upon his tin bowler.

"Come in," I said. "This is the place you want. I presume you have come to take over?"

About midnight, the Orderly-room Staff filed through the ghostly streets of Albert, to the music of innumerable big guns working up to their final spasm. At their head marched a silent major and a preoccupied assistant adjutant.

Next morning, just after dawn, the Second Royal Covenanters went raging to the opening attack of the greatest battle yet fought in the history of warfare. We were led into action by our Commanding Officer, Eric Bethune.

CHAPTER XI

ENFIN!

If those years brought unprecedented misery to the human family, they had their compensating moments—especially for those most deeply concerned. Lovers, for instance—true lovers. When two people really love one another, and are limited by inexorable circumstances to rare and brief periods of companionship, each one of which may be the very last—and each succeeding day of those four years saw some six hundred British soldiers of all ranks go back from Leave never to return—their love is lifted to heights, and breathes an atmosphere, of which ordinary workaday lovers can know nothing. Poor peace-time lovers—sitting holding hands in a conservatory, or spooning on a golf course—what do they know? Faced by a future all their own (and the enervating consciousness that there will probably be a good deal of it), what do they know? What do they know of the blind rapture of Six Days' Leave?

Roy's telegram preceded him by exactly one hour, so Marjorie had little time to get excited. She merely embraced Liss, changed her frock, embraced Liss again, changed her frock again, and dashed off to Victoria. After that her recollection of events went out of focus a little. She had watched the arrival of the Leave-train so often merely as a benevolent spectator, that sudden and personal participation in that function disarranged her perspectives.

She caught sight of Roy almost at once—singling out his glengarry from among the flat caps and steel helmets. He was politely resisting the importunity of an elderly gentleman in a grey uniform and a red brassard, bent on luring him to a free ride upon the Underground Railway. Next moment, Marjorie had slipped her arm through his. After that, neither of them remembered anything much until they found themselves sitting hand in hand in a taxi, gliding stealthily through the darkened streets of London, both feeling a little constrained and embarrassed. Re-united lovers, especially of our nation, do not always spark immediately on contact. We are a highly-insulated race.

"They keep this old place pretty dark," said Roy, peering out of the cab window. "Zeppelins, I suppose?"

"Yes. We had some last week."

"Have you ever seen one?"

"Rather!"

Roy laughed, constrainedly.

"It's funny you should have seen something in this war that I haven't," he said. "Where are we going?"

"To my flat."

Roy turned and surveyed Marjorie's profile in the dim light of the cab.

"I shall be able to see you properly then," he announced with satisfaction. "It's as dark as the inside of a cow here. Have you changed at all, I wonder?"

"You will find I am quite a big girl now," replied Marjorie, laughing constrainedly.

Roy laughed too, and his face came closer to hers. Her hair brushed his lips. Next moment their arms were about one another.

Five minutes later, they groped their way mechanically upstairs to Marjorie's landing, while a slightly incredulous taxi-driver, with one of the newly-invented pound notes in his oily palm, drove hurriedly away before somebody came out of the chloroform.

"You are thinner, dear, and older—much older," was Marjorie's verdict when they found themselves under the lamp by the sofa. "You look more like thirty than twenty. I expect things have been pretty awful sometimes, haven't they?"

Roy nodded. "Yes, sometimes," he said. "I'll tell you about it one day." Then, suddenly and boyishly: "Dearest, you look wonderful!"

It was no more than the truth. Marjorie had felt tired enough a couple of hours ago; but now her cheeks were pink, and her eyes glowed. Her hair had suddenly recovered its lustre. For the first time in six months she looked what she was—twenty. But she realised that the old Roy could never come back to her. Her smooth-cheeked schoolboy was gone, and in his place she had a man—thin as a lath, healthily bronzed, and curiously grave. The Western Front lost no time in making a man in those days—or breaking him.

They kissed again, with absolute lack of shyness this time. Suddenly a thought struck Marjorie.

"Good gracious!" she cried. "What time is it?"

"Seven o'clock. Why?"

"My dear—the theatre! I'd forgotten all about it. I am an honest working girl, and the curtain goes up at eight-thirty!"

"By gum!" said Roy, who of course knew all about "Too Many Girls." "*Absent from parade when warned for duty*, eh? That will never do. What about it? Can't you get a night off?"

"I might," said Marjorie doubtfully. "Most of the girls send a doctor's certificate. But I don't think it's the game. They overdo it so."

"Quite right!" said that young disciplinarian, Lieutenant Birnie. "But it's a bit rough, all the same."

A key rattled loudly and tactfully in the outer door, which then opened with mature deliberation, and Liss appeared.

"I hadn't meant to butt in," she explained, after introductions, "but I just want to say that I have seen Lancaster, and he says you can have the night off. I told him about you," she explained to Roy, "and he said you could have her this evening if you promised faithfully to send her back for to-morrow's show."

"I will bring her back myself," replied Roy, "and buy the whole front row to watch her from!"

"Righto! Good-bye, children! Enjoy yourselves!" said Liss, and vanished, like a diplomatic little wraith.

After that, Roy and Marjorie sat down to make plans.

"First of all," began Roy, "I must hop off to the club and order a bed and have a hot bath—a real hot bath! *Sah vah song dearie,* as we say at the Quai D'Orsay. My last one was in a little house somewhere behind Albert, in a sort of zinc coffin in front of the kitchen stove, with the family sitting tactfully in the scullery. But I am digressing: let us resume! After that, we will go and dine somewhere. By the way, I suppose there is still plenty of food to be had in these days?"

"There is a shortage of potatoes at present, I am sorry to say," replied Marjorie in her best canteen manner. "But—"

"We can worry along without potatoes," said Roy. "What I chiefly want is to dine off a table covered with a white cloth instead of a newspaper; and drink out of a glass instead of a tin cup. I think the Carlton will meet the case. Oh, my dear, my dear! I can't believe it all yet! Are you *really* here?" ...

At this rate of progress it was nine o'clock before they sat down to the feast, which was served to them by an obsequious neutral in a corner of the big restaurant. It was a luxurious dinner for war time, though bully beef and stewed tea would have served equally well. Reunited lovers are not, as a rule, fastidious.

They talked steadily now, unfolding reminiscence after reminiscence. Roy had most to tell; for Marjorie's adventures had been faithfully recorded in her daily letters, while Roy, as previously noted, had usually confined himself to breezy irrelevance.

"Uncle Alan is in command now," he said. "I suppose you heard that the Colonel had been knocked out?"

"Colonel Bethune? Yes, I saw it in the paper." To her own annoyance, Marjorie felt her colour rising. But Roy noticed nothing.

"Yes, he stopped a five-point-nine with his left arm on the second day of the Somme show, and went home without it. We were in a pretty tight place at the time, and it was a bit of a job getting him away. But I hear he's all right again now, though short of a fin. Have you seen him by any chance?"

"Not since April," said Marjorie. "He was in London then, on leave." She was feeling thoroughly self-conscious, and despised herself for it.

"They gave him a bar to his D.S.O.," continued Roy. "He deserved it too, for what he did."

"What did he do?" asked Marjorie jealously. She was a little critical of a system which gave a decoration to a man for getting wounded and coming home, and nothing to those who had to remain and carry on.

"We were right up in the air," explained Roy, "uncovered on both flanks. We did not know where we were; Brigade Headquarters didn't know where we were, so couldn't reinforce us; and the gunners didn't know where we were, so couldn't fire for fear of hitting us. The only person who really knew where we were was the Boche—a well-informed little fellow, the Boche!—and he gave it to us good and hard. But the Colonel was wonderful. We had no cover in particular, beyond a kneeling-trench which we had scooped out for ourselves. There was no room for any officer to pass up and down, so we all stayed where we found ourselves, as ordered, and controlled our fire as well as possible. But the Colonel came walking to us across the open from Battalion Headquarters—an old mine-crater about a hundred yards in rear of us—and strolled right along our whole front from end to end, with Boche snipers taking pot-shots at him all the time; looking as if he had just come out of his tailor's—he had *gloves* on!—stopping here and there to talk to the men, and telling them that no battalion of the Covenanters had ever been known to go back, and that reinforcements were coming up, and how pleased he was to see us so steady. (We weren't feeling a bit steady, really.) The trenches were full of wounded men whom we couldn't get away. He stopped and spoke to them all—by name!—and gave them cigarettes. The result was that when the Boche attacked, our fellows fought like tigers. It was after the attack got round our undefended flanks that the hard time began. Finally, their gunners got our range, and simply blew us out of the trench. Even then the C.O. wouldn't give in. He stood on the parapet, giving fire orders as cool as you please, and telling us how well we were doing. Finally he was hit. They carried him away on a blanket, insensible, and Uncle Alan took command. By this time we were surrounded on three sides—enfiladed, and everything. Uncle Alan passed word along that we were to fall back slowly to our proper place in the line."

"Your proper place?"

"Yes. I forgot to tell you about that. We had overrun our objective, it seemed. Everybody else in the brigade was snugly dug in about half a mile behind us, on a continuous line, except for a gap that we ought to have been filling. We got there at last, but it was a pretty awful walk. We got all our wounded away, though."

"Were there many?"

"A good lot. It was bad luck getting into that position at all. However, we got a tremendous pat on the back from the Divisional Commander afterwards. Apparently there had been some misunderstanding about orders. Now let us talk about something else."

And that was as much as was ever told of the story of how Eric Bethune's lofty contempt for the "book of the words" led a fine battalion into a skilfully baited death-trap.

After that they talked, as lovers will, of the present. They even spoke of the future—a subject upon which, in those days, few young people cared to hazard conjecture in cold blood. But to-night their blood ran hot and high. The world was theirs—for six days.

"To-morrow morning," continued Roy, with an air of immense authority, "I shall take you out and buy you an engagement ring. It is perfectly scandalous your going about with me in this way without one! (Still, I suppose you will have to wear it round your neck on a string, anyway!) After that, a little shopping! I suppose there will be no harm if I buy you some things—long gloves, and high-heel shoes, and silk stockings, and things like that? We'll throw in a nice sensible umbrella, as a chaperon! Then in the evening we will dine early, so as to give you plenty of time to get to your show."

Marjorie laid her slim fingers upon Roy's brown paw.

"Darling," she said firmly, "to-morrow morning I am going to take you to a railway station, and you are going to take the train to Scotland, to see your father!"

Roy's face fell ludicrously. Then the smile he had inherited from his mother came suddenly back. He was all contrition.

"Good Heavens! You had me there, dear. I own up! For the last twenty-four hours my noble parent has entirely escaped my memory. As soon as they told me that I could go on leave I simply grabbed my haversack, asked the Buzzers to send a wire, and then sprinted for the railhead. Poor old dad! Of course you're right. I haven't had a line from him for six weeks, by the way. I'll send a telegram to Baronrigg at once, and start to-morrow." Then he added anxiously:

"How long must I stay?"

Marjorie considered.

"Your father doesn't know anything about *me*, of course?" she said.

"No; nobody knows. It's our secret—ours, and no one else's!" The impulsive pair squeezed hands upon the secret, instantly revealing it to the obsequious neutral aforementioned. "Still, perhaps it would be as well if I told him, eh? Then he couldn't object to my coming back here pretty quick."

"Supposing he doesn't approve?" said Marjorie doubtfully. "He doesn't know me—nor my people, so far as I am aware. Or perhaps he does, which might be worse!"

"My old dad's a white man," said Roy stoutly. "He'd understand. He knows what it is for a fellow to have to go without. He once had to endure seeing his girl—my mother—engaged to another man for several months. He'll understand, all right!"

"I never knew that," said Marjorie. "Who was the other man?"

"Colonel Bethune. Of course he was only a subaltern then."

"*Who?*" Marjorie was fairly startled out of herself this time.

"Eric Bethune, our C.O. I thought that would surprise you! I never knew myself until a few months ago. Uncle Alan told me. The Colonel has always been rather heavily down on me—I never knew why—and one day when I was more than usually fed up with things in general, having just been informed by my commanding officer that I was not fit to hold the King's Commission, old Uncle Alan told me all about it. He explained that the Colonel didn't really think me a dud soldier; he was only peeved at not being my father. Fancy disliking a fellow for that! It's a queer world!"

Queer indeed! Marjorie, better informed than Roy, mused upon the diabolical trick of fate which had caused a man to be baulked of the only thing that really matters by two successive generations—first by the father, then by the son. For the first time she felt a genuine pang of pity for Eric Bethune. But it passed, in a flash. Eric was "heavily down on" Roy—her Roy! All her generous soul revolted at the pettiness of such a revenge.

"I often wondered," continued Roy, "why my mother broke it off. I don't believe Uncle Alan knew. Why was it, do you think?"

"I don't know," said Marjorie. But she did.

Five minutes later they arrived at the theatre where the musical comedy—or musical tragedy: you never know—of their choice was in progress. The vestibule was deserted, but Roy held open the swing door and ushered Marjorie into the darkened auditorium. A blast of hot air and a concerted feminine screech greeted them.

"The curtain's up," said Roy. "Come along! Our seats are in the back row, on the gangway. Rotten, but convenient!"

They slipped unostentatiously into their places. The company were massed upon the stage; the orchestra was in full cry; the young persons of the Chorus were in a state of unwonted animation. In the centre, a lady of ravishing beauty was melting into the arms of a distinguished-looking individual just over military age. Humourists supported either flank.

"This is going to be some show!" announced Roy, groping for Marjorie's hand, and surveying the chorus with all the appreciation of a Robinson Crusoe of six months' standing. "I shouldn't mind being Adjutant of *that* battalion! Not that any of them could walk down the same street with you! Hallo, hallo! What's all this? The interval! We must have come in late."

The curtain fell, and the audience, with one accord, rose to their feet and made for the doors. The band offered a hurried tribute to the Crown. Roy looked at his watch, and turned to Marjorie with a comical grimace.

"Eleven o'clock!" he announced. "We must have sat over dinner a bit longer than we thought. The show's over! Does it matter?"

"Nothing in the world matters—this week!" said Marjorie, taking his arm.

CHAPTER XII
TOM BIRNIE
I

Roy was duly despatched to Scotland the following morning.

"When does your leave end?" Marjorie asked, as they waited for the crowded train to start.

"Let me see—this is Friday. I go back by the leave-train next Wednesday afternoon—"

"Then travel back here on Sunday night," said Marjorie; "unless, of course, you can persuade your father to come back with you at once."

Roy pondered.

"I don't know," he said, "that it wouldn't be better to stick the week-end out at Baronrigg, and then come back alone, and have you all to myself."

Your true lover is an uncompromising egotist. Marjorie at once recognised the superiority of Roy's view.

"All right," she said. "There's the whistle! Get into the train, little man. Send me a telegram when you arrive."

She watched the long train crawl out of sight, and went back to the flat with a hungry heart. Six days! And she had to give him up for three of them! Still, it was the game.

But she had not to wait so long. Roy burst into the flat about noon the very next day—to the entire *bouleversement* of Liss, who was a dilatory dresser. Redirected by her (from behind the bathroom door) he sought Marjorie at the canteen, dragged her almost forcibly out to lunch, and communicated his news in a breath.

"Baronrigg is closed up tight! Has been for six weeks! Dad put all his affairs into order at the beginning of last month, and disappeared!"

"Disappeared? What do you mean?"

"Well, he simply shut up the house, gave what servants were left by the war a year's wages, walked to the station, and took the train for London. He hasn't been heard of since."

"But where has he gone?"

"Nobody knows!"

"Was he ill, or anything?"

"No. By all accounts he was as hard as nails and as fit as a fiddle."

"But didn't he leave any message?" asked Marjorie, bewildered.

"Yes," replied Roy, unbuttoning his tunic pocket, "he did. This letter, for me. I got it from old Gillespie at the Bank. I expect Dad knew I'd pop in there!"

"But doesn't it explain?" asked Marjorie.

"I don't know," said Roy calmly. "I haven't opened it yet."

"You have had it for a day and a night, and haven't opened it?"

"No. I wanted to wait until you and I could read it together."

"But weren't you dying of curiosity?"

"I was, rather. Still, I said to myself—"

Marjorie slipped her arm impulsively into his.

"Roy, dearest," she said, "*I* could never have done that!"

It was the first and last time Marjorie ever admitted to Roy that her sex was in any way inferior to his. They returned to the flat and read the letter together. That is to say, Roy read it aloud to Marjorie:

My dear Son,

You will remember that when the war broke out I was among those who thought it might have been avoided. I was also numbered among those who thought it would be a short war. I was wrong in both views.

My errors did not end there. I was not in favour of the raising of a great army. My opinion was that we should limit our efforts to the efficient policing of the seas, the supplying of munitions and equipment to France and Russia, and the enforcement of a great commercial blockade against the enemy. Neither honour nor interest, I said, demanded more of us. When our young men left all and followed the Colours without, as it seemed to me, pausing to reason why, I was inclined to regard them as hysterical Jingoes.

"I remember him saying that," observed Roy. "We had quite a battle before he would let me apply for a commission."

The war has now been in progress for two years. My first purpose in writing to you is to acknowledge to you that in your conception of national duty you, my son, were right and, I, your father, was wrong.

"It was decent of him to put in that," said Roy, looking up again.

I realise now that not only was the war inevitable, but that unless we make a superhuman effort as a nation we shall not win it. That realisation, unfortunately, is not universal in this district. Most of our people have done magnificently, and I shall always be proud to think that my only son was among the first and the youngest to volunteer.

"This," commented Roy, "is darned embarrassing to read aloud."

"Go on!" commanded Marjorie: "I love it!"

Indeed, the effort has been too great. Too high a tax has been levied on spontaneous loyalty. The general enthusiasm of the country has not been maintained. Consequently the best of our stock, both gentle and simple, is bearing the burden alone, at a cost which is ruining the future of the country.

That brings me to the second thing I have to say to you. In this very neighbourhood there are many blind optimists, many drifters, many irritating phrase-mongers, and a certain number of so-called Conscientious Objectors to warfare.

"He must have met Amos!" said Marjorie.

These latter are not dangerous: their very cowardice makes it easy to deal with them. Far more pernicious are the optimists, the drifters, and the phrase-mongers. Yesterday, at a meeting of the Territorial Association, I met a typical specimen—Mr. Sanders, of Braefoot. You may know him.

"I do," said Roy, grinning. "A celebrated captain of industry, now a county magnate—Nineteen-Thirteen vintage!"

This man said to me: "Sir Thomas, what I like about the situation is the way we are all doing our bit. I, for instance, have been working overtime on Government contracts for two years. I have bought nearly one hundred thousand pounds worth of War Bonds, and I have given seven nephews to the Army. Pretty good, eh?" By what authority, or with whose knowledge, he had presented other men's sons to the Army he did not explain.

Roy, I am ashamed of such people. But who am I to be ashamed of anyone but myself for not realising sooner—as soon as you—that in this sacred cause of ours there is only one thing that counts, and that is personal service? I am sound in wind and limb, and I have no helpless dependents. To-morrow I am going to London to join the Army. As an earnest of the fact that I do so in the spirit of humility and contrition, and not from any desire to pose or advertise, I shall communicate my intention to no one but yourself. I shall enlist as a private soldier, but in a unit where I am not likely to meet any one I know; and I pray God that he will enable me to serve my country as effectively as my own dear son.

Roy's voice shook a little. He had just made his father's acquaintance.

Should I not come back, you will find my affairs in perfect order, and Baronrigg waiting for you. Your trustees are Lord Eskerley and Alan Laing. Should neither of us come back—

"Don't read any more, dear," said Marjorie.

"All right!" replied Roy. "That's practically all now." He folded the letter and put it away in his tunic.

"I wish," he added thoughtfully—"I wish fathers and sons could get to know one another a bit better while they have the chance!" Then, "I wonder what regiment he enlisted in! I wonder if we shall ever meet out there! I'm sorry he didn't see you before he went. You'd have liked him, I think."

"I like him now," said Marjorie, with shining eyes. "I think he's splendid! And"—she broke into a happy laugh—"I like him particularly at this moment, because he has given you to me for four days more instead of two!"

"Let's go shopping!" said Roy, rising importantly.

II

After a gloriously deliberate start, the six days, as usual, gathered momentum. The last forty-eight hours whizzed by like an eighteen-pounder shell.

On Wednesday morning Roy, once more equipped in mud-stained khaki and bristling with portable property, appeared at the flat for breakfast at nine o'clock. Marjorie was ready for him. Liss joined the party a little later. For all her feather-head, she was no mean tactician. Having conscientiously effaced herself throughout the week, instinct now told her that her presence at the parting breakfast would be a good thing. So she uprooted herself from her beloved bed, and entered upon the task of distracting the lovers from the contemplation of the immediate future.

"I thought it was just time," she announced to Roy, "to bring myself to your notice a little. I am here, you know! I have been here most of the week, only I don't think you observed me very much."

"Oh, yes, I did," replied Roy gallantly. "Who could help it?"

"Well, you could—and did! I don't much like being in the same room with people who don't know I'm there. It's not safe. You walked straight through me the other afternoon, when you called to collect Marjorie. And the day before that, when I opened the door to you, you wiped your feet on me! I've had a wonderful week!"

With such blunt shafts of wit as these Miss Lyle ultimately provoked the lovers to a smile.

"That's better!" she said. "Now, next time you come home on leave, give us longer notice, and I will warn Leonard, or somebody, for duty. Then I shan't feel such an outsider."

Roy promised to do so.

"You will take care of Marjorie, won't you?" he added.

Miss Lyle favoured him with a gaze of withering wonder.

"You have been trying to take care of her yourself most of this week, haven't you?" she demanded.

"I have been doing my best," admitted Roy, cautiously.

"Very well, then! What happened? How did it end?"

74

"It ended, I think," confessed Roy, "in her taking care of me!"

Liss nodded her bobbed head triumphantly. "That's it," she said. "That's what always happens to people who try to take care of Marjie. She grabs them by the neck, puts them in her pocket, and keeps them there! That's what she'll do to me again, when you're gone. It's no good my pretending I ever do anything for her."

"Nonsense!" said Marjorie.

"But I'll tell you what," continued Liss: "I'll see she doesn't take care of anybody else while you're away—if I can. That's her trouble: she'd take care of the whole army, and navy, and munition people, and Red Cross, and everything, if she was let! But I'll watch her, and save the leavings for you!" She glanced at the clock, and rose. "Now, children, your Auntie Liss is going to leave you! Tactful—that's me! When is your train, General?"

"Two o'clock," said Roy. "I fancy we sail from Folkestone about six."

"Then," inquired Liss, playing a carefully hoarded ace of trumps, "why not go down to Folkestone *now*, both of you, by the morning train? That way you would have her until nearly six, instead of two. It's all right; don't thank me!" she concluded pathetically, as Marjorie, without a word, dived into the bedroom for her hat, and Roy began to struggle madly into his equipment.

III

They spent the bleak November afternoon on the Leas at Folkestone. At their feet lay the Straits of Dover, across whose waters British soldiers had come and gone for twenty-six months, and continued to come and go for twenty-five more, without the loss of a single soldier's life. But they could not see their feet that afternoon: their heads were in the clouds—private clouds, to which we will not presume to follow them.

As the autumn darkness fell, they took an early dinner in an almost empty hotel hard by the harbour, talking cheerfully of things that did not matter. Roy ordered champagne, and they drank a silent toast with a fleeting glance over the rims of their glasses.

"When does my train start?" asked Marjorie at length. "Don't forget that I have to be back for the evening performance."

Roy would inquire.

"Half-past five, from the Town station," he announced on returning. "That's some way from here. I have ordered a car, and if we start now I can go with you and see you off. That will give me just time to hop into the official leave-train coming down from London. It stops at Folkestone Town to turn round, and then backs right down to the boat."

Once more the parting was staved off. However, one cannot go on pilfering minutes eternally. This time it really was good-bye. It was half-past five; and they stood on the Town station platform.

"This is your train," said Roy, "standing here. Mine is due at the other platform now. There goes the signal! I must skip across the bridge. So—"

He drew Marjorie behind a friendly pile of luggage.

"It has been wonderful, Roy dear—wonderful!" For a moment she laid her head on Roy's breast. "But we did one stupid thing."

"What was that?"

"We ought to have got married!"

"I never thought of it," said Roy simply. "We were so happy, there didn't seem to be anything else."

"But we'll remember next time!" said Marjorie.

75

"I will give the matter my personal attention!" Roy assured her. "So-long, and take care of yourself!"

CHAPTER XIII

ALBERT CLEGG

In the early summer of Nineteen-Seventeen Uncle Fred paid a prolonged visit to Netherby—ostensibly to renew family ties, in reality for reasons not altogether unconnected with air-raids on London.

For the moment the fortunes of the war were back in the melting pot. The Battle of the Somme had bundled Brother Boche right back to the Siegfried Line, and enemy morale on the Western Front was low. The British army, fortified by twelve months of conscription, was blundering forward in characteristic fashion upon many fronts. The navy had swelled to a size undreamed of by any, and known only to few. Over the British coast alone nearly three thousand vessels of all sorts and conditions were keeping watch. The "Q" boat, too, with its crazy crew of immortals, was abroad upon the face of the waters, and the hunter had become the hunted.

But there was much to be set down upon the contra side. The spring offensive of the French army, after a brilliant beginning, had faltered, then halted. There had been recriminations, inquiries, resignations; and Pétain, the saviour of Verdun, had succeeded the gallant Nivelle. To keep the enemy from benefiting by the sudden relaxation of pressure on the Chemin des Dames the British army had flung itself into the premature Battle of Arras, and once more the casualty lists had shot up.

At home, the talk was mainly of Gothas—the Zeppelin was entirely *démodé*—and ration cards. The war was costing us six million pounds a day. Income tax at six shillings in the pound was teaching the man of moderate means the meaning of war; super-tax and excess profits tax were subjecting the capitalistic waistcoat to a not unsalutary reduction. Labour—or rather what was left, now that all that was best and soundest in Labour was away fighting—was going on strike periodically and with invariable success for more adequate recognition of its efforts to furnish the sinews of war to its wasteful and unproductive brothers in the trenches.

In Russia the Empire, battered from without and all corroded within, had collapsed upon itself; and an earnest but unpractical gentleman named Kerensky was rapidly undermining what was left of Russian staying-power, and, with the enthusiastic assistance of the German General Staff, paving the way for those great twin brethren, Lenin and Trotsky. One jaw of the vice which had been crushing the Hun to death was relaxed for good.

Still, there was no weakening on the Western Front. The Messines Ridge had recently "gone up," with a bang which had warmed the heart of every schoolboy in that schoolboy army, the British Expeditionary Force. The Salient of Ypres, that graveyard of British soldiers and German hopes, stood more inviolate than ever. Bagdad had been captured: Palestine was being freed. And in France, down in the Vosges, within the great quadrilateral formed by Chaumont, Toul, Vittel, and Ligny-en-Barrois, huge cantonments were being run up, and roads and railways laid down, by long-legged, slim-hipped, slow-speaking, workmanlike young men from a vast continent overseas—the forerunners of an army of indefinite millions which had pledged itself to come and redress the final balance at no very distant date.

But all this did not prevent London from being an extremely uncomfortable, not to say unsafe, place of residence for a high official of the noble army of Bomb-Dodgers. Finally, after a Gotha raid over London in broad daylight one bright morning in July, in which fifty-seven people were killed, Uncle Fred decided that it was no longer either just or prudent to risk a valuable life further, and went to Netherby, where he succeeded without any difficulty whatever in outstaying his welcome by a considerable margin.

Netherby itself was not over-cheerful, even though the master of the house was absent a good deal. Albert Clegg spent most of his time in those days on Tyneside, making himself liable to excess profits tax. Amos, his eldest son, who from early boyhood had cultivated the valuable habit of keeping one ear to the ground, was by this time in Glasgow, safely embedded in a convenient stronghold labelled "Civilian War Work of National Importance." Brother Joe was far away, as happy as a sandboy—and living like one—assisting General Allenby to construct a military railway from Beersheba to Dan. The younger members of the family were occupied in making unserviceable articles for the Red Cross, and complaining of the shortage of sugar. Mrs. Clegg faithfully attended committee meetings and gatherings where bandages were rolled and inside information imparted. Craigfoot lay remote from the tumult of war, though Edinburgh to the north, and Tynemouth to the south, had each been soundly bombed. Still, there was no lack of military atmosphere. Colonel Bethune himself—minus an arm, and with a bar to his D.S.O.—was back in command of the depot, an object of respectful worship to the entire community; and was always ready and willing to enlarge upon the situation, whether to an attentive mess or to a casually encountered ploughman. His august mother, Lady Christina, specialised upon the crimes of the Government, and had it on reliable authority that the counsels of the Cabinet were now entirely directed from Potsdam. Men on leave came and went, with tales of glory and gloom. Many of the girls were in London or in France; and there were countless letters to quote. Mrs. Clegg sat and listened to the babble of rumour and conjecture, shyly contributing here and there an excerpt from Palestine. Joe had never been home since his clandestine enlistment, but as the event had proved that conscription would have claimed him in any case, his father had decided to forgive him.

Marjorie's name was never mentioned at Netherby, by decree of the master of the house. With Mrs. Clegg—gentle, submissive, colourless—to yield in act was to yield in opinion. She possessed the faculty (recently enjoined, with indifferent success, upon an entire nation) of being "neutral even in thought." She accepted Marjorie's excommunication as she would have accepted her death, or any other form of irrevocability.

It was the last day of Uncle Fred's hegira. On the morrow he was to return, to face the dangers of Dulwich. Evening prayers had been concluded, and Albert Clegg was setting the markers in the Bible for to-morrow morning's exercises. Suddenly he looked up, and spoke:

"Fred!"

"Yes, Albert?"

"When you return to London I shall be obliged to you if you will make inquiries about my daughter."

Uncle Fred sat up—his back perfectly straight for the first time for many years. Mrs. Clegg's knitting dropped from her fingers. No one else was present. Only children remained at Netherby, and they had gone to bed.

"I have been thinking matters over," announced Albert, in measured tones. "I try to be a just man in all my dealings. It is one year to-day since the news came to me that my daughter had taken to—her present ways. By this time her punishment has possibly begun. It is not my intention to intervene between her and her Maker; but I have decided that there can be no harm in taking steps to ascertain what has become of her."

Mrs. Clegg caught her breath. Uncle Fred, utterly dazed, wagged his beard weakly.

"That's very handsome of you, Albert," he said respectfully.

"Handsomeness has nothing to do with it!" snapped Albert, among whose rare and austere amusements none was more prized than that of keeping his younger brother in his place. "I am simply doing what I consider to be right and just. Now, when you return to London I want you to institute inquiries as to where my daughter is to be found. If you are successful, I wish you to visit her. I should not like to think that she was actually destitute. Of course, she can never return here, but I can see that she is provided for."

There was silence. Then Uncle Fred inquired, after the fashion of all feeble folk:

"How should I set about finding her? London is a big place. I suppose the police—"

"I will not have the police brought into the matter until absolutely necessary," thundered Albert. "You must search the theatres!"

It was a magnificent suggestion, but too daring for Albert's audience—certainly for Uncle Fred.

"I have never been inside a theatre in my life," he objected.

"Neither have I. But you need not go inside. Enquire at the door whether my daughter is employed there. Demand to see the manager!"

"Do you think he will tell me?"

"Threaten him with the law if he won't. These fellows are usually under police observation, in any case. They won't dare to fight."

"Perhaps a word with the stage-door keeper—" suggested Mrs. Clegg timidly.

"There's no need for Fred to get mixed up with the dissolute crowd that hangs round stage-doors," was the stern reply. "He'll go in by the front!"

Uncle Fred, flattered on the whole at being still regarded as a potential profligate, hastened to associate himself with this sentiment. But at heart he felt a little ashamed. There were elements of the dare-devil about Uncle Fred. Still, he reflected, he could take his own line of action when he got back to London. He propounded another conundrum.

"Supposing she isn't in one of the theatres—what then? Would it be any good trying the churches? She may be attending some place of worship regularly."

"If she is, it is bound to be Church of England; and I don't intend to be beholden to that body for *any* help!" replied Albert firmly. "You might try the Salvation Army. Their rescue work brings them in contact with every walk of life—the West End restaurants and clubs, and haunts of that kind."

The implied spectacle of Uncle Fred, assisted by a contingent of Hallelujah Lasses, raiding the Athenæum or The Popular Café, for a lost niece was not without its humour; but the paths of humour and righteousness converge too seldom, to their mutual detriment.

"When you find her," concluded Albert, "ascertain quietly what her circumstances are, and report to me. I will then decide what it is best for me to do."

Uncle Fred, duly uplifted, wagged his head with increased solemnity.

"I must say, Albert," he announced, "even though it angers you, that you are acting in a very generous manner."

"Yes, father," added Mrs. Clegg wistfully.

In a watery way, her heart yearned over her daughter.

"Nothing of the kind!" said Clegg. "I am merely acting as my conscience directs me. These are demoralising times for the best of us"—perhaps Albert's excess profits were pricking him—"and we must make certain allowances. Of course, having acted the way she has, after her Christian upbringing, she can never expect forgiveness. But—well, I shall wait until I hear from you, Fred."

CHAPTER XIV

TWO SPARROWS

I

Marjorie was one of those who were "able to proceed to their own homes after receiving surgical aid." Others were not so fortunate. The Mouldy Old Copper—badly wounded by splinters of glass, and excoriating the entire Teutonic race with a failing tongue but unabated spirit—was borne off to St. Thomas's Hospital, followed by others. The canteen had been moderately full at the time, and more than one soldier home on leave had had his leave indefinitely prolonged by the visitation. Providentially, no one was killed; the bomb had fallen just too far down the street.

The raid took place on a Sunday evening, during Marjorie's one period of night duty in the week. (In this way, she gave herself one clear weekday for fresh air and exercise.) They kept her at the hospital until she had breakfasted, then dispatched her homeward, with instructions to return daily as an out-patient until further notice.

She walked across Westminster Bridge in the morning sunshine, feeling badly shaken, but not a little proud. Few of us ever outgrow a childish thrill at finding our arm in a sling. Not only was Marjorie's arm in a sling, but her right shoulder was bandaged. ("Just missed your carotid artery, my dear," had been the comment of the elderly house surgeon.) She felt gloriously conspicuous. A 'bus-load of convalescent soldiers in hospital blue recognised her as one of the elect, and inquired affectionately whether she had been out in a trench raid. She waved her sound arm in cordial acknowledgment of the pleasantry. Roy would be interested to hear about this. On second thoughts, no. Roy never told her when he had had an escape; she must maintain Roy's standard of reticence.

She walked jauntily into the flat, and sat down, a little suddenly, upon the feet of Miss Elizabeth Lyle, who, as already noted, was usually insensible until about eleven a.m. Liss rolled over with a resigned sigh, poked her *nez retroussé* out from under the sheet, and remarked meekly:

"All right! Give me just five minutes more, and I promise—My goodness gracious, Marjie, what *have* you been doing to yourself?"

Marjorie described the raid. She told the tale as lightly as she could, with humorous touches here and there; for she had seen human blood flow freely, and was feverishly conscious of a desire to get the picture out of her mind. Gradually the narrative became more frivolous, the touches more and more humorous. Finally, the narratress grew so amused with the recollection of her own experiences that she threw her head back and laughed loud and long.

Liss slipped hurriedly out of bed, put both arms round her uproarious friend, and laid her by main force in the place which she had just vacated.

"You stay there, dearie," she said. "They ought never to have let you out."

"The hospital was so full!" Marjorie was shivering all over now, and battling with an inclination to tears. "They said that they were very sorry—*very* sorry—very sorry indeed—but—"

"That's all right!" said little Liss soothingly, covering her up, and patting her undamaged arm. "I'll make you a good, strong cup of tea, and then you will have a nice sleep, and you'll wake up as right as ninepence! I'll slip round to the theatre and tell them they needn't expect to see you again for a week or two. The show is going to close soon, anyhow."

"I don't care if it does!" murmured Marjorie, her head on Liss's pillow. She did not even trouble to cross the room to her own bed. "I have learnt one thing in the last year, and that is that I am not cut out for the stage. It bores me. I was meant to stay at home, and look after little people like you—and Roy! *That's* what I—"

She settled down like a tired child, and fell sound asleep. Liss snatched some apparel from a chair, padded out of the room in her bare feet, and closed a door gently for about the first time in her life.

II

Marjorie woke up in the afternoon—herself again, but stiff and bruised. She rose, and entered the sitting-room. Liss was lying on the sofa, reading the *Daily Mirror* and smoking a cigarette. She sprang up on seeing Marjorie, and flew to her, stopping just in time.

"Sorry, duckie!" she said. "I must remember that arm of yours. Are you feeling all right again?"

"Splendid!" said Marjorie. "What time is it?"

"About four."

"Let us have some tea then, and I'll go round to the hospital and get my arm dressed again. Hallo, it's raining!"

"Yes; it has been pouring ever since eleven o'clock this morning," said Liss; and coughed.

Marjorie turned upon her sharply. Liss was one of those persons to whom coughing is a forbidden luxury.

"Liss," she cried, "you're soaking! Every rag you have on is sticking to you! What's the matter?" She began to fumble at the back of the child's blouse. "Here, undress yourself! I have only one hand."

"I got a bit wet when I went out to the theatre," said Liss airily.

"But why on earth didn't you—" Marjorie glanced towards the bedroom door, and stopped abruptly. She understood. "I see," she said, "you didn't want—? Was that it? How long have you been like this?"

"Oh, not long," Liss assured her; and coughed again.

III

Marjorie, returning from her alternative role of out-patient to resume that of head nurse, walked into the flat, and sat down heavily on Liss.

"How are you feeling this morning, Baby?" she inquired.

"Top-hole!" replied the invalid.

Three weeks had passed. Liss was now convalescent; but congestion of the lungs is not a malady to be taken lightly, especially by little wraiths with weak chests. Marjorie herself had nearly shaken off the shock-effect of the raid. Her arm was still lightly bandaged.

"It's a lovely day," she said. "I will take you for a bus ride this afternoon, if you're good. Meanwhile, I want to have a pow-wow with you." Marjorie had picked up this expression from Roy, and was rather proud of it.

"What about?"

"Well—have you any money?"

"I thought there'd be a catch about it," said Liss, reaching out to the little table beside her bed for the bag in which the young woman of to-day is reputed to keep everything but the kitchen stove. "Let me see!" she said. She laid out on the counterpane a cigarette-case bearing a regimental crest, a match-case bearing another, entirely different, a long cigarette-holder, a powder-puff box, a lip-stick, and a diminutive handkerchief. "Now we're getting down to business!" she announced encouragingly. "Here's a shilling—a threepenny bit—and four pennies. Wait a minute! Here's a crumpled up thing here that might be a Bradbury. No, it's a note from Reggie. I suppose I oughtn't to keep that now!"

Liss tore up the *billet-doux* with a sentimental sigh. It may be noted in passing that her engagement to Master Leonard had terminated some months previously by mutual and violent consent. A subsequent contract of eternal fidelity to a young gentleman in the Royal Flying Corps—one Reginald Bensham—had recently been dissolved, by unanimous vote. At present Miss Lyle's affections were disengaged.

"One and sevenpence!" she announced. "You can search me for more!"

"That's rather a blow," said Marjorie.

"Are we running short?" asked Liss. "Of course we must be, both having been out of a job for three weeks. But I thought—"

"So did I," replied Marjorie. "I thought we had a nest-egg in the bank at my home in Scotland. I haven't touched it for a year, because I wanted it to accumulate for a rainy day. On Monday I came to the conclusion that our present days were rainy enough—there's the doctor's bill, for one thing—so I wrote to Mr. Gillespie, the manager, and asked what my balance was. I got his answer this morning."

"I hate to ask—but what is the balance?"

Marjorie smiled dismally.

"That's just it! There isn't any balance at all! Just a few odd shillings. My father seems to have cut off my allowance about a year ago. I wonder why? At least, if he was going to do it at all I wonder why he didn't do it in the very beginning. However, we won't worry about that. The situation is, that you have one and sevenpence, and I have about two pounds ten."

"Two pounds ten, and one and sevenpence—that's about two pounds fifteen," announced Liss, after a brief calculation. "We can live for weeks on that. Before it's gone we shall be back in a job again."

"I shan't let you take a job again for a long time, my dear," said Marjorie. "They won't have much use for me, either; I can't lift my arm above my shoulder at present. How could I hold up the Torch of Liberty in the last act?"

"We'll rub along," announced the small optimist in the bed. "If the worst came to the worst, I could always get engaged again. There's a perfectly sweet boy in the Tanks—"

But Marjorie's hand was over Liss's mouth. "Baby, remember you don't get engaged again without my permission!"

"All right!" mumbled Liss. "Have it your own way! But what about your Roy? Can't you raise a small subscription out of him? That would be quite O.K., wouldn't it? You're going to marry—" Suddenly Liss sat up in bed, for she had caught sight of Marjorie's face. "Why, what's the matter, dear?" she asked.

"I haven't heard a word from him for five weeks," said Marjorie in a low voice. "I'm most awfully unhappy, Liss."

Liss forgot all about herself at once, and put both arms round her protector.

"Think what a lot of letters must be lying waiting for you somewhere," she said. "You'll get a whole bunch one morning. Now I'm going to get up, and we'll go on that bus ride."

They lunched frugally at an A.B.C. shop, and having boarded a Number Nine bus sped westward along Piccadilly. A communicative man with a broken nose, wearing the silver badge of a discharged soldier, leaned over their shoulders from the seat behind them.

"Sir Dougliss 'as done it again, ladies!" he announced importantly, thrusting an evening paper before them. "Look! *Fifteen-mile front—twelve villages—five thousand prisoners*! That's the stuff to give 'em!"

The girls read the report eagerly. It described the opening British attack of the Third Battle of Ypres. (In the first two, the attack had come from the other side.) Woods and villages, long familiar in daily bulletins as German strongholds, were at last in British hands—Hollebeke, Sanctuary Wood, Saint Julien, Hooge—and the advance was still continuing. Marjorie's heart quickened—then faltered. Great victories mean big casualties—and she did not even know where Roy was. When last heard of she had gathered that he was in a rest-area somewhere behind Amiens. But that had been five weeks ago.

"Do you know that district?" Liss was asking.

"Know it? I should think I did, miss—like the back of me 'and! I copped a sweet one there in 'fifteen—near Cambray."

"But Cambrai is not in the Salient," observed Marjorie.

The communicative man conceded the point immediately.

"Neither it is, miss—not in that *Salient*. My error! They rushed us up and down that Western Front so fast, no wonder a feller gets mixed! I was hit in both places, though. Well, 'ere we are in good old 'Ammersmiff. This is where I 'ops off. Good-day, ladies! Keep the paper, and welcome."

"It's big news, isn't it?" said Liss, continuing to skim through the heavily leaded paragraph.

"I wonder why that man thought Cambrai was in the Salient," remarked Marjorie.

"Swank, I expect," said Liss. "Probably he hasn't been out at all—*or* wounded!"

"But he was wearing a silver badge," objected Marjorie, to whom all military geese were swans.

"Perhaps he pinched it," suggested Miss Lyle, who harboured few illusions concerning the male sex.

Her theory received entire corroboration a moment later. On folding up the newspaper before descending they discovered that Marjorie's vanity-bag, which was lying on the seat between them, had been neatly slit open and its entire contents extracted.

The pair turned and regarded one another silently. Liss was the first to speak.

"That brings us down to one and sevenpence," she remarked. "No wonder he didn't know where Cambrai was!"

IV

"Luncheon is served," announced Liss.

"What is there?" asked Marjorie.

"The same as breakfast, with Willie and John thrown in. Also the rest of the day before yesterday's loaf. Pull up your chair, dear."

As breakfast had consisted of nothing at all, the prodigality of this menu can be readily gauged. Willie and John, by the way, were the last two sardines in the tin.

"You take Willie," said Liss. "Here's your half of the bread. Oh my, but I'm hungry! Good-bye, John dear! Marjorie, what are we going to do next?"

Marjorie bent her brows judicially.

"Let me see," she said. "I've tried the theatre, and they don't begin rehearsing the new piece for a fortnight. It was no use trying the canteen, because it isn't there any more—at least, nothing worth considering. And as it happens, I don't know anyone else in any other canteen."

"We haven't got an account at any shop," continued Liss, "because we've always been to the cheap cash places. I don't know a living soul in London, except my family; and if I go back to Finchley I know I'll jolly well have to stay there for the duration."

"And I," supplemented Marjorie, "know no one except Uncle Fred, in Dulwich. And I'd rather die than ask *him* for help!"

"No one at all?" exclaimed Liss. "Do you and I mean to sit here and tell each other that we know no one in London, except the people at the theatre, and the people at your canteen, and one or two dud relations? Why not call on your old Lord Eskerley?"

Marjorie hesitated.

"I don't think I can," she said. "I have no particular claim—"

"No claim? Didn't you drive his silly old car in all weathers for nearly a year? Didn't he tell you to come back and see him whenever you had time? It's no use being modest when you're starving. If you don't go and see him, I shall."

"Then I may as well tell you, dear," announced Marjorie, "that I have been already."

"Why didn't you say so before?"

"I didn't want to disappoint you."

"Why? Were you chucked out?"

"No. He's away in Paris, on an indefinite mission. The butler was very nice about it, but he had no information as to when his lordship would be back. I hadn't been entirely forgotten, though. There was a message for me. It had been lying there for weeks."

"What did it say?"

"It was just a scribbled note in an envelope with my motor licence, which I had left behind in the garage." Marjorie crossed the room to her little bureau. "Here it is! It says:

My dear late lamented Habakkuk,—I enclose your licence, which you have inadvertently left on my premises. No doubt you will need it again some day.

With kind regards,

Yours sincerely—

There's a postscript," she added:

Apropos of motor licences, let me offer you a piece of advice. Always keep an adequate sum—say a pound or so—folded up and tucked away between the covers of the licence itself. This expedient, when you get held up in a police-trap, and the minion of the law examines your credentials, may obviate a public appearance before the local Beaks. Verb, sap.! Very useful. Don't say I told you.

Marjorie laid down this characteristic effusion, and laughed.

"I don't think we are likely to tie up any capital in that way at present!" she said, finishing the last crumb of her bread. "We are down to fourpence now. We had better keep that for to-morrow, and go without supper to-night. No, we'll spend threepence on biscuits, and have a biscuit apiece at bed-time!"

"By golly, we do go it, don't we!" Liss looked round the room hungrily. "Isn't there *anything* left that we can pop?"

"Nothing, I'm afraid. My jewellery is all at Netherby. I have my engagement-ring, of course—"

"That stays!" announced Liss firmly. "It was lucky," she went on with more cheerfulness, "that my little Leonard did not want his back! Not that we got much for it; I always *said* he bought it at a stationer's! Now, if it had only been the one Reggie gave me, that would have been a different story; his was a beauty. But the little beast practically grabbed it back from me. Marjie, I *really* think I'd better get engaged again. I could wire Toby, at—"

"You will do no such thing!" said Marjorie. "Besides, you can't send a wire for fourpence."

"I suppose," continued Liss (whose motto in life was "Anything Once!") "it wouldn't do to go and sit about in a restaurant somewhere, and get taken out to dinner by an Australian, or somebody? All right, I was only joking! Well, we must just hang on till Saturday; then there will be lots of our nice boy friends in town for the week-end, and we can make up for lost time. Meanwhile, let's go round and see if we can't get a job directing envelopes, or something. Carry on, partner!"

V

Towards evening our two hungry sparrows forgathered again, footsore and faint, but still smiling. Liss, who ought by rights to have been in bed consuming chicken-broth, was as white as wax.

"What luck?" she enquired.

"Nothing doing!" sighed Marjorie. "They will take me on at an office in Holborn as soon as my arm is well enough to write, but they wouldn't give me an advance of pay. They just told me to report at nine o'clock on Monday."

"And to-day's Thursday! Thank them for nothing!"

"Did you get anything?" asked Marjorie.

"No—except that I went round to the theatre again, and they are putting on the new show a little sooner. There's a call for rehearsal on Saturday. That doesn't mean any salary for a long while, but I ought to be able to borrow a shilling or two from the girls. Not that it will be easy: they all need the money themselves these days, poor things! I'm cold. Let's have our biscuit and go to bed."

"I wonder what time it is?" said Marjorie, getting up from her chair.

"About eight, I should say." (Watches had been hypothecated long since.) "It's a bit early."

"*Qui dort, dine,*" quoted Marjorie.

"What does that mean?"

"It's what Lord Eskerley used to say when he'd been to the House of Lords. Let's go to bed; I'm comfortably tired. London's a big place to get about in—when one hasn't a bus fare!"

They shared Marjorie's bed that night, for misery loves company.

"I say," suggested Liss suddenly, "couldn't we go round and get a meal from the Red Cross, or somebody?"

Marjorie, who was just dropping off to sleep, replied with great firmness:

"The Red Cross can only assist people who have been wounded in action. If they go beyond that, the Geneva Convention allows them to be fired on; and then Roy might— No, we *can't* ask the Red Cross—unless we get hit in another air-raid!" she added hopefully.

Having no more suggestions to offer, Liss dropped off to sleep in her favourite attitude—with her head under the pillow. Marjorie lay awake for a long time, pondering many things in her heart—speculating mainly as to whether she could last out until Baby's flock of plutocratic second lieutenants came to town on Saturday. She decided immediately that she could, adding a mental rider condemning persons who, like herself, worried about their own personal comforts when there was a war on. She also wondered, again and again, what had become of Roy. She wondered whether he were hungry too. Presumably not. He had assured her that the British Army on the Western Front were grossly overfed—in fact, the inevitability with which the Army Service Corps got the rations up and through bordered on the uncanny. No, she need not worry about Roy's diet. His safety was another matter. Five weeks! She dropped into a troubled sleep.

CHAPTER XV

THE EXPLORER

Meanwhile, in a crowded street just off the Strand, in the fading light of a July evening, an elderly gentleman with a goat's beard, spectacles on nose, was diligently examining the framed photographs exhibited outside a very popular theatre. His attention was particularly directed to a large chorus group—an ensemble of attractive young women in costumes attuned to the economical spirit of wartime.

Aware of a sudden interference with the not too abundant supply of light, the elderly investigator turned round, a little guiltily, to find that he was being assisted in his investigations by three hard-breathing members of His Majesty's Forces—an English Sapper, a Highlander, and a Canadian of enormous bulk.

"And very nice, too!" observed the Sapper. "But Grandpa, not at your time of life, you didn't ought to—reely! 'Op it—there's a good boy!"

"Awa' hame!" added the Scot severely—"or I'll tell on ye tae Grandmaw!"

Bitterly ashamed at having his motives thus misconstrued, Uncle Fred hurried away. His course now took him westward along the Strand, which was packed from end to end with seekers after diversion—mostly soldiers and their adherents. He plodded steadily through the press, with the air of a man who has a definite goal before him. This was the second week of his search for Marjorie, but he had considerably modified the plan of action laid down for him by his elder brother. His attempts to call upon the theatrical managers of London, *seriatim*, for the purpose of compelling them to disgorge his niece, had resulted in a sequence of humiliating reverses at the hands of stunted but precocious children in the outer office. Uncle Fred had now evolved a plan of his own. He had observed that theatres were accustomed to stimulate the appetites of their patrons by displaying samples of their wares—in the form of large framed photographs—outside the entrance to the theatre. Good! He would resolve himself into an investigating committee of one, visit each theatre in turn, and examine photographs until he had located Marjorie. After that, the stronghold itself must be penetrated. A somewhat hazardous enterprise, he decided, but not without its romantic side. As already noted, there was the making of a man-about-town in Uncle Fred.

His self-imposed quest had been in progress for several evenings, and, as yet, had borne no fruit. Uncle Fred was not familiar with the life of the West End—his knowledge of social life in London, like that of too many Members of Parliament, was limited to the tea-room of the House of Commons—and he had wasted a good deal of time hunting for photographs outside establishments where chorus girls are not usually to be found— Maskelyne and Cook's, for instance, and the Polytechnic. Also, it required expert knowledge to distinguish the humble home of the Drama from the palace of the Movie Queen. But he was learning rapidly. Assisted by the advertisements in the daily press and a District Railway map of London, he had now charted out the whole of theatre-land, and had very nearly completed a most methodical survey thereof. He knew the name of every revue and musical comedy in London, and could have given points, in his familiarity with the features of professional beauty, to the average Flying Corps subaltern.

He crossed Trafalgar Square, and headed for the Shaftesbury Avenue district. A hurried reference to the map, in a quiet corner behind the National Gallery, confirmed him in his bearings. Presently he found himself before another theatre. It was nearly nine o'clock; but, thanks to the Summer Time Act, it was still daylight. The name of the current attraction of the house, as stated on the bill-boards outside, was *Too Many Girls*. Diagonally across each bill-board was pasted a printed slip which said, a little ambiguously, "*Last Week*."

"That's a pity," mused Uncle Fred. "But I can slip inside and find out what they are doing this week and next. There's some sort of entertainment going on: I can hear it."

Thrusting his beard well forward, Uncle Fred marched boldly into the vestibule of the theatre. The framed photographs had been taken in for the night, and were ranged round the wall on easels. Uncle Fred set his spectacles in position, and began his usual methodical tour of inspection, at his regulation range of six inches.

A stout lady, confined in a gilded cage in one of the walls, engaged in counting change, suspended operations to watch him. She caught the eye of the commissionnaire who stood at the swing-door leading to the stalls, and coughed delicately. Certainly Uncle Fred, in his semi-ecclesiastical frock-coat and Heath Robinson tall hat, crouching astride his umbrella in a strained endeavour to scrutinise the very lowest row in a large photographic group of chorus girls, fairly invited comment.

"Boys will be boys!" observed the commissionnaire, to no one in particular; and the siren in the cage giggled.

Suddenly Uncle Fred came to a dead point opposite the very last photograph in the last row. Feverishly reinforcing his spectacles with a pair of eye-glasses, he made a confirmatory examination, and then rose to an upright position—looking as Stanley may have looked when he found Livingstone. Then, for the first time, he became aware that he was not alone.

"Naughty, naughty!" said a wheezy feminine voice.

"Haw, haw, haw!" roared the commissionnaire.

"I'm ashamed of you, little brighteyes!" declared the accusing angel in the cage.

"Outside!" added the commissionnaire, recalled to a sense of duty by the appearance at the swing-door of an authoritative-looking person in a dinner jacket.

Uncle Fred, shamefully misunderstood and deeply wounded, hurried out. In the street he hesitated.

"Those people might have given me some useful information," he reflected. "But I won't go back now, to be insulted! I think, after all, it would be best to see the caretaker at the stage door. I suppose that will be somewhere at the back."

A voyage of circumnavigation brought him to the dingy portal which early training and settled conviction had always represented to him as giving direct access to the Infernal Regions. With a guilty thrill he crossed the threshold, and found himself confronted by an unshaven man slumbering in a glass box. Uncle Fred coughed nervously. The man opened his eyes, and pushed open a glass shutter.

"Well?" he enquired.

"I want to ask a favour," began Uncle Fred. But the man cut him short.

"What is it? Temperance, or Christian Science? You can't put up no notices on our call-board. Management don't allow it."

"I have reason to believe," pursued Uncle Fred, with feeble dignity, "that a young woman is employed here—"

"We employ thirty-six of 'em," said the stage-door man.

"I have just seen her likeness—in a group—round there"—explained Uncle Fred, waving his umbrella vaguely towards the front of the house.

"It very often starts that way," remarked the stage-door man. "But why not pay for a seat, like a little gentleman, and go in front and see the gel?"

"She's my niece," explained Uncle Fred.

"They always are," said the stage-door man. "Or else cousins! Good night, Tirpitz!"

86

He shut the little glass shutter in the investigator's face, and recomposed his features to slumber. But Uncle Fred, though not a dashing person, possessed some elements of the dogged persistence of the Clegg family. He rapped on the window-pane. The stage-door man opened it again.

"Now, you run away!" he said. "'Op it! Sling yer 'ook, or I'll set the cat on you!"

"Is my niece here to-night?" asked Uncle Fred, employing the handle of his umbrella as a lever of the third order. "I am very anxious to have a few words with her, on a domestic matter. I see a notice outside, saying that the present entertainment concluded last week. But it has occurred to me that it is still possible—"

The stage-door man slid from his stool, came out of his den, and laid a heavy hand, not unkindly, on the orator's shoulder.

"What you want to do, ole friend," he said, "is to 'ire the Albert 'All, and make a night of it! That'll get it out of your system nicely. Good-bye!" He gently impelled his guest in the direction of the street.

"I want my niece's address," gasped Uncle Fred, clinging like a limpet to the door-post.

"Go along, you silly old sinner!" said the stage-door man, disengaging him. "I'm ashamed of you."

"I will pay you!" said Uncle Fred desperately.

The stage-door man relaxed at once.

"Now you're *talking*!" he announced.

Five minutes later, after a sordid commercial wrangle, Uncle Fred emerged from the stage door with a slip of paper in his hand. He walked straight into the arms of three members of His Majesty's Forces. They recognised him, and drew back in affected horror.

"What, again?" cried the Canadian. "My God, he's a Mormon! Come along, boys!"

CHAPTER XVI

THE GREAT PRETEND

"And the sweet?" enquired Marjorie, pencil poised.

"*Méringues!*" said Liss firmly.

"Well, I would say chocolate *soufflé* every time—with whipped cream, of course!" replied Marjorie. "But have it your own way. Now for the savoury!"

"We don't want a savoury," said Liss.

"Remember," Marjorie reminded her, "that there will be gentlemen present."

"I was forgetting the gentlemen. Well—what?"

"*My* gentleman friend," said Marjorie, "is very fond of angels-on-horseback."

"All right! You can put them down if you like; only don't ask me to eat them: I expect I shall be stodged by that time, anyhow. Oh Marjie, if only it were true!" Liss hugged her hungry little self, longingly.

"There, that's the complete *menu*," said Marjorie. She laid down her pencil, took up the writing pad, and began to read:

"*Oysters!*" She took up her pencil again. "By the way, we can't have oysters."

"Why not?"

"You can only have oysters when there's an R in the month."

"Well, it's August!" said Liss. "And as they aren't going to be there anyhow, they may as well stay in!"

"No," said Marjorie. "This dinner is going to be things we would order here and now—just supposing we could. So don't let us spoil it by putting down impossible things."

Liss at once recognised the logical consistency of this view.

"All right!" she said. "No oysters! *Hors d'oeuvres*, instead. Then nice hot soup!"

"Yes—*Potage à la reine*."

"It sounds a bit watery; but I don't mind, so long as it's hot. Oh, how *lovely* it would be!"

"*Sole meunière*. That's Roy's favourite."

"Oh—Roy's to be there? That's your pretend, is it?"

Marjorie nodded over her hypothetical menu.

"That's a good idea. Who shall I pretend my man is? Toby?"

"All right."

"In that case, we shall want more than one bottle of champagne. You know what that child is! But never mind that just now! Read out some more food."

"*Duckling*—"

"And green peas, of course?"

"Of course!"

"What then?"

"That brings us to the *méringues*."

"Good! That should be enough. We will have coffee and *crème de menthe* afterwards, of course?"

"We will have cognac as well. You see, Roy—Oh, Liss!" For a moment Marjorie's fortitude forsook her. Her face sank into her friend's fluffy hair.

"Liss, dear," she murmured, "if *only* I knew!"

"It's Friday afternoon now," said Liss cheerfully. "We'll get lots to eat to-morrow, when the boys come up to town."

"I wasn't thinking of food," said Marjorie—"just then!"

"Well, I was! Oh, my *dear*, I'm hungry! I didn't know it was possible to be so hungry. What time is it?"

"About five, I think."

"Well, let's have a nice drink of water, and eat a couple of biscuits, and go to bed. It's the best way."

"Very well," said Marjorie listlessly. She was the more exhausted of the two; for Liss was of the ethereal type that seems to thrive on a diet of next-to-nothing. Neither girl had touched food, except a few biscuits, since the previous evening. This afternoon they had endeavoured to maintain *morale* by indulging in one of the oldest pastimes known to children of the world—the game of "Let's pretend!"—sturdily endeavouring to hold a fire in their hands by thinking on the frosty Caucasus.

Suddenly there came a tapping on the outer door. Both girls started up.

"Who on earth can that be?" said Marjorie, hurrying automatically to the mirror above the mantelpiece.

"I wonder if it is anybody with any money!" remarked Liss, hastily removing herself from the couch, where she had been stifling the pangs of hunger by lying on her front.

"Go and see!" commanded Marjorie, busy at the mirror.

Liss went out into the little vestibule, and reappeared, followed by a visitor. Her face was a study.

"This gentleman wants to see you, dear," she said solemnly. "I will leave you together!"

Marjorie turned hastily round.

"No—stay!" she commanded. "How do you do, Uncle Fred?"

"I am very well, thank you," said Uncle Fred in a low voice. Apprehension was written upon his features, and his large, weak mouth trembled. This adventure was trying him high. To penetrate into the boudoir of an actress—two actresses, apparently—was practically equivalent to visiting a theatre dressing-room, which he knew to be the last station before perdition.

Marjorie shook hands.

"Sit down," she said. "I am afraid we are not quite dressed for callers. Do you mind?"

Uncle Fred shook his head feebly, guiltily conscious that he did not mind enough. His niece was dressed in a very simple blue serge frock, with touches of scarlet at her waist and wrists. She was thinner and paler than when he had last seen her. Late suppers, of course. She had done something theatrical but undeniably becoming to her hair, which, instead of being discreetly piled upon her head, framed her face in a sort of aureole. In order to shake hands with him she had deposited upon the mantelpiece, without any attempt at concealment, a small powder-puff, with which she had obviously been tampering with that infallible symbol of respectability, a shiny nose. She wore very thin black silk stockings and patent leather shoes, with dangerously high heels. One of the shoes had a hole in the sole, but Marjorie kept that sole glued to the floor throughout the interview. The silk stockings had lisle tops, but naturally Uncle Fred did not know this. Blinking feebly, he turned his attention to Marjorie's companion. In the obscurity of the vestibule he had not particularly noticed her. He did so now. His pale blue eyes bulged.

Before him he beheld a small, fluffy creature in a flimsy garment which she would have called a *negligée*, but which to Uncle Fred looked suspiciously like a nightgown. On her feet were padded pink satin bedroom slippers. Her lips were bright red, and were directing a dazzling smile upon him. There were dark hollows under her large grey eyes. Uncle Fred resolutely averted his gaze, and turned again to his niece.

"This is Miss Lyle," announced Marjorie. "We share the flat. Liss, dear, this is my uncle, Mr. Clegg. Well, Uncle Fred, how are you? I'm sorry we can't offer you tea, but we—we have practically all our meals at a restaurant. Don't we, Liss?"

"We simply live there!" affirmed Liss.

"Will you have a cigarette?" continued Marjorie, offering a box. "Don't mind about that being the last one! There are plenty more."

"I do not smoke," replied Uncle Fred coldly.

"Throw it to me, Marjorie!" chirped the vision in the *negligée*. A moment later, genuinely oblivious of the sensation she was causing, Liss was lying back in the arm-chair, blowing smoke rings up to the ceiling.

Marjorie proceeded to make conversation.

"Have you been at Netherby lately?" she asked. "I haven't heard a word from anybody there since I left. I wrote to father and mother, but neither of them answered, so I gave it up. I was sorry, all the same. I hear from Joe, of course. Have they conscripted Amos yet? How are the children?"

This was neither the tone nor the temper that Uncle Fred had anticipated from the prodigal. He had expected either flamboyant defiance or broken-hearted contrition—most probably the latter. This resolute, cheery, ladylike—yes, he had to admit it, ladylike—bonhomie was making his mission more difficult than he had anticipated. He cleared his throat.

"I was at Netherby during July," he began. "Your father and mother are well, though borne down with sorrow, over—over—"

"Over what?"

Uncle Fred, who had meant to improve the occasion, baulked at his first fence.

"Over this wicked war," he substituted.

"Well, they haven't much to worry about," said Marjorie composedly. "Joe tells me that he's in no particular danger, except from odd long-range shells. Amos—I suppose he has kept out of it all right?"

"Your brother is in Glasgow," said Uncle Fred, "doing civilian war work of national importance."

"I thought so," said Marjorie. "Trust Amos!"

"Your father," continued Uncle Fred, "commissioned me to ascertain your whereabouts in London—"

"How *did* you find us, by the way?" asked Marjorie. "It was rather clever of you."

"I set an investigation on foot," replied Uncle Fred with a not very successful assumption of grandeur.

"Quite a little Sherlock Holmes!" remarked an approving voice.

Despite himself, Uncle Fred looked round. The small siren in the arm-chair was regarding him with obvious interest. Doubtless she was taking his moral measure, with a view to ultimate conquest. As a matter of fact, Liss was wondering whether it would be feasible to borrow five shillings from him.

"How *did* you set about it?" Marjorie continued.

"I decided not to question the police. We were anxious to have as little scandal as possible—"

Marjorie rose with some deliberation, and took her stand upon the hearthrug exactly opposite her diplomatic relative.

"What did you do?" she asked.

"I began by instituting inquiries among the London theatrical managers."

"Then you knew I was working on the stage?"

"Yes. Your mother recognised your likeness in some periodical."

Marjorie nodded her head.

"So that was why father stopped my allowance!" she said. "I was wondering. Well, go on. Father has sent you to see me? What for?"

Uncle Fred had carefully rehearsed the little address which he proposed to deliver to his errant niece. Marjorie's point-blank query gave him as good an opening as he appeared likely to get.

"Your father," he began, settling down to work, "is a just man—"

"Yes; I think you're right there," agreed Marjorie. "He tries to be, anyhow; but he's too ignorant and narrow to succeed. That was why I left home. Go on!"

"Your father," reiterated Uncle Fred, who was of that brand of orator which finds it easier, when interrupted, to go right back to the beginning, "is a just man—"

"Yes; I know. You said that before," said Marjorie.

"*No Encores, by Request!*" added Liss.

"Your father suggested that when I returned to London I should institute inquiries as to your whereabouts. He was anxious to know if you had been spared during these years, and—"

"That was very kind of him," said Marjorie. "No!"—as Uncle Fred took another breath—"don't go back to the beginning again! 'If I had been spared'—yes?"

"And, if so, what your circumstances were."

"Why?"

"Your father said he would not like to feel that you were in actual destitution, and—"

"Oh! *And?*"

"I was to tell him if you were."

"And if I were?"

"He did not say; but he practically gave me to understand that if you would send him your assurance that you were truly and humbly repentant, and would endeavour in future, by Divine Grace, to raise yourself from your present condition"—Uncle Fred was settling comfortably down now to his pulpit manner—"he was prepared on his part, to temper justice with mercy. You would be provided for. Of course, you would never be permitted to return home. There are the children to think of—"

Next moment, Uncle Fred had the surprise of his blameless and dreary existence. A small figure in a tempestuous *negligée* whirled into his field of vision, and Liss—white-faced, stammering, passionate—stood over him.

"What do you mean?" she screamed. "You silly old blear-eyed devil, what do you mean by it? What do you mean by crowding into this flat where you weren't invited, and insulting my Marjie? How *dare* you! Get out before we throw you out—do you hear? You psalm-singing old nanny-goat, for two pins I'd pull your rotten little beard off!" She flew to Marjorie, and threw an arm round her shoulders. "And to think that real men are dying in this war every minute—and the finest women in the world killing themselves with overwork—just to keep insects like you *alive*! Why, I—*Oh!*" She choked.

Marjorie restored her small, hysterical, half-famished champion to the arm-chair.

"That's all right, Baby," she said placidly. "He means well, but he's had the same upbringing as father—poor old man! Sit down! Sit down too, Uncle Fred!" (The dazed ambassador was groping for the door.) "I want to talk to you."

The symposium resumed its session. Uncle Fred was so benumbed by his recent experience that when his late assailant deliberately renovated the scarlet of her lips in his presence he made no protest at all. How quickly a man can become a *roué*, even at fifty-nine!

"You can tell father," announced Marjorie, "that you gave me his message, and that I know him well enough to understand his point of view. In a way, there's something rather fine about it. I have seen enough of life in the last year or two to know that this world would be none the worse for a touch of good old-fashioned, Old Testament, discipline. Also, that many of my sex aren't to be trusted with a latch-key. But you can remind him, from me, that I am his daughter—and quite capable of taking care of myself!" She sat down again.

"Now, I will tell you exactly what I have been doing during the last two years. Like every decent, able-bodied person in this land, I have been doing what I could in the way of war work. I wasn't able to do as much as I wanted, because my education had been completely neglected; also, as most war work is unpaid, I had to work for my living at the same time. That was why I went on the stage. By working at night I had my days free to serve in a canteen. I have been in the canteen for more than a year now. I am not working at present, because I had a slight accident to my arm. I have also driven a motor-car, for a cabinet minister, liberating a man for active service. That was why I bobbed my hair, so that I could put my service-cap on and off my head easily. Most of us have done it; no one has time to waste over doing hair these days. We girl chauffeurs and munition makers have set quite a fashion. But, of course, you aren't interested in fashions. Besides, bobbed hair doesn't really prove anything. What you want is some direct evidence of what I have been doing." She thought for a moment. "I'll tell you what—I'll show you my motor-driver's licence. I know I put it away somewhere."

She crossed to the bureau, and took the licence out of a drawer.

"Here it is," she said, unfolding it. "You will notice it hasn't been renewed. That was because—"

Her voice died away. Liss glanced up, saw that her friend had turned white, and was swaying on her feet. She ran impulsively to her aid; but in a moment Marjorie had recovered herself, walked across to her flinching relative, and proffered the licence.

"There—you see!" she said. "I drove a car during all that time. It was war work, all right."

Uncle Fred examined the document mechanically, and handed it back.

"That seems quite in order," he muttered.

"Father is a business man, I know," continued Marjorie, with a cheery smile; "and I know business men like to see evidence in black and white. You can keep that licence, if you like, and send it to him from me, as a certificate of character, and tell him that I am very well—*and* busy—*and* happy—*and* respectable—and don't require providing for in any way whatever. And you can give my love to mother."

Uncle Fred rose to his feet, and held out his hand hesitatingly. Down in his puny soul he dimly felt himself in the presence of something rather unusually big.

"I will tell your father I have seen you," he said, "and what you have told me. And I'm—I'm sorry, if—"

Marjorie cut him short.

"That's all right!" she said, with great cheerfulness. "It was a difficult mission for you, I know, and I'm not surprised you made a mess of it. Now," she added briskly, "I feel terribly inhospitable at not having given you any tea. Liss and I are just going out to dinner. It's—it's—rather a special occasion with us, and we are going to have an extra good one. Won't you join us?"

She crossed to the bureau again, and picked up the writing-pad.

"We are going," she announced, resolutely avoiding the bulging eyes of Miss Elizabeth Lyle, "to have *Potage à la reine, Sole meunière, Duckling, Méringues*—"

But Uncle Fred was down and out.

"I can't accept," he replied, almost piteously. "I must be off to Dulwich. But thank you kindly!" He moved to the door. "I will write to your father. Good-bye, my girl!" He nodded nervously towards Liss. "Good-evening, all!"

Next moment the vestibule door had clicked behind him, and the girls were alone.

Liss threw her arms round Marjorie's neck.

"O magnificent, wonderful angel! How you stood up to that silly old Nosey Parker! How you put him in his place! How you bluffed him! But, darling, what a risk! Supposing he had accepted—what then?"

"What then?" Marjorie laughed unsteadily. "We would have taken him round the corner to Savroni's, and *given* him his dinner—every bit of it—that's all!"

Liss looked timidly up into her idol's face.

"Dearest," she enquired apprehensively, "are you feeling *funny*, at all? I don't like the way your fist is clenched. Relax!"

"I'm not feeling funny," Marjorie assured her, relaxing the fist in question. "Unless it's funny to be rich!" She held out her hand. "Look! Look what I found inside the pocket of my motor licence! I might have guessed, after that message. Dear, kind old man! I might have guessed—bless him!"

In her upturned palm lay a neatly folded bank-note.

Liss's eyes goggled.

"How much?" she whispered.

"We'll see." Marjorie unfolded the rustling treasure-trove. "Ten pounds! Now wasn't I right not to put down oysters? Oh, Baby, if only, only, only we had the guests!"

But Fortune, once she veers round, seldom does things by halves. There came a knock on the outer door.

"Hallo!" cried Liss. "Surely it's not that old Nanny back again?"

It was not. It was a soldier—or rather, an elderly civilian in uniform. He saluted, with all the elaboration of the newly initiated. Both girls surveyed him in perplexity. Then Liss screamed:

"It's Uncle Ga-Ga!" and embraced him forthwith.

Uncle Ga-Ga it was. With his hair dyed a new and awe-inspiring colour, and an almost convincing set of false teeth, he did not look a day over forty-five. He held his old head proudly erect, and offered a hand to each of the girls, with a gallant gesture.

"Yes, ladies," he said; "I have the great happiness to inform you that I have this day been accepted as a member of His Majesty's Forces. I wear the uniform of King George the Fifth." His right hand went to the salute. "The King—God bless him! I have only just put it on, and I came round here at once to show myself to you—my two kind friends and unfailing supporters! There were some of my colleagues"—his mild eyes flashed—"men who should have known better—who derided my pretensions—who said that the King had no need of my services! But not you, ladies! You knew the King better than they did! Now, behold me! It is a common triumph for us all!"

"And we are going to celebrate it!" announced Liss. "You are coming straight out to dinner with us—isn't he, Marjorie?"

"Most certainly he is!" said Marjorie.

"We are going," proclaimed Liss, "to have *Potage à la reine; Sole meunière—*"

Uncle Ga-Ga laid his hand upon his heart, and made a courtly bow.

"Ladies," he announced, "you overwhelm me! But before I accede to your most hospitable invitation, pray read this: it may affect your immediate plans. I found it lying thrust under your outer door."

He proffered an orange-coloured envelope. It was addressed to Marjorie.

Telegrams in war-time take tense priority over everything else. Marjorie seized the envelope, ripped open the flap with one feverish movement, took out the message, and carried it to the window to read. Then, very deliberately, for the first and only time in her life, she slid down upon the floor, with her head on the window-seat, in a dead faint."

"Oh, God!" cried Liss, running to her—"it must be something about Roy!"

They carried her to the sofa, and laid her down. Her eyes were closed, but began to flutter again almost immediately.

"The telegram—should we read it? Would it be right?" asked Uncle Ga-Ga.

"Oh, yes!" said Liss: "I'd forgotten about it." She turned back Marjorie's closed fingers, extracted the crumpled message, and smoothed it out. Then she gave a little sudden chuckling sob.

"Listen!" she said; and read the message aloud....

"Sent off from Folkestone," she added breathlessly, "at four-forty. What time is it now?"

"About half-past six, I think."

"Then he will be here any minute!" cried Liss, in sudden panic. "We must get her to for him," she added, in the mysterious syntax of her kind. "Help me, Uncle!"

"A lovely face!" observed Uncle Ga-Ga, respectfully, as he assisted Liss in administering to Marjorie what they both firmly believed to be First Aid—"but pale, and thin!" He sighed gently. "It is rather beautiful to think that people can still swoon for joy."

"Not joy," said Liss, panting—"starvation! But she'll have her guest at dinner, after all. (She's coming to now.) It's been a great pretend! (Darling, lean your head on me.) She'll be as right as rain to-morrow. In fact, she's jolly well got to be. It's her wedding day!"

CHAPTER XVII

THE UNDEFEATED

This morning I went to church, in a real church—the parish church of Craigfoot. After more than three years, I found myself once again in the Baronrigg gallery.

Of late, I have become accustomed to performing my religious exercises in the open air, in a boggy field of Flanders or Picardy, struggling, in company with a choir of some hundreds of devout, mud-splashed "Jocks," armed to the teeth and insufficiently supplied with hymn-books, to produce a respectable volume of psalmody; or listening resignedly, in an east wind, to a sermon replete with apposite references to the canker-wurrum and the pammer-wurrum, delivered with gusto by an untimely young chaplain newly out from home.

I shared the Baronrigg pew with the Matron of the Eskerley Auxiliary Military Hospital, and some half-dozen restive convalescents in hospital blue. It was January, and bitter cold, but no fire burned in old Neil Carrick's grate at the back of the gallery. The coal ration—like the thermometer—hovered near to zero in those days.

Of the rightful occupants of the pew there was no representative. The son of the house was commanding his company somewhere in the neighbourhood of La Bassée: at least, that was where I had left him last week. The master—well, there I was no wiser than the rest. All I knew was what I had read in the letter which he had written me at the time of his disappearance—a letter very similar in substance and temper to that received by his son.

My eyes wandered over the familiar scene below. Here, too, were changes: even the immutable ritual of a Scottish parish church had been affected by forty-one months of war. Doctor Chirnside was still in command. He was preaching the sermon now—on a text from his beloved Isaiah—more gaunt, more eagle-eyed, more uncompromising than ever. The parish, I knew, were of the opinion that "the auld man was failing." Still, there he was, sticking to his post.

"The most practical way," he had declared recently to a tactfully inquisitive Kirk Session, "to maintain national efficiency at a time of abnormal national wastage is for those of us who are spared to increase our output; to work longer hours—longer years, in my case—in order to make good the loss of those who have been called from our midst. So, though I have laboured long in the vineyard; though I have lingered long in the arena, and am now perhaps *dignus rude donari*, I shall remain at my post until God giveth the Victory. In other words, Gentlemen, you may whistle for my resignation!"

Still, the influences of the time seemed to have affected the Doctor like the rest of us. He was more human, less Olympian. The First Prayer—in which, it may be remembered, the Doctor was accustomed to commune with his Maker to the pointed exclusion of the congregation—was now much shorter. The Second Prayer—the Prayer of Intercession—was considerably longer, and very moving to hear. In that prayer, week by week, the progress of the Great War was reviewed—reviewed from the standpoint of an obscure but not altogether undutiful little parish in the Lowlands of Scotland. Not a boy from that parish, be he laird's son or herd laddie, fell in action on this front or that but the fact was duly noted, with sorrowful pride and amazing tenderness, in the Prayer of Intercession in the Parish Kirk of Craigfoot on the following Sabbath.

There were many such events to record. The Roll of Honour, fluttering in the draughty porch outside, bore witness to that fact. So did the composition of the congregation. Most of the men present were forty-five years old and upwards. Those below that age were mainly in khaki. But it was the women who told the most eloquent tale. The three tall daughters of Sir Alistair Graeme—The Three Grenadiers—still sat side by side in the Burling pew, to all appearances unchanged except for their V.A.D. uniforms. Yet I knew that each of those girls had been made a wife and widow within three short years. Mrs. Gillespie, the Bank Manager's wife, on the other hand, made no pretence of being the same woman: her son Robert, the Divinity student, had died of dysentery in Mesopotamia. Of the Misses Peabody, only the elder now sat in the pew. The younger was dead—dead of overwork as a ward-maid in a Base Hospital. None disputed her claim to be of the elect now. Little Mrs. Menzies, the wife of Lord Eskerley's late factor, was changed too—but only in name. She had done her bit—by becoming the widow of a D.S.O. and promptly marrying a C.M.G.

Looking further afield, I observed that old Couper and his wife were almost crowded out of their pew by a string of grandchildren, billeted upon Abbotrigg until such time as a newly-widowed daughter-in-law could adjust her compasses again. I missed the kindly vacant countenance of my friend Jamie Leslie, our organ-blower, which had usually been visible, on pre-war days, peering furtively round the red rep curtain which screened the organ-bellows from view. His place was now occupied by a bucolic young gentleman of thirteen. Subsequent inquiry on my part elicited the news that Jamie had at last achieved his heart's desire and been accepted for the Army, the authorities having very properly decided that what was sauce for the Staff was sauce for the rank-and-file.

In a back pew under the gallery I noticed old Mrs. Rorison, accompanied by her giant son, Jock, the Scots Guardsman—discharged, permanently unfit, with a crippled foot. I had met the pair in Main Street the day before.

"That's bad luck, Jock!" I had said, noting his crutches.

"It's naething of the kind!" replied Jock's mother, tartly. (She usually replied for Jock.) "See him, sir! Sax feet fower—and gets himsel' shot in the fit! I doot he was standing on his head in they trenches!" concluded the old lady bitterly. "Trust him!"

Eric was sitting in the Buckholm pew, with his lady mother: I was to lunch with them presently. I surveyed my friend's handsome profile, his empty sleeve, and the medal ribbons on his uniform. I thought of our regiment—which I now commanded and which he himself had led. I thought of the day, eighteen months since, when we had carried him away insensible, followed by what was left of our personnel, from that tight corner opposite Beaumont Hamel. Eric was home now with a decoration and a soft job—the idol and the oracle of the country-side. I had not been decorated, or even mentioned in Dispatches, but I had, so far, preserved a whole skin—which was far better—and been confirmed in my rank. Though lean and grizzled, I still felt fighting fit, and had no desire to change places with any one. I was staying at The Heughs—a sober household in those days, for my brother Walter had lost his eldest boy at Gallipoli. Of the other two, John was helping to navigate one of His Majesty's Destroyers, while the youngest, Alan, my namesake and particular crony, was consuming his impatient young soul—to his mother's private relief—at Sandhurst.

"*Finally, my brethren*"—began Doctor Chirnside; and I knew that we were within five minutes of the end of the sermon. The maimed men beside me wriggled in relieved anticipation, then settled down again; and I hastened to conclude my church inspection.

I glanced across to the Netherby pew. Mr. and Mrs. Clegg were both there, with the younger children. The two grown-up sons were absent: I remembered having heard vaguely that one of them had enlisted and that the other had secured a "cushie" job somewhere. The fair daughter was nowhere to be seen. I was sorry, because a thing of beauty is a joy for ever—especially during a long sermon. I wondered what had become of her—and Master Roy's infatuation. I had once or twice, during the early days in France, made playful allusion to the lady in Roy's presence, but my pleasantries had not been well received, and had been discontinued.

I gave a final glance round the church.

"*Plus ça change*—!" I said to myself.

But I was a little too quick in my judgment.

"*They that wait upon the Lord shall renew their strength; they shall mount up with wings as eagles; they shall run, and not be weary: they shall walk, and not faint.* May God sanctify to us this poor exposition of His Word; and to Him alone be the glory and the praise!"

The last sentence, at least, was familiar enough. It had rounded off every one of Doctor Chirnside's sermons, to my certain knowledge, for the last thirty-five years. The congregation came to life: the organ-bellows began to pump, almost automatically, for the last hymn. The elders of the kirk fumbled under their seats for the collection-bags.

We rose on a triumphant chord from the little organ, and sang the hymn—stoutly enough, and with that prickly sensation at the back of the nose which attacks undemonstrative people engaged in a slightly emotional exercise; for the hymn was "Onward, Christian Soldiers"! I learned afterwards that it had been sung (alternately with the hymn For Those at Sea), at the close of morning worship every single Sunday since the regular casualty lists had started. Then, in good Scottish fashion, we remained standing for Doctor Chirnside's patriarchal and impressive Benediction.

"*May the Peace of God, which Passeth All Understanding...*"

His old voice died away; and I was on the point of stooping down to grope for my glengarry, when I became conscious of a gradual stiffening in the attitude of the congregation. The organ began to rumble again. (I could see the young organ-blower working as if to crack every muscle in his back.) Then, suddenly, explosively, with every pedal and stop in action, it crashed into "God Save the King"!

Instinctively I came to attention. But though my head was immovable, I fear I allowed my eyes to stray downward to the scene below. Here was an unexpected test of war spirit.

Our National Anthem is a curious canticle; you never know what it will do with you. It may cause you to feel merely ridiculous—as when an orchestra of aliens in a restaurant drags you to your feet in the middle of your soup. Too often it elicits a purely perfunctory acknowledgment. But there are occasions when the sound of it grips the very heart of you; when you are conscious, deep down in your well-ordered British soul, of a sudden, tremendous, irresistible wave of passionate loyalty to the Sovereign who rules you and the thousand-year-old tradition for which he stands. Here was such an occasion. Here, in this little church, was our battle hymn being thundered forth, after more than three years of battle, to a community who had been paying the maximum price for their participation therein. How would they take it?

My field of vision was naturally constricted, but without moving my head I could command a fair view. Eric Bethune, of course, was standing as straight as a ramrod. So was the elder Miss Peabody—also the three poor Grenadiers. The wounded men beside me stiffened their twisted bodies proudly: evidently it was incumbent upon them to teach the rest of the congregation something.

Finally, my eyes fell upon the Abbotrigg pew. Old Couper and his wife were standing side by side, with bowed heads. I saw that they were holding hands. Beside them, in order of size, were ranged five small figures in black—three boys and two girls—the grandchildren whose father had fallen in action six days ago. They did not look too well-fed—milk and meat were not over plentiful in those days—but they stood shoulder to shoulder in a perfectly aligned row, emulating the soldiers in the gallery above. It was difficult to believe that they had not rehearsed the formation. (Probably they had, under the personal direction of a martinet home on leave.) Each small head was held resolutely up; each small chest—situated rather low down, as is usual when we are very young—was thrust resolutely forward; each small pair of arms pointed rigidly to the floor; and each pair of round eyes gazed fixedly and unblinkingly into space.

Suddenly, I saw nothing more. But I remember feeling reassured about things.

CHAPTER XVIII

THE OLD ORDER

After church I joined Lady Christina and Eric, and was conveyed in a very ancient victoria—her ladyship had "put down" the motor, owing to petrol difficulties—to Buckholm for luncheon. I noticed that my friend Bates no longer attended to the front door; he was now, I gathered, guarding our coast from invasion somewhere in Suffolk. His deputy was a grim-looking crone in a black skirt, silver-buttoned coat, and yellow waistcoat, which made her look something between a female impersonator and a prison wardress. I seemed to have encountered her in a previous existence hanging washing on a line on the drying-green behind the Buckholm orchard. She relieved me of my glengarry, gloves, and stick, and demanded my ration-book.

"There will be meat for dinner," she explained.

I handed over the emergency ration-book with which soldiers on leave were supplied in those days. It was returned to me when I left the house, lacking not only one full meat coupon, but all the butter and sugar coupons as well.

"Her leddyship said you would no be needing them," explained the wardress, and I meekly acquiesced. If Lady Christina said that I did not need a thing, who was I to say that I did? In any case I was due to rejoin the best-fed Army in the world in a few days' time.

The luncheon party consisted of Lady Christina, as bolt upright as ever, at the head of the table; Eric, at the foot; Lord Eskerley; and a weather-beaten Lieutenant-Commander of the Royal Naval Volunteer Reserve, named John Wickersham. Five years ago he had been mainly known to fame as a prominent King's Counsel, a superb bridge-player, and a fair-weather yachtsman. Now, for three years or more, his converted pleasure-craft, navigated by its owner and enrolled an original member of a certain silent, unadvertised brotherhood of the sea, had been keeping grim vigil over our island coast, with such effect that German submarine crews were breaking into open mutiny rather than face that flotilla of terror any longer. John Wickersham was ashore on long leave, for the first time for many months.

Doctor Chirnside, who seldom missed his Sunday luncheon at Buckholm, had been called away, to say what he could to a girl-wife who had just received a telegram from the War Office.

Having consumed its meat ration and sugarless apple tart, the company proceeded to mitigate the austerity of Lady Christina's war-time régime with a glass of port. Then, after a perfunctory and short-lived struggle, we yielded to the inevitable and settled down to the topic of the military situation. It was a curious experience for me, who had heard little round that peaceful table since boyhood but hunting shop and county gossip, to find myself involved in the same eternal debate as was exercising every mess, billet, and dug-out on the Western Front—a debate distinguished in both cases by extreme personal bias and entire ignorance of essential details. It is hardly necessary to mention that Lord Eskerley, the one person who could have enlightened us, offered no contribution.

Naturally we concentrated upon the rumours of the knock-out blow which Germany was preparing to deal her arch-enemy in the early spring—a blow which came near, in the actual event, to driving a wedge between the armies of France and Britain, and establishing a German base on the English Channel. But in January, nineteen-eighteen, when we had not lost a field-gun or a trench system since the First Battle of Ypres, and had been steadily winning back the soil of France and accumulating German prisoners for more than three years, no one took such a possibility seriously. Eric was particularly sanguine.

"A good thing, too!" he said. "Let them come! Then we can sit well back, and make a clean job of the lot, instead of getting hot and dusty going to look for them! This war will end when we have killed enough Boches; and if the Boches will help us by coming along to get killed—and you know what the Boche can do in that way once he gives his mind to it—there will be no complaints on our side. I feel—"

This characteristic pronouncement was interrupted by Lord Eskerley.

"It's only human nature, you know," he said. "You can't blame them. Naturally they think of their own front first. Must!"

This did not seem to fit in well with the rest of the conversation—a not altogether unusual feature of his lordship's table-talk.

"Napoleon was right," he continued. "Or was it Hannibal? Said he would sooner fight two first-class generals collaborating than one single-handed second-rater. It works out this way. Tweedledum says to Tweedledee: 'You must take over more Front.' Tweedledee says to Tweedledum: 'It can't be done! Look at my casualty list for the last three months!' Tweedledum replies: 'But you are only holding about half as much line as I am.' Thereupon Tweedledee produces statistics to show that although he holds the shorter line he has sixty-seven and a half per cent. of the enemy massed against him. And so it goes on. The old game! I believe that in Bohemian circles it is known as 'Passing the Buck.' A colloquial but apposite expression! I picked it up from an American *attaché* in Paris. In due course we shall come to the only solution—a Supreme Commander, responsible for the safety of the whole line. But, as usual, we shall pay in advance—through the nose!"

The import of the old gentleman's ruminations was now tolerably apparent to all; that is, to all but our hostess.

"Eh, what? What's he talking about?" she inquired sharply of me. (Of late, Lady Christina's hearing has deteriorated a little.) "What's he talking about? Tell me; he mumbles so! What's all this nonsense about Tweedledee and Tweedledum? Who are Tweedledee and Tweedledum? They sound like people out of Punch—two of those wretches in the Government. In German pay, every man-jack of them! Do you know what Bessie Brickshire told me last week? She went to Downing Street—"

"Your leddyship's coffee is up the stair," announced the deep voice of the prison wardress; and a libellous and irrelevant anecdote was nipped in the bud.

Lady Christina rose, informed us that she proposed to take her coffee in her own room, and, with a passing admonition to her son to be sparing of the saccharine, left us to ours.

We lit cigars and stretched ourselves, like schoolboys relieved of the pedagogue's presence.

"How do they feel about things in general up at the top, Eskerley?" asked John Wickersham. "We never hear any news in our job. Are they all quite happy and comfortable?"

"Not at all!" replied his lordship brusquely.

"What's the trouble?"

"Not enough troops."

"How? The number of Divisions on the Western Front hasn't been reduced, has it?"

"Oh, dear, no. We are as strong as ever—on paper. But instead of going frankly to the Labour bosses and telling them that another half-million men must be released from civilian employment, our politicians have reduced the personnel of each Division from thirteen battalions to ten—nearly twenty-five per cent. It's an admirable scheme, because it satisfies so many people. It satisfies the politician, because it saves his face; it satisfies the slacker, because it saves his skin; and it satisfies the Boche, because it's going to save him a lot of trouble when he makes his spring offensive. The only people who are inclined to criticise it are the insignificant individuals who are responsible for the safety of the Western Front. In fact, they are crying out to Heaven for more men. But, of course, nobody takes any notice of recommendations from such a prejudiced person as a soldier. His turn will come later, when the scapegoats are being rounded up." The old gentleman sighed. "That's one of our worries. The other is that we have too many Allies."

"I see! Too many cooks—eh?"

"Precisely! I spend all my working hours nowadays propitiating plenipotentiaries from countries whose existence I had never heard of two years ago. By the time I have recognised the status of this Ally, and soothed the susceptibilities of that, the day is over and there's no time left to get on with the war. I sometimes sigh for the era when the French and ourselves muddled along by rule of thumb without having to expend any tact upon anybody, except a periodical slap on the back to Russia. *We few, we happy few, we band of brothers!*—and so on. Life was simple then. Now it is a perpetual Pentecost, without the feast. Give me a forlorn hope and a lone hand every time; that's an invincible combination—eh, Alan?"

"I agree," I said. "In the first year or so there was a sort of cheerful, simple, all-in-the-same-boat feeling about everything. The French liked us; there was not too many of us; and what there were were perfectly disciplined—old Regulars and the pick of 'K's' Army; or else Indian troops, with the manners of Hidalgoes. Now, the average French citizen never wants to see an ally again—"

Lord Eskerley nodded.

"Exactly!" he said. "And I can't say I blame him. I sometimes feel that way myself. We're a fairly promiscuous lot. We may be a host of modern crusaders, but we're a *crowd*! I feel like old McKechnie at the revivalist meeting here five years ago, who refused to stand up and be 'saved' with the rest because he objected to going to heaven 'with a d——d Cheap Trup!' Still, we mustn't be ungrateful. Our post entries may have complicated the machine, but they have made it a pretty reliable piece of mechanism."

"What I complain of," interposed Eric, "is that we, upon whom the whole burden fell at the start, are almost forgotten now. Most of us have ceased to exist, and the rest are lost in a mob of amateurs."

"The wrong attitude entirely!" announced Lord Eskerley promptly.

"What's the right attitude, then?" asked Eric, who hated correction almost as much as Lord Eskerley delighted to administer it to him.

"The right attitude," replied the old man, with sudden seriousness, "should be a feeling of pride that We were fortunate enough to find ourselves Original Members of the

Brotherhood—to hold Founders' Shares. When the edifice is completed—and completed it will be—the world won't be able to see the foundations. But they will be there all right! And we shall know who laid them—the Old Order!"

"What do you mean by the Old Order?" asked Eric. "The landed gentry?"

"Far more than that. I mean the people to whom this country, as such, has always really meant something; I mean every mother's son who felt the ancient spirit of our race wake in him, perhaps for the first time, when the challenge came in Nineteen Fourteen. I don't care who he was—squire's son, parson's son, miner's son, poacher's son—it was all the same. If he was conscious then of that single blind impulse to get up and play the game, just because it was the game; just because it was impossible to do otherwise—without any dialectics about Freedom, or Altruism, or Democracy, or whether his job would be kept open for him or not; simply because the Blood told him to—then he belonged to the Old Order! He held a Founder's Share, all right!"

"Of course," the old man continued presently, "the more one has to give the more one is expected to give, at a time like this. And as a rule it seems to be the best that is taken. *'This is the heir; come, let us kill him!'*—that has been the general attitude of the War Gods. Only the very best would suffice—only the very best!"

We sat silent again. Lord Eskerley himself had lost his two sons, and his only grandson. After him, what was to become of the ancient title—of the "Big Hoose" and its "policies"—of the family which had served the State for three hundred years? *"This is the heir!"* How true that was. I thought of my brother Walter's eldest son. Fortunately in this case there were two more. And Roy? What would become of Baronrigg, if—

But Lord Eskerley was speaking again—more to himself than to us.

"The Old Order! The Willing Horse! There's hardly an estate, or a farm, or an allotment, in this country-side, or in any part of Scotland or England, that has not changed hands, prospectively at least, during the last three years. And what with designedly disruptive death duties, and income tax on the same scale, levied on people who have no personal income—only a few precious, ancient, barren acres—the old estates are passing right away from the original owners—one half sold to pay the charges on the other half. It seems a queer way of rewarding people who have given everything— to sell them up because they have nothing more to give! Still, one has the supreme satisfaction of having played the game. Our record stands—" He broke off. "I apologise: I was sermonising! Bad habit!" He looked at his watch. "Three o'clock! I must go; a trunk call comes through from London every afternoon at four. Alan, I will give you a lift."

A few minutes later I found myself rolling home in an unaccustomed motor.

"I still get twenty gallons a month," explained Lord Eskerley. "Business of State, and so on. Going back soon?"

"Thursday," I said.

"Well, enjoy the war while you can. When it is over there will be no peace for anybody. After the Boche has given his last expiring kick we are going to sit down to a Peace Congress in comparison with which the Congress of Vienna will take rank as a model of sagacity and altruism. The Millennium that we are all composing cantatas about is not coming—yet."

"Are we going to have more wars, then?" I asked, gazing rather dejectedly at the red, wintry sunset.

"We are always going to have more wars," replied my companion testily—"and then more! (The final war will be between men and women. Even that won't really settle anything, because there will be too much rendering aid and comfort to the enemy going on.) By the way, how is Roy?"

I reported favourably upon my nephew's health and service record.

"I suppose you know," I remarked, "that Tom Birnie appointed yourself and myself Roy's trustees and executors?"

"Yes. Tom wrote me a letter to that effect before he enlisted."

"He did enlist, then?"

"I believe so."

I did not press for details. Lord Eskerley has means at his disposal of discovering most of the secrets of this world—which is not to say that he is accustomed to pass these on to third parties.

"Have you seen Roy," I continued, "or heard from him of late?"

"I have not seen him, and he has not favoured me with a single line since he went out for the first time. By the way, I observe she received a decoration the other day—for conspicuous bravery during an air-raid."

"Who?"

"Who? The girl!"

"The girl? You mean—the Netherby girl? Is that *affaire* still—?"

"Yes. Name of Clegg. You know what became of her, I suppose?"

"No. Roy has never been communicative on the subject, although I believe he used to maintain a correspondence with her. The junior members of the mess were quite intrigued about it. I had almost forgotten her existence. What became of her?"

"She couldn't stand Papa's peaceful principles, so ran away from home and came to London. I employed her to drive my car for some time; but she left me. Said the work wasn't hard enough. She now supports herself on the stage, so as to have her days free for some sort of drudgery in a canteen."

"And you think that she and Roy still—

"Married, last August!" replied his lordship simply.

"*What?*"

"On the quiet—registry office! Wonderful, heavenly secret, and all that! How the young love a clandestine romance! And some of us never grow up!" added the old man complacently.

CHAPTER XIX

THE LAST THROW

"I'm sorry, gentlemen," said the Divisional Commander, "but I can't possibly let any unit proceed to rest areas at present. Our orders are to stand by, day and night, and be ready to move in any direction at an hour's notice. By the way, this is quite an informal meeting, so ask any questions you like."

"What is the latest news of the tactical situation, sir?" inquired the senior Brigadier, articulating the question that was on every one's lips.

We were gathered together at a Commanding Officers' Meeting. The Division had just emerged from four months of winter trench-warfare in the north—only to be diverted from its search for well-earned repose by an urgent summons to repair southward without delay to its ancient stamping-ground behind Albert. We had marched all night, to be intercepted at dawn by orders to bivouac where we stood. I myself was summoned to the meeting, hastily convened in a village school five miles farther on.

"It's a pretty sticky business all round," said the General frankly. "The situation appears to be this. As you know, it has been obvious for months that the Boche has been meditating a tremendous offensive against some part of the British front. The

Commander-in-Chief, not having sufficient troops to give adequate protection to the whole of his line—

"Why *hasn't* he sufficient troops?" inquired a voice—the voice of the C.R.A., a fiery old gentleman with a monocle. He was a coeval of the General's, so was qualified to act as cross-examiner for us lesser lights.

"It's not my business to explain, or ours to wonder. I can only give you the facts. Last year the British Army had, roughly speaking, one million casualties. This year the British Army is fighting in France, Belgium, Italy, Saloniki, Palestine, Mesopotamia, the Indian frontier, and East Africa; so you can imagine the clamour for reinforcements that is going on all over the globe. Thirdly, the French, not long ago, asked us to take over another twenty-eight miles of line. We did so; with the result that the C.-in-C. found himself in the position of having to decide, since he hadn't enough men to hold all the line securely, where he must hold on at all costs, and where he could afford to take chances. Obviously, he had to make the Straits of Dover impregnable; so the northern part of the line got the lion's share of troops. Down here, the Fifth Army were strung out to a beggarly bayonet per yard. North of them, the Third Army had about three bayonets to two yards. Opposite this line, during the past few weeks, the Boche was known to have accumulated a force averaging seven bayonets per yard—" A low murmur ran round the crowded little school-room. It was fully light now, and we could see one another's startled faces. "In other words, sixty or seventy divisions. Against that force we had available twenty-two divisions in the line, with twelve infantry divisions and three cavalry divisions in reserve. The attack opened six days ago. The Boches, as usual, had the Devil's own luck with the weather—thick mist—and were on us in a solid phalanx before we saw them at all. I may add that they were backed by the most terrific concentration of artillery fire on record, and raised unexpected Sheol in our back areas by a new very long range gas-shell. By all the rules they ought to have wiped us right out. But they didn't. We were bowled over again and again; but we always managed to re-form some sort of line—until the want of reserves began to tell, and brigades and divisions, thinned out to nothing, began to draw in upon themselves and leave gaps on their flanks. The cavalry worked like heroes to cover the intervals; but they couldn't be everywhere, and one position after another was outflanked and had to be given up. Noyon has gone; Péronne has gone; Monchy has gone; the whole Somme battle-field of Nineteen-Sixteen has gone. Even Albert"—there came a groan here from all of us who had fought in the Somme battle—"has fallen into Boche hands. Yes, I know! But things might be worse. Arras is holding fast; and the good old Vimy Ridge is still standing right up to them. It's tolerably certain now that the Boche was booked to get Amiens in three days. He hasn't got it; and if we can continue to make him pay his present price he will never get it at all."

There was small comfort in this. The very fact that Amiens had become a Boche possibility was a staggerer in itself. We thought of the Hôtel du Rhin, and other haunts of ancient peace, and sighed.

"How is morale?" asked the C.R.A.

The General held up a paper.

"Here is the Commander-in-Chief's latest dispatch," he said. "Listen to this, gentlemen!"

At no time was there anything approaching a breakdown of command or a failure of morale. Under conditions that made rest and sleep impossible for days together, officers and men remained undismayed, realising that for the time being they must play a waiting game, and determined to make the enemy pay the full price for the advantage which, for the moment, was his.

We broke into applause. We could not help it.

"Naturally," continued the General, "the strain has been awful, because we are employing tired men, fighting without reinforcements against ever fresh bodies of troops. However, more divisions are coming down from the north—you are one of the first arrivals—and Foch has taken supreme command, which means that hereafter the Allied forces will be more evenly distributed and the line stabilised. The long and short of it all is that the enemy has been frustrated, for the time being, in his amiable attempt to drive a wedge between the British and French armies."

"Still," said the voice of the C.R.A., "I suppose the situation is pretty critical?"

"Critical isn't the word! But the line is still intact, though badly bent, and we have beaten all our previous records for Boche-killing, which is saying something. And if they fail to break through—good-bye Germany! It's their last throw. A German who knows he cannot win is a German beaten. Now, gentlemen, you will understand why it is that you cannot go into retirement at present. That's all, I think! To your tents, O Israel—and breakfast! But be ready to move at an hour's notice."

Roy and I jogged wearily back across country to the field where the men were bivouacking. Roy was my senior company commander, and I had brought him to the meeting in preference to the adjutant, who was very young and already bowed down with regimental routine. Roy, a seasoned Ironside of twenty-two, with two-and-a-half years continuous active service to his record, was now my shield and buckler and right-hand man.

We had little to say to one another. We were both dog-tired, and were suffering in addition from that unpleasant form of reaction which comes from hope deferred. We were thinking, too, of the men. They had completed four months of exhausting and expensive trench duty, working by "internal reliefs," which really means no relief at all; each man staying his dour dogged heart with the only two consolations available in those days—the humdrum certainty of ultimate relief by another division, and the ever present possibility of a "Blighty" wound. And now, when they had actually packed up and removed out of the shell area, with a spell of rest and relaxation well within their grasp, they found themselves pulled back into the line. That sort of experience is a severer test of morale than an intensive bombardment. The danger was that they might go stale—just as I had once seen a highly-trained college crew go, when the races were postponed for a week owing to ice on the river.

"We will call a pow-wow when we get back," I said to Roy, "and tell the officers to explain matters to the men as well as they can. They must sing the usual song about our trusty old indispensable Division, the prop and stay of the weaker brethren, proudly filling the breach and saving the situation, and so forth."

"They'll respond all right," said Roy confidently. "They are a wonderful crowd."

"They certainly are; but it will break their hearts if they are shoved back for another spell of trench duty. Of course, if we go right into the scrap, with a fair chance to get above ground and grab the Boche by the ears, they won't mind at all—quite the reverse. It will be a perfect tonic."

"If half of what His Nibs said is true, they'll get all the tonic they want!" remarked my sage young companion. "We're for it, this time!"

He was right. Even at that moment our task had been assigned to us; for when we reached Battalion Headquarters—a G.S. waggon in the corner of a field, in the middle of which certain incurable greathearts were playing football—we found that the telephone had outstripped us, and that our orders were waiting.

We gobbled breakfast, with that curious mingling of sentiment and satisfaction which comes to men who are not sure if they will ever see a poached egg again. Then I summoned my officers. I passed on to them the substance of the General's statement, and spoke of the gaps that were being created in the line by lack of reinforcements.

"Such a gap," I explained, "has occurred almost directly in front of us, along the crest of a low ridge called Primrose Hill. (The Adjutant will give you the map reference in a minute.) The gap is being filled at present by a rather raw battalion of newly-arrived Territorials, rushed up from Corps Reserve. It is a very important point, and we are to go in and stiffen them. Written orders will be issued to you immediately; but it may save time if I mention that I propose to march the battalion direct to the back of Primrose Hill, deploy, and advance in lines of companies until we strike the trench system which the Royal Loyals are holding. In that way we ought to be able to plug any possible gap in the shortest possible time. We may have to advance through a barrage; but that, of course, is all in the day's work. Company commanders will take such precautions as are possible to ensure the safety of their men, but they must not waste time on this occasion looking for covered lines of advance. In other words, the situation is critical, and must be tackled bald-headed. The point of deployment, as at present fixed, is a blacksmith's forge on the road running direct from here to Primrose Hill. It is marked in the map, *Michelin Forge*; there's a big motor-tyre advertisement on the western gable, the Brigade Major tells me. I shall go there now myself, and establish temporary headquarters. Companies will move off independently in succession, A Company leading. Company commanders will report at Michelin Forge for further instructions. Later, after we have deployed and advanced up the reverse slope of Primrose Hill—it is a mere swelling in the ground, as a matter of fact—Battalion Headquarters will be established, if possible, in a *point d'appui* just behind the crest, called Fountain Keep. It is a ruined ornamental garden, I believe, with the wreck of a fountain in the middle. I hope you'll all arrive there in due course—and find me there! That's all! Good luck to you!"

My officers saluted in a manner that warmed my heart, and hurried off to their duties. I felt sorry I had not been able to give them a more stirring harangue: I felt sure that Eric would have done so. Still, harangue or no harangue, I knew they would lead their men to the crest of Primrose Hill. I looked after them affectionately. Most of them I never saw again from that hour. But I remember them all to-day—their faces, their voices, their characteristics. They were of many types—the variegated types of a whole nation at last in arms. There were Public School and Sandhurst products, like Roy; there were promoted rankers, with permanently squared shoulders and little waxed moustaches; there were professional and business men verging on middle-age, who had long shed their stomachs and acquired a genuine passion for army forms and regimental routine. The last two figures that caught my eye were those of my machine-gun officer, a Mathematical Fellow of an ancient Cambridge college, and Adams, second-in-command of B Company, who in a previous existence had officiated as under gate-porter in the same foundation. The British Army in those days was one great ladder, up which all men, gentle or simple, might climb if they had the character and the will. In that army at the end of the war there was a Divisional General who had been editor of a newspaper; there was a Brigadier-General who had been a taxi-cab driver; another who had been a school-teacher. Numbered among that exclusive hierarchy, the General Staff, were an insurance clerk, an architect's assistant, and a college cook. A coal miner, a railway signalman, a market gardener, and countless promoted private soldiers commanded battalions.

A few minutes later I rode off with my adjutant, young Hume-Logan, in the direction of Michelin Forge. My faithful orderly—a gigantic, inarticulate Lowland hind named Herriott—jogged along in rear of us. It was a distressing ride. A badly mangled terrain, restored to France and cultivation by Hindenburg's operatic retirement to the Siegfried line, was being overrun once more: and the plucky, industrious peasant population, which had been so busily employed for the past twelve months in rebuilding their villages and re-ploughing their emancipated soil behind the traditionally sure shield of a British trench line, found itself uprooted and cast forth for the second time. The panic-stricken flood of refugees had now subsided; but along the road we encountered sights which wrung the heart and tweaked the conscience—here, a pitiful little cart loaded with worldly possessions which hardly seemed worth salving; there, a tired woman struggling along a muddy roadside with her children

Respiciens frustra rura laresque sua

—as Ovid used to say in the Repetition Book. I felt somehow, perhaps unjustifiably, but none the less poignantly, that for once the British Army had failed in a trust.

But presently I saw something which inspired me. Down the road came a big elderly peasant woman wheeling a barrow, piled high with household furniture. (You have to invade French peasant territory very suddenly and very early in the morning indeed, if you expect to find so much as an orange-box left to sit down upon.) We looked down on the barrow as it passed.

"She doesn't seem to have forgotten anything, sir," observed Master Hume-Logan.

I gave Madame a respectful salute as we rode past. Her hard features never relaxed. Instead, she set down her barrow by the roadside, turned round, and started back in the same direction as ourselves: in fact, she outstripped our two horses, which were walking delicately amid the puddles.

"She seems to have forgotten something, after all," I said.

But I was wrong. She had forgotten nothing. Two hundred yards along the road stood another wheelbarrow. In it—mute, helpless, patient—lay a very old man. The old woman seized the shafts of this barrow and began to wheel it after the first. In so doing she met us again—and again I saluted her. We turned in our saddles and looked after her. At her original halting-place she deposited the second barrow as close to the side of the road as possible, turned again to the first, and trundled it forward, without a moment's rest, another hundred yards or so. When last we saw her she was coming back—grim, resolute, invincible—for the old man. She *was* France—La Patrie, incarnate!

At last we penetrated beyond what we may call the refugee zone, and arrived at Michelin Forge. There was little of it left save the western gable, which was still decorated by a tattered presentment of two pre-war friends, the Bibendum Twins. The low ridge of Primrose Hill defined the horizon about a mile or two ahead of us. It was nothing of a hill; it looked no higher than its namesake in distant "N.W." A quarter-of-a-mile away from us enemy shells were falling with Teutonic regularity of interval into a group of poor houses, clustered round a cross-roads. Over the ridge itself shrapnel was bursting intermittently. Away to our left a large canteen hut was burning fiercely: probably it had been cleared and set alight to save it from falling into enemy hands. To the right of the forge a battery of our Four-point-Five Howitzers was firing salvoes—securely dug in, and screened from aeroplane view by nets interwoven with leaves and twigs. When, to the great content of our horses, this performance ceased, I rode over and sought out the young officer in command. He had not shaved for a week, and his quite creditable beard was encrusted with mud.

"Yes, sir," he said, "I can tell you a little. The enemy are in force just beyond that low ridge—Primrose Hill. We are strafing them now. Our F.O.O. is somewhere in Fountain Keep, which is a strong point just behind the crest, with one or two observation posts stretching over it. He has direct observation; his last telephone-message said that the enemy were massing again behind their own second line. I haven't heard from him since: that's why I stopped firing. Something gone wrong with the works, I expect."

"What's the distance from here to the ridge?" I asked.

"Well, we are firing at a range of four thousand three hundred; but that, of course, reaches Boche territory. The range to the crest is about three thousand five hundred."

"I see; a brisk country walk of about two miles? I shall deploy here. Has the Boche been shelling the reverse slope of the hill at all?"

"Not lately. But yesterday afternoon, during a big attack, he put down a heavy barrage from end to end of it."

"Hum! That means that when he attacks again he will put down another heavy barrage. The sooner we get to the crest of that hill the better."

I was turning away, when the gunner said:

"There's a sunken road over there, sir, behind that hedge. It runs straight towards Primrose Hill for nearly a mile, and ends where the gradient really begins. If you followed that you could get shelter for a bit, and need not take open order quite so soon."

"That's good advice," I said. "I will have a look at it. Is there much going on in the air at present?"

"They set one of our sausage-balloons on fire early this morning. The observer got down all right in his parachute; but I fancy the heavies behind us are a bit in the dark about things, in consequence."

"How are the gas-works?"

"They put mustard down with their last barrage."

"Any aeroplanes been over?"

"One Boche machine came over at dawn, but our Archies hunted him back. This battery hasn't been spotted so far; but I expect we shall have to limber up and do another Hindenburg act presently; we have been doing nothing else for a week. A fortnight ago we were in rest billets about here, running about and playing football and going to the pictures! It's a bit thick!" he grunted ruefully, through his mask of dirt.

"We are to go in and stiffen the line ahead of us," I said. "You stay where you are, and back us! Here's my leading company coming up now. Good-morning!"

"Good-morning, sir, and good luck!"

The gunner hurried back to his camouflaged emplacements, and I turned to find Roy at my elbow.

"A message came through from brigade, sir," he said, "just after you left, to say that the enemy were massing heavily opposite Primrose Hill, and that we were to get up as soon as possible."

"Right! Let us have a look at a covered approach I have just heard about."

We crossed a meadow and looked over a hedge. Sure enough, at our very feet lay a deep cutting, following the line of the hedge towards Primrose Hill.

"Bring your company over here," I said, "and start them up this thoroughfare for all they're worth. Have the signallers arrived?"

"Yes, sir; they came with me."

"Tell the signal sergeant to establish telephone communication with Brigade Headquarters as quickly as he can." I turned to that faithful shadow, my adjutant. "Notify the other companies as they arrive—to this effect." I scribbled an order. "Explain to Major Wylie"—Major Wylie was my second in command—"that I have gone ahead with A Company. He will take charge of affairs here and maintain communication as far as possible from front to rear. Is that quite clear?"

"Yes, sir."

106

"Good! Ah! here is Captain Birnie, with A Company. Now, Roy, young fellow-my-lad, what about it?"

Five minutes later Roy and I were heading up the sunken lane, followed by A Company, with steel helmets adjusted and gas-masks at the ready.

"By rights," I grunted, "I suppose I ought to be sitting in Michelin Forge maintaining touch with Brigade Headquarters. But I think this is going to be one of those occasions upon which a C.O. is justified in leading his regiment from the front. I am fed up with this Duke of Plaza Toro business."

Roy did not reply. He struck me as a little *distrait*, which did not altogether surprise me, considering that we were both going, in all probability, straight to an early demise. In fact, I was feeling a little *distrait* myself. But this was no time for preoccupation. Progress along the lane was not too easy. There was a good deal of traffic coming the other way—stragglers, stretcher-cases, walking wounded, and dispatch-riders urging their reluctant motor-cycles through a river of mud. Phlegmatic cave-dwellers in dug-outs in the banks of the lane, mainly signallers, looked out upon us, exchanging grisly jests with my followers. Sappers, imperturbable as ever, were running out wire across an open space to the right. A water-party met us, jangling empty petrol-cans. At one point we passed a row of our dead, awaiting removal. On nearly every sleeve I noticed one, two, or even three gold stripes. It seemed desperately hard that The Willing Horse, healed three times of his wounds, should have gone down for good so near the end—as the event proved it to be—when others had never left the stable.

Presently we overtook a slow-moving procession, advancing with that injured bearing and gait which mark Thomas Atkins when employed upon an uncongenial job. They were a fatigue party, carrying enormous trench-mortar bombs.

"We can never get past this crowd," I said to Roy. "We'll climb out here, and deploy to the left."

Roy gave the order, and soon A Company were advancing in extended formation with their faces set towards Fountain Keep. Roy and I tramped ahead of them: the ridge of Primrose Hill was barely a thousand yards away now. The morning mists had cleared away, and we could see it quite distinctly.

Suddenly Roy turned to me.

"Uncle Alan," he began—

But he got no further. There came a roar and a shock that shook the ground. Five hundred yards ahead of us the brown face of Primrose Hill broke into a spouting row of earth-fountains, intermingled with the smoke of shrapnel and whizz-bangs. The evening's barrage had begun. The line of men behind us recoiled for a moment, then pressed stolidly forward.

"We have got to get through that," I announced—a little superfluously.

Roy replied—somewhat unexpectedly—right in my left ear, at the top of his voice:

"Uncle Alan, I want to tell you that I am married!"

"So I have been given to understand!" I bellowed. The din was growing louder.

"Who told you? Old Eskerley?"

I nodded; halted; and sniffed the air,

"I thought so," I said. "Gas-masks, Roy—quick!"

Roy turned and waved an order to his company. In a few seconds we were advancing again: each man had transformed God's image into a goggled deformity, and was breathing God's air from a box of chemicals through a jointed tube.

Roy and I adjusted our masks last.

"Come along," I said, with a glance ahead of us: "the longer we look at it the less we shall like it!" I tried to fit my mask to my face, but found that Roy was shouting into my ear again.

"Uncle Alan—"

I inclined my head towards him.

"Well?"

"*I am a father!*"

I nodded my hideous head, and smiled congratulations as well as I could.

"I only got word this morning," I heard him bawl as his face disappeared into his mask. "BOY!" And with that he led his company into the barrage.

I felt convinced if we got through it Roy would tell the first German he met about the baby.

CHAPTER XX

FOUNTAIN KEEP

Of the next half-hour my recollection is mercifully blurred. All that I know is that most of us got through the barrage and foregathered at the back of Fountain Keep, which proved to be a circular *point d'appui* intersected and honeycombed with trenches, saps and tunnels.

"Carry right on with the company," I said to Roy. "I think you will find some hand-to-hand work going on just over the ridge; so your men will be welcome. I will try to find the Headquarters of the Royal Loyals. Take care of yourself, laddie!"

Our gas-masks were off again by this time, so we could smile at one another as we parted.

Ultimately Herriott and I discovered the Headquarters of the Fifth Royal Loyals—a dug-out at the back of the Keep, occupied by a slightly hysterical second lieutenant (apparently the adjutant) and a telephone orderly vainly trying to make connection with a Brigade Headquarters which we learned afterwards had been shelled out of existence twenty minutes before.

"The battalion are cut to pieces, sir," gasped the second lieutenant. "They are fighting more or less in the open.... There are hardly any trenches.... The C.O. was killed half an hour ago.... Most of the company commanders have been scuppered too. The line's broken in two or three places, and we are fighting in small groups.... They are putting up a wonderful kick.... But there's hardly anybody left ... no platoon commanders or anything. I seem to be in command of the battalion!" He giggled, foolishly. "I came back here to try and telephone for help.... All the numbers seem to be engaged, though!" He began to sob. He looked barely twenty.

"That's all right," I said. "I have sent a company of my Jocks to stiffen your front line, and three more are coming up. Here, take a pull at my flask, and then show me the way through this Keep of yours! Looks like the Maze at Hampton Court, doesn't it? We must hold on to it whatever happens: it's the key to the whole business. Who's in command up in front, by the way?"

"A corporal, I think."

"*A corporal?* Come along! The sooner we reinforce him the better."

But the boy was too badly shell-shocked to guide me, so Herriott and I went on alone. We plunged into the depths of the Keep, and followed its deep mazes as best we could. Here and there I noticed traces of the ornamental garden. We passed by the wrecked fountain, with a broken stucco figure lying across its basin. Once our road took us through an artificial rockery, reinforced with sandbags. The trenches were deep, and we could see nothing but the sky above our heads. Everywhere was the old familiar reek—humanity and chloride of lime. The noise was terrific now. Our own shells were whistling over our heads: evidently my grimy friend with the four-point-fives had got to work again. Enemy artillery was silent, probably through fear of hitting its own men; but bombs and trench-mortars were busy.

The windings of the Keep were tortuous, and we wandered more or less at random, stepping here and there over some obstruction—an abandoned case of ammunition, or a dead soldier. Suddenly we emerged into what was obviously a firing-trench. It was lined with men, mounted on the step and maintaining a steady fusillade. From their deliberate movements I saw that they were fighting well within themselves. Some were Roy's men, others members of that sturdy Territorial unit, the Fifth Royal Loyals. There were other details—cyclists, signallers, Labour Corps men—all contributing. Evidently some organising influence had been at work. A few yards along the trench to the right I observed a sort of projection, or bastion, in which a Lewis gun team were maintaining enfilade fire along the wire to their own right.

Realising that I had reached the forward edge of Fountain Keep, I was about to hoist myself on to the firing step in order to see what was happening on the other side of the parapet, when my attention was attracted to the man who appeared to be in general charge of the sector. It was difficult to discern his rank, for he was in his shirt sleeves, like many of his comrades. (Tommy Atkins has a passion for *déshabillé*.) Obviously he was not an officer, for he wore the unæsthetic boots and grey flannel shirt of the rank-and-file. His steel helmet had fallen off, and I could see that his hair was quite grey. His face, like those of most present, was framed in a six days' beard, with a top-dressing of dirt; but he was an undoubted leader of men. When first I saw him he was directing the Lewis gun team. Presently he came down the trench towards me, throwing up fresh clips of ammunition and shouting encouragement to the men on the firing-step—though in that hellish din I doubt if they heard much of what he said.

He passed the mouth of the communication trench in which I was standing without noticing me, and disappeared round a traverse on the left, evidently on his way to stiffen morale in the next bay. I found myself gazing after him with an interest for which I could not quite account. Probably he was the corporal of whom the shell-shocked boy behind us had spoken....

I became suddenly conscious that Herriott was stiffening to attention. This meant that Herriott desired permission to deliver himself of a remark.

"Well, Herriott?" I said.

"I beg your pardon, sirr—"

"Yes? What?"

"Yon, sirr, is—"

At that moment a German trench-mortar bomb came sailing over, and burst some thirty yards to our left. Fortunately our bay was screened from the effects by a stout island-traverse. However, I fear I missed the purport of Herriott's statement. In fact, I doubt if I heard it at all, for at that moment Roy appeared round the corner on the right, followed by an orderly.

He was bleeding from a scratch on the cheek, and held his Colt automatic in his hand.

"We have just pushed them back on the right, sir," he announced. His eyes were blazing. "They tried to rush a bad bit of our line about a hundred yards along; but our boys were splendid, and very few Boches got as far as the parapet. They simply withered up when they got to the wire."

I pointed to the bastion, where the Lewis gunners were recharging magazines.

"Those are the fellows you have to thank," I said. "How is the situation generally?"

"The Boche has gone back everywhere, for the moment," Roy replied. "I fancy he will give us a dose of trench-mortars and H.E., and then try again. I am going along the line now, to see if all the men are in place."

"You will find a very efficient understudy round that traverse," I said—"a corporal. I found him handling this bit of line like a field-marshal."

Again I was aware of the dour presence of Herriott at my elbow.

"I beg your pardon, sirr—" he began again.

Again the words were taken out of his mouth. Round the corner of the traverse to our left struggled a pitifully familiar group—two stooping men supporting a third between them. The wounded man held an arm resolutely round the neck of each supporter, but his feet dragged in the mud. It was the grey-headed corporal.

"Stretcher-bearers, there!" cried one of the men gruffly.

"How did they cop you, Corporal?" inquired a Royal Loyal, leaning down sympathetically from the firing-step.

"That last trench-mortar!" gasped the grey-haired man, as they set him down on the floor of the trench, just below the Lewis gun emplacement. He turned his head feebly in our direction, and our eyes met for the first time. At the same moment Roy gave a cry and started forward.

Then I understood what Herriott had been trying to tell me. Tom Birnie lay dying before our eyes—at the feet of his own son.

Roy, very white, dropped on his knees beside his father. A stretcher came, and we did what we could. Tom had a dreadful wound in his side; plainly it was only a matter of minutes. I remember seeing Roy unbuckle his own equipment, take off his tunic, and wrap it round his father's shoulders. Tom's eyes were closed; his breathing was laboured; he recognised no one.

For a moment the tempest of battle around us seemed to stand still. The crowded trench was silent; the men on the firing-step looked down curiously. Roy still knelt beside his father, motionless. Herriott, who had worked on the Baronrigg estate ever since he could walk, stood rigidly at attention at the foot of the Laird's stretcher, with tears trickling down his cheeks.

At last Tom's eyes opened. He smiled and said faintly:

"That you, Roy? Good boy! I was expecting you.... I carried on as well as I could, until you came to take over.... I knew you would come.... I knew! Give your father a kiss, old man."

Roy bowed his head....

Next moment, with the shriek of an express train emerging from a tunnel, a German shell whirled out of the blue and exploded against the traverse a few yards away.

When I came to myself I was being carried in Herriott's arms—and I weigh nearly fourteen stone—back through the mazes of Fountain Keep in the direction of the first aid post. After more than three years of continuous seeking I had achieved the soldier's ambition—a "blighty."

That night, as I passed on my jolting way to the base, with a smashed collar-bone and a damaged skull, my rambling dreams ran naturally on one subject—that strange meeting between father and son; and the spectacle of the one passing on to the other, as it were some precious inheritance, the safe custody of Fountain Keep.

CHAPTER XXI

IDENTITIES

I

Night had fallen on Fountain Keep; for the moment the guns were silent and the battle had died down. To-morrow the Boche would come again—and again. But he would get no farther. The high-water mark of the great spring offensive of Nineteen Eighteen had been reached—in this region at any rate, though none knew it. To the right the long, attenuated British line had been pressed back to the village of Villers Bretonneux, within sight of Amiens; the Australians were destined to do historic work here six weeks later, when the bundling-out process began. On the left, before Arras, despite massed attacks and reckless expenditure of German cannon-fodder, the line had held fast. On every side, for the moment, the enemy had sullenly withdrawn, to lick his wounds. He would try again later on further north, in the flat plain of the sluggish Lys—only to create a second spectacular and untenable salient in the British line, with the Vimy Ridge standing up invincibly between the two, like a great rock splitting the force of a spring spate.

Fountain Keep was very still and silent. It lay once more well within the British lines. It had been captured by the enemy in a massed attack at three o'clock that afternoon, despite the gallant defence put up by A Company and the great-hearted remnants of the Royal Loyals—to be recaptured in a most skilfully directed counter-attack just before nightfall by the three remaining companies of the Royal Covenanters. With the key position restored, a gallant rally had taken place all along the line, and once more the whole of Primrose Hill was in British hands.

Out in front weary men were consolidating the position—replacing sandbags and running out wire. Fountain Keep itself, lying snugly behind its restored trench-line, had resumed its proper function of *point d'appui* and battalion headquarters. But British prestige had been restored at the usual prodigal cost. Stretcher-bearers were everywhere, stumbling about in the darkness from shell-hole to shell-hole, where wounded men usually contrive to drag themselves. Many of those wounded had seen khaki puttees, then German field-boots, then khaki puttees pass over their heads that day.

They were nearly all collected by this time; our own particular Alan Laing had passed through the field dressing-station hours ago. Now the battle-ground was occupied by other search-parties, whose business lay with those who had been delivered for ever from the pain of wounds and the weariness of convalescence.

Such a party was at this moment employing itself in Fountain Keep, under the direction of a conscientious but not over-imaginative sergeant, named Busby.

"We'll go along the front parapet first," he announced; "that's where most of 'em are.... Yes, 'ere's one—a Jock; lance-corporal, by his stripe. Get his pay-book out of his pocket, 'Erb. Not got one? Well, he *ought* to 'ave, that's all; it's in Regulations. Look at his identity-disc, then. Read it out, and read it slow; my pencil's blunt. *Number Seven-Six-Five-Fower-Eight—Private J. Couper*—been promoted since he got that—*Second Royal Covenanters—Presbyterian.* Righto! Now, this one—No, never mind 'im, it's only a 'Un; no need to take *his* number! Pass along, boys! Get a move on; we've got a lot to do."

The little procession moved on, performing its grim duties with characteristic sang-froid, lightened by the incurable, untimely, invaluable flippancy of the British soldier. Presently they came to a place where a bastion of sandbags had been improvised as an emplacement for a Lewis gun. The gun itself lay twisted and earthy on a heap of burst sandbags; below the emplacement lay the gun's crew.

"One shell got the lot, I fancy," remarked Sergeant Busby. "Switch on your torch, Alf; there are four or five of 'em here. Lift them clear of one another, boys."

Four bodies were lifted, not irreverently, and laid side by side on the ground behind the emplacement, with sightless eyes upturned to the twinkling stars. One remained—a long-legged figure in shirt-sleeves, lying with face turned to the parapet.

111

"Help me to turn this feller over, 'Erb," commanded the sergeant. "Seems to have lost his toonic; Government property, too! Well, he can't be brought up for it now. Hallo! ... *'Strewth*! ... Did you see that, 'Erb? It give me a turn for a minute. 'Alf a tick!" He bent down hurriedly, and listened. "He's breathing! There's a stretcher-party round that traverse; you, Richards, double off and bring them, quick!"

Five minutes later the insensible form of the man who had mislaid Government property was borne away, and Sergeant Busby proceeded with the identification of his less (or more) fortunate companions. 'Erb, the *littérateur* of the party, read off the identity-discs one by one.

"*Smith—Turner—'Opkins*," repeated the sergeant, labouring with the blunt pencil. "That's the first lot of Loyals we've struck. There must be a heap more somewhere; we'll find 'em presently. What's the name of this last one? Give us his number first. *Six-O-Four-O-Two; Private T. Birnie*—spelt with two I's—right! Royal Loyals, I suppose? *Religion*? Eh, what's the trouble now?"

"Sergeant," interposed 'Erb, in a puzzled voice, "look 'ere! This ain't no private; it's an orficer! Look at his tunic—three stars, and all!"

Sergeant Busby flashed his electric torch once more. It revealed a grey-haired man, with a captain's tunic wrapped round his shoulders, tied by the sleeves.

"Yes," he announced judicially, "he's an officer, all right; and what's more, he's an officer in a Jock regiment. I know a bit about uniforms, my lad; and no English officer wears a cutaway tunic like that, or his pips in that position. And there's his collar-badges! He's not a Loyal at all, this feller; he's a Covenanter."

"What about his identity-disc?" inquired 'Erb, respectfully. "That says 'Private.'"

The sapient Busby pondered. Then—

"He was a private once," he explained, "in the Loyals; then he got his commission and was gazetted to the Covenanters; but he never got himself issued with a new identity disc. Economical that's what he was. Real Scotch, I expect! Well, if he's an officer, we needn't worry with his regimental number; that goes out." The blunt pencil thudded. "I'll just put him down as *Captain Birnie, Royal Covenanters—Presbyterian*; that's enough. Carry on, boys!"

The heavy-footed procession filed away through the mud, round the traverse, and out of this narrative.

And that was how it came to pass that Sir Thomas Birnie, Baronet, of Baronrigg, who in the humility of his heart had enlisted as a private and died as a corporal, was buried next day, with absolute justice, as the officer and gentleman that he really was.

II

Meanwhile Roy, with his stout young skull almost riven by a glancing Boche nose-cap, lay tossing and muttering in a Base Hospital.

One dream beset and obsessed him for weeks. He, Roy Birnie—the soldierly, the punctilious, the immaculate—had been haled by an escort of overwhelming numbers and terrifying appearance before his commanding officer—Uncle Alan, swollen to enormous size and invested with Mephistophelean eyebrows—upon the charge of coming upon parade improperly dressed. It was not merely a question of an unbuttoned pocket, or a pair of badly-wound puttees; he had paraded in his shirt-sleeves—minus his tunic! And in his dream, try as he might, poor Roy could not for the life of him recall, in response to the nightmare cross-examination of his satanic superior and relative, what he had done with it.

All he could recollect was that he had wrapped it round someone—someone who appeared to have lost his own and to be badly in need of another; because he was lying on

112

the ground in the mud. Roy had fitful glimpses of the face—the face of a man dying in great pain, but in great peace—a strangely familiar face. Roy had tried to converse with its owner; but in his dreams their intercourse was limited chiefly to intensely affectionate smiles. Then, suddenly, he had recognised the face, and was stooping, in an awkward, boyish fashion, to kiss it, when something happened, and he remembered no more.

III

Gradually these troubled visions faded, and with the steady healing of his wound came healthy sleep and tranquillity of mind. Finally he came to himself; and one bright morning in May was carried on board a hospital ship and transferred, across the most efficiently guarded strip of water in the world, to a convalescent hospital in a great country house in Kent.

That night he slept in a little room in a long passage full of doors, behind each of which lay a boy, seldom older than himself, who had squandered his youth, mayhap a limb, too often his whole constitution, in the service of his country.

Next morning, when he awoke, the sun was streaming down the passage. All the doors stood wide open, and the air was rent by a raucous and irregular chorus, proceeding from the doorways and beginning:

Nurse, Nurse, I'm feeling rather worse;

Come and kiss me on my little brow!

Words of rebuke were audible, and the riot died down. A majestic young woman, admirably composed, presented herself at Roy's door.

"Good morning, Captain Birnie. I hope you slept well."

"Thank you, I did," replied Roy. "Are you the Sister?"

Across the passage came a voice:

"Let me present you, sir, to Little Lily, our Cross Red nurse! She—"

The lady indicated whirled round upon the offender, whose grinning face, partially obscured by a patch over one eye, could be discerned upon the pillow of the bed in the room opposite.

"Mr. Abercrombie," she announced, "if you can't behave I shall report you to the Matron."

Mr. Abercrombie was all contrition at once.

"All right, Nurse!" he announced. "I apologise! I only want to warn you, sir," he added to Roy, "that she's married! But she never tells us that until it's too late! *Do* be careful!"

Little Lily, the Cross Red nurse—otherwise the Lady Hermione Mulready—turned an unruffled countenance to Roy. It was true that she was married; she possessed what Mr. Abercrombie would have called "a perfectly good husband of her own" in the Irish Guards. She had once possessed two brothers also, somewhat akin in appearance and disposition to the effervescent Abercrombie. Perhaps that was why she suffered his impertinences so readily.

"Here is your breakfast, Captain Birnie," she continued. "The Matron says you can't have bacon yet; but if you are good you may reach an ordinary diet next week."

Roy thanked her.

"After breakfast," he asked politely, "may I write a letter—just one? And see a paper? I'm a bit behind with the war, and—"

"You can have anything you want, in reason, so long as you lie still and don't fidget. We have enough babies in this place already!" announced Little Lily, with a withering glance in the direction of the room opposite where Master Abercrombie was acting foolishly.

"It's all right," Roy assured her. "You will have no trouble with me. I'm quite an old man, really: a kind husband, and an indulgent father, and all that," he added, with a curious little air of pomposity.

His nurse looked down upon him with quickened interest.

"Are you a father?" she asked.

"Yes. Only just, though! I—I—haven't seen It yet!" His voice quivered suddenly, to think how near he had gone to not seeing It at all.

"I am glad you came through," said Little Lily quietly; and handed him *The Times* to read with his breakfast.

Roy poured out his tea, stretched back luxuriously, and unfolded the paper. Like most of us in those days, he turned first to the casualty list. The names of the officers alone filled two columns.

"I wonder if my old cracked cranium has figured here yet," he ruminated. "What a nice little thrill if it's in to-day!"

He glanced down the long list of wounded.

"No, nothing doing! It has probably been in already." He turned in more leisurely fashion to the previous column, and began to read the names of the killed. But his eye got no further than the first name. There were no A's to-day: this began with B.

He laid the paper down, and grinned to himself.

"I'd rather read it than be it!" he reflected.

Then, suddenly, a blinding thought smote him.

Marjorie! What if she had seen it? He sat up excitedly, as a further probability occurred to him.

"She must have been notified privately by the War Office long ago. Then, of all times!" He was talking to himself now, in a low, agitated voice. "My God! I wonder where she is! The old man never told me when he wired; but he'll know." His voice rose. "Nurse! Nurse! Nurse!"

"Great Scott!" announced Mr. Abercrombie from the opposite room: "The lad has succumbed already! And I *warned* him!"

But already Lady Hermione's tall figure was framed in Roy's doorway.

"Here I am," she said. "Don't shout, please. You will find a bell-push under your pillow, if you look.... Why, my *dear*, what is it?"

Roy handed her the paper, pointing dumbly.

"My wife!" he whispered. "She'll think I'm— And I don't even know where she is—to contradict it! Have you a telephone here? Could you ring up Lord Eskerley's house in London? He'll know! He knows everything! He knows—"

Lady Hermione laid a cool hand upon his bandaged forehead.

"Don't get flustered!" she said. "Get up, and put on your dressing-gown. I will show you where the telephone is."

Next moment, with Roy swaying on her arm, she was sailing down the passage in the direction of the office in the front hall.

"They're keeping company already! Quick work! Quick work!" commented Master Abercrombie, admiringly.

CHAPTER XXII

THE MILLS OF GOD

"He must have left a will of some kind," said Lord Eskerley.

"He made one before he went to France," I replied; "but that has been invalidated by his marriage. It doesn't really matter; because everything—the baronetcy, Baronrigg, and so on—will pass automatically to the child."

"Still, you know what lawyers are when a man dies intestate! There will be nothing left worth scraping up if we don't provide something of a documentary nature for them to bite on. Didn't they find anything in his pockets, when they—found him?"

"Nothing but his cigarette-case, and Marjorie's last letter."

We were standing in the outer library of Lord Eskerley's great house in Curzon Street. It was a bright morning in May, and the sun, streaming between the heavy window-curtains, made the rest of the room look more than usually funereal by comparison. At one end, double doors opened into his lordship's *sanctum sanctorum*, where few but the faithful Meadows ever presumed to track him. At the other yawned a great empty fireplace, with a curiously carved mantelpiece, over which hung Millais' radiant portrait of Lady Eskerley as a bride.

Beside the fire-place stood the secretary's own particular writing-table. To the wall just above it was fixed an incongruously modern-looking telephone switch-board. Lord Eskerley's eye fell on this; and he was off in a moment down one of his usual by-paths.

"Private wire, and so on!" he explained. "Meadows had it put in. He just pushes a few buttons, and puts a plug in a hole; and I can telephone not only to the outside world but direct to the office, or the War Cabinet, or to my own bathroom. Wonderful invention! Wonderful fellow! It's the devil, though, when he goes out for a walk: I'm no good at it myself. I tried to ring up the P.M. the other day, and found myself breathing private and confidential war secrets to my own laundry-maid. By the way, have you looked through those things yet? You may find what you want there."

He pointed to the corner of the room, where a mud-stained, sun-bleached Wolseley valise of green Willesden canvas lay rolled and strapped. It had once been Roy's, and had arrived the previous day, forwarded to me as next-of-kin, bearing that pitiful designation: "*Deceased Officers Effects.*"

"I will go through it this morning," I said, "and report. Eric is coming along; he'll help me. By the way, how is Marjorie to-day? Eric is sure to want to know."

"Why should he want to know—eh? Why this solicitude?"

"I don't know. He always does. Why shouldn't he take an interest in her, like the rest of us?"

But plainly my old friend was not quite satisfied.

"To take an interest in a beautiful young widow is right and proper," he said—"especially if you happen to be an eligible D.S.O. But not too premature an interest, please! Bethune is a gallant soldier; but fine feeling never was his *forte*." Suddenly the old man blazed up. "Good God! Has he realised that the poor child doesn't even know she is a widow?"

That Eric should be taking, or ever have taken, a more than fatherly interest in Marjorie was news to me. I am not very perceptive in these matters; but the possibility of such a thing explained a good deal to me—Eric's persistent dislike of Roy, for instance. Still, I had no desire to pursue the topic; and switched accordingly.

"I am afraid she will have to be told now," I said. "It's in the paper this morning. People will be writing to condole, and so on."

"I know," said Lord Eskerley. "I shall tell her myself—this afternoon." He shook his white head sorrowfully. "It will be pretty awful, though: a woman ought to do it really."

He glanced up at the portrait of his long dead wife. "We will give her one more morning, poor little soul! Hark!"

The door into the hall stood open; so, apparently, did the door of Marjorie's room, on the first floor above us. As we stood, we could hear her voice uplifted in a somewhat exaggerated apostrophe to her own son; also that self-satisfied infant's gurgling reception of the same. Mother and son, by the way, had been in the house for more than three weeks, having been conveyed thither from a nursing home in Kensington, where, thanks to the timely warning of a flamboyant but attractive young person named Liss Lyle, we had been constrained to look for them. Miss Lyle was now our constant visitor, and had completely enmeshed the hitherto impregnable Meadows.

"Extraordinary gibberish, baby talk!" remarked Lord Eskerley. "Primeval, of course, and quite unaltered through the ages." Then, suddenly:

"Poor child, she's had a hard time! Three years of exhausting self-imposed drudgery—then maternity! And now she has to be told that she's a widow. My God, Alan, how I hate Wilhelm sometimes! And he once dined in this house!"

"What is the news, by the way?" I asked.

"Good, decidedly good! I think we have the Boche cold at last. Internally Germany is on her last legs. Only one thing could have braced her up—a spectacular success last March. As things turned out, that enterprise went off at half-cock—though it gave us a most salutary scare. Now our morale is returning: Foch has the situation well in hand. I fancy he will encourage the enemy to attack a little longer: then, when he has blown a few more swollen salients in our line, come right back at him and puncture them one by one. That and the arrival of the Americans—they are splendid troops, I hear, and are being rushed over at the rate of three hundred thousand a month now—should put the last nail into the Teutonic coffin." The old man paused, and sighed. "Not before it was time, though! Our casualties passed the three million mark the other day, Alan! Still, our tribulations of the past three months may have been worth while. They have taught us two things: firstly, that this blundering, flat-footed old country of ours retains its ancient staying-power; secondly, never to be too cocksure about winning until you have won! What time is he coming?"

"Eleven o'clock," I replied, concluding that this lightning reference was to Eric.

"Umph! I have to be at Downing Street at twelve. Meanwhile, I shall be in my own inner chamber if you want me. Good-bye! There are cigarettes in that box. Poor little girl!"

The double doors closed, and I was left alone.

I unstrapped Roy's valise without much difficulty—my comminuted collar-bone was mending nicely, though I had been warned that I might never be able to wield a salmon-rod again—and emptied out its jumbled contents on to the floor. At the same moment Eric was announced.

"Come along," I said, "and get that new tin arm of yours to work. Sort out everything in the shape of papers from that mess, and let us go through them."

"Are we looking for anything in particular?" asked Eric, reluctantly setting to work. He always hated drudgery.

"Roy's will."

Eric nodded; and laid a heap of documents on the table. There was a tattered sheaf of battalion orders; an old field dispatch book, a number of maps; and a bundle of letters.

"I fancy the letters are from Marjorie," I said. "We need not bother to read them."

"How is she, by the way?" asked Eric, looking up.

"Getting along, I believe."

116

"One would like to show her any little kindness that is possible," Eric continued. "One has sent her flowers, of course, and so on. Is there anything else? I wonder if she would like to see me? It would probably do her good."

It was the old touch. I smiled despite myself.

"I wouldn't suggest it at present, if I were you," I said. "She is to have some news broken to her this afternoon."

"You mean—?"

I nodded.

"It's in the paper this morning," I said. "The War Office telegram we could keep from her; but not that."

Eric was silent, and began to turn over the papers.

"These maps had better go back to Ordnance," he remarked. "They ought to have been taken out at Battalion Headquarters, by rights. Some of these old Orders are interesting: they have a musty flavour now. Listen to this":

The C.O. has observed that N.C.O.'s and Men are falling into the habit of washing their gas-helmets.

"Do you remember those noisome old flannel jelly-bags, Alan?"

"I do! They were abolished, as far as I can remember, about the middle of nineteen sixteen."

"Yes, that's right. They were about as much use as the sick headache which they produced."

Officers Commanding Companies will see that this practice is discontinued at once. Helmets so washed are entirely useless against a gas attack.

"Still," I commented, "if you wore them unwashed you died whether there was a gas attack on or not; so altogether, I don't blame the washers!"

"Hallo," continued Eric; "here's a *billet-doux* from Corps Headquarters."

"What is it?"

Eric grinned.

"*Mules, Brief Notes on the Treatment of.* They do manage to think of things on Olympus!..."

The mule is much more dainty about what he drinks than about what he eats.

"I think that's true: my last consignment ate seventeen nose-bags and three pack-saddles in a single night."

The mule is not really of a vicious disposition; he is only shy and nervous, and is very responsive to petting—

"So am I, for that matter! But let's get on, Eric. Here's a field despatch book. It has been lying in a puddle, I fancy: these carbon duplicates have run a bit. Never mind! I don't suppose there is anything of importance inside it."

"The only legible despatch is the last one," said Eric, turning over the pages. "A pretty stately epistle, too! Listen!"

To O.C. 7th Battalion, the Grampian Regiment.

Sir,—Reference your FZ/357, in which it is stated that the one hundred picks and shovels which this Battalion was directed to hand over to yours on the 16th inst. were handed over deficient five picks and four shovels; I am to inform you that an N.C.O. was duly sent in charge of the picks and shovels in a G.S. Waggon to Bluepoint Farm at seven a.m. on that date, and there handed over the full number of picks and shovels to an

N.C.O. of your Battalion, who counted them and gave a receipt for same, a copy of which I now enclose.

Your obedient servant,
R. T. C. Birnie, Lieut.,
For Lt.-Col. Commanding
2nd Battalion, Royal Covenanters.

"That fairly puts it across the Grampian Regiment!" was Eric's verdict. "I congratulate you!"

"It was Roy who was responsible," I said. "He got me out of a nasty mess with the C.R.E. by producing that receipt. He was a grand adjutant, bless him!"

Eric continued to turn over the leaves of the despatch book.

"There is nothing in the shape of a will or testament here," he said at last. "No; wait a minute; there's something in the pocket of the flap."

He held the pocket open, and shook out its contents on to the table cloth—two faded slips of pinkish paper.

"These don't look very promising," he said. "Field telegraph despatches!"

He unfolded the first slip, smoothed it out, and read aloud:

The expression "Dud" will no longer be employed in Official Correspondence.

He laughed. "There's Staff work for you!"

"Eric—!" I began suddenly. Some inward monitor had jerked an alarm-cord in my brain. Where had I heard that message before? And in conjunction with what? I leaned across the table and stretched out my hand; but already Eric had unfolded the second despatch, and was smoothing it out with the wrist of his artificial arm. I noticed that a covering slip was pinned to the despatch.

Passed to you, read Eric—*for immediate compliance, please.—J. E. F.*

"That was old Forrester, the Brigade Major. It sounds quite urgent; I wonder what it is all about."

"Eric—!" I said again. Then, suddenly, I held my peace. Who was I, to interfere with God?

"Hallo," continued Eric—"here's my name!"

Lieutenant-Colonel E. F. B. Bethune, D.S.O., Commanding Second Battalion Royal Covenanters—

He stopped suddenly—as I knew he would. I looked up, and watched his face go white, as he read the message to the end. I saw him re-read it, again and again. Then he examined the date, and hour of despatch. Then came a long, deathly silence.

At last he lifted his face to me—the face of a man suddenly aged. He pushed the pink slip in my direction.

"Have you ever seen that before?" he asked, in a hoarse voice.

I read the message mechanically through, though I knew it by heart. It said:

Lt.-Col E. F. B. Bethune, D.S.O., Commanding Second Battalion, Royal Covenanters, will return home forthwith, and report to War Office.

CHAPTER XXIII

THE SOUL OF ERIC BETHUNE

How long we sat there I do not know. But at last I was conscious that Eric was speaking again.

"When did Roy Birnie get this?"

118

"Immediately after you had moved off with the battalion—that afternoon at Caterpillar Farm, before the Somme show. He and I stayed to clear up, you remember?"

"Yes, yes!" he muttered, staring at the paper. "I remember. But—but why didn't he give it to me? Didn't he realise what it meant?"

"Yes, he realised all right. That was why he didn't give it to you."

Eric took up the despatch in his shaking hand.

"Roy Birnie deliberately held that back?" he said.

I nodded.

"And you?"

"Don't ask me about it," I replied, lighting my pipe and feeling thoroughly uncomfortable. "It's no part of a second-in-command's duty to supervise the adjutant's correspondence."

"But—didn't he show it to you?"

"Now you ask me, he did."

"But—but—it would have put you in command of the battalion!"

"My dear sir," I explained gruffly, "a man can't take command of a battalion if the adjutant neglects to publish the order which appoints him." I felt horribly mean, but this seemed to me to be a case where the dead could most conveniently bear the responsibility.

Suddenly Eric rose to his feet. I glanced at him, and flinched, for I knew what was coming. The colour had come back to his face, and his blue eyes were aglow. He was "up in the clouds." He came round to my side of the table, and laid his hands on my shoulders. It was strange to feel the lifeless weight of his artificial arm. I flinched again, and made a testy reference to my comminuted collar-bone.

But Eric was not to be denied. He had been exposed to himself as an incompetent and a failure; but what mattered more—solely—to him was that the world did not know about it; Roy and I had saved him from that. All that was grateful in his nature had been roused by that infernal telegram. He sat down beside me and took my hand in his. I felt very ridiculous.

"My God, old man," he said, "you saved me! You two saved me from being broke! You, who might have commanded the battalion—and young Roy! Young Roy! After what I had done to him—and—tried to do to him!"

"Oh, come!" I said. "You were a bit of a martinet, sometimes—the heavy C.O., and all that—but there's no need to reproach yourself over Roy."

Eric let go my hand—greatly to my relief— and began to walk about the room. Suddenly he turned to me.

"Alan, old man," he said, "do you know exactly what I did to Roy? I tried to take his girl away from him!"

I looked up. Lord Eskerley had been right, as usual.

"You mean—Marjorie?"

"Yes—Marjorie! Not once—nor twice—not accidentally—nor casually; but deliberately and continuously! Listen!" He was in the flood-tide of confession now, and I knew that in that mood he was not apt to be reticent.

"I made love to her at Craigfoot—in a 'you're-a-nice-little-girl' sort of way—while Roy was at Sandhurst. I made love to her in London, when I was on leave and he was in France—took her out to dinner and lunch, and so on—"

"Why not? It was up to her to refuse."

"She didn't refuse."

"In that case, she must have found your society agreeable."

"No, she didn't! I am pretty vain about myself, Alan; but I could see she didn't!"

"Then why did she accept your invitations?"

"I fancy it was because it gave her a chance to talk about the regiment—which meant Roy. Not that she ever mentioned him; but—I see it now! My God, what a cad I was! I let her sit there, while I crabbed him—talked patronisingly of him—belittled the good work he had always done for me and my battalion. Ugh!"

"Did you really care for her?"

"I was fascinated by her for the time. She is a glorious creature!"

"She certainly is."

"But I think that in the main it was jealousy—jealousy of Roy's youth, and the fact that instead of being my son, as he might have been, he was my rival. It was a mad business altogether. Finally, I asked her to marry me."

"She turned you down?" It was an unnecessary remark.

"Of course she turned me down! But she did it very sweetly. She was rather apologetic about it; said she was engaged already, and perhaps she ought to have made that fact a little clearer to me from the start; only she never suspected, and so on."

"She didn't mention Roy's name, I suppose?"

"No! I half thought that she would, just to score me off. It would have been a real slap in the face for me, his Colonel, if she had. But she didn't: she just said she was very, very sorry, but that she was engaged to some one else!"

"Well, there was no great harm done," I said, wishing he would stop. But he had not finished yet.

"And then—oh Lord, Alan!—do you know what I did then? I turned round on her, like a spoiled child, and accused her of having flirted with me, and led me on! And, not content with that, I turned on the pathetic tap. I said something rotten about expecting a little more consideration from her, seeing that I was going back to the trenches to-morrow—and muck like that! And she just looked at me, and said, quite quietly: 'He is there, too—now!' As if I didn't know! Oh, what a miserable rotter I was—and am!"

He dropped into a chair, and buried his face in his arms. He was "doon in the midden" now. I puffed wretchedly at my pipe and longed, from the bottom of my heart, for an air raid. I found myself wondering whether Marjorie had ever told Roy of this incident. I decided that my Eve would not have done so; and therefore probably not Marjorie.

Presently Eric began to talk again, with his forehead still close to the table.

"And this very morning," he said bitterly—"with Roy's death hardly made public—I came to this house fooling round Roy's widow with flowers, and silly old man's messages! I believe I was actually jealous of the dead, Alan! Well, that's over now. I needn't insult her any more—or him!" He sat up again, and took the pink slip. "This has killed my conceit at last—and perhaps saved my soul. Thank God I came across it! It has brought me to myself. And thank *you*, old friend"—Eric turned swiftly to me, and his face broke into the smile that I loved—"for what you did for me! You saved me from being sent home! Yes, and you provided me with a far more creditable exit from my soldiering career than I ever deserved!"

"That's all right," I said. "Let's clear up these papers."

But Eric was not listening. He had fallen into a rare mood—gentle and frank. He talked on—more calmly now.

"Men are queer mixtures. And, oh Lord, how truly some women judge us! Marjorie saw through me from the start, I believe. So did Diana. Did you ever know why she broke off our engagement?"

I shook my head. I had not heard Eric mention Diana's name for twenty years.

"Eve and I never spoke of it," I said.

"No, of course; you two wouldn't—being you two. Well, Diana said to me, quite suddenly, one day: 'Eric, I want to tell you that I can't marry you after all.' Just that! Of course, I asked her why."

"That was probably a mistake."

"It was. She asked me not to press her; but, being me, that only made me more unreasonable. So finally she told me.

"'Eric,' she said, 'I am very fond of you; I always shall be—more than I care to think about. But you have one fault that I can't get over: you have a mean streak in you. I would take you with every other fault in the world—but not that! So—good-bye!' They were the last words she ever spoke to me. You know, she was like that. I took my medicine with a smiling face, as you may remember; but it hurt like hell—and it taught me nothing! Well"—he tapped the telegraph form—"here is my second dose! It has got home this time. I *have* a mean streak in me, and I know it at last! Still"—he rose to his feet and held up his right hand: he could never resist the dramatic touch—"it's not too late. I am still on the right side of fifty; and I am going to spend the rest of my life eradicating that yellow streak from my system. I think I can do it. A thing's never dangerous once you know it's there." Suddenly he leaned over towards me. "Alan, old boy, I'm not a *hopeless* outsider, am I? Tell me! You know me! What am I?"

"You are what I have always thought you," I said—"a very brave soldier, with a weakness for facing difficult situations with both eyes shut! Also, you are my oldest friend. Now, for goodness sake, let's clear up this mess, and report entire lack of progress to Eskerley!"

The telephone bell rang sharply.

CHAPTER XXIV

THROUGH

The double doors at the end of the room swung back, and Lord Eskerley appeared. The bell was still ringing. A tiny hinged metal flap on the switchboard had fallen open, revealing a white disc with a number on it. His Lordship gazed absently down upon the apparatus.

"The inestimable Meadows is still taking the air," he said, "so I must tackle this contraption myself. Let me think; what is the combination?"

He peered at the vibrating flap and the revealed number.

"Three!" he announced. "Aha! I haven't the faintest notion what that implies. Let us stop this noise, anyhow."

He pushed up the flap again, and the bell stopped ringing.

"Shall we retire?" I asked.

"No, no, no! If it's desperately confidential I will switch it through to the instrument in my room; but I don't expect"—he put the receiver to his ear—"Who wants me? What wants me? ... Caperton? Never heard of him! Oh, an exchange? A locality? A trunk call? Very well! *Rien ne m'étonne!* Carry on!"

Lord Eskerley's back was turned to us. Suddenly I saw his shoulders stiffen; he caught his breath sharply. As this was the first sign of emotion that he had betrayed, to my knowledge, for the last thirty years, I watched him with quickening interest.

"Yes!" he said ... "Yes, yes! This is Lord Eskerley ... Louder, please!" Then came a pause, while the receiver squeaked steadily. Then, a little unexpectedly: "Praise God from Whom all blessings flow!"

Eric was watching too, now. The old man steadied himself, grasping the end of the mantelpiece with his disengaged hand. Then he looked round over his shoulder at us, peering over his spectacles.

"A most interesting communication coming through here!" he announced. "Forgive my demeanour!" His voice was as harsh as ever, but there were tears in his old eyes. He turned to the instrument again.

"Yes," he said, "I concur. Such a rumour would be *most* prejudicial to your future career. Shall we contradict it? You are quite sure it's incorrect?" ... He chuckled; so did the receiver. Then he continued:

"Eh? ... Oh! Naturally! You would like to do that at once? ... Yes, I think I can put you in communication with the party in question.... When? Oh, within a fairly reasonable interval of time, I hope. Let us say next week—" He moved the receiver a few inches away from his ear. "I can hear you quite easily in your ordinary voice, thanks!"

He chuckled again, laid down the receiver, and brooded once more over the switchboard. Then, after a brief mental calculation, he selected a plug at the end of a wire, thrust it into a hole, and pressed a small ivory button.

A bell rang faintly upstairs, then ceased sharply. Our noble operator took up the receiver again.

"That you, Habakkuk?" he inquired.... "Good! Some mysterious individual in Kent wishes to speak to you on the telephone. Wonderful invention!"

The old gentleman made a final adjustment of the switches on the board, and spoke for the last time—apparently to the person in Kent:

"You still there?"

The telephone vibrated stormily.

"All right! You are through to her—dear boy!"

He hung up the receiver, and left them together.

THE END

CPSIA information can be obtained at www.ICGtesting.com
Printed in the USA
BVOW06s2307140915

417981BV00012B/130/P